Europa, in the second half of the twenty-first century. The administrations of all countries have broken down due to extreme environmental changes. Europa's countryside has been divided into small fiefdoms ruled over by bands of outlaws. The only hope for humanity lies now in the north of the continent, where the climate has become more attractive due to global warming. The influx of new arrivals is changing the demographics, creating problems for the local population and the environment.

Erick, a former soldier, who retreated into the tundra wilderness fifteen years ago, finds himself suddenly under siege from a disaffected band of marauding soldiers. Having teamed up with a young woman, previously freed from slavery, he is wounded during their escape, consequently being forced to amputate his right forearm. During his recuperation, he hears about a mysterious cybertech plant specialising in producing prosthetic limbs. To reach that plant, he and the young woman must travel through the now devastated continent to get its location in Paris. Along their travels, they will endure the extremes of the changing environment and life-threatening encounters.

SAVAGED LANDS

VOLUME I

MICHAEL CHAPUS

Savaged Lands

Published by The Conrad Press Ltd. in the United Kingdom 2023

Tel: +44(0)1227 472 874

www.theconradpress.com

info@theconradpress.com

ISBN 978-1-915494-41-2

Copyright © Michael Chapus, 2023

All rights reserved.

Disclaimer: This is a work of fiction. Names, characters, places, and incidents either are the product of the author's imagination or are used fictitiously. Any resemblance to actual persons, living or dead, events, or locales is entirely coincidental.

Typesetting and Cover Design by: Charlotte Mouncey, www.bookstyle.co.uk

The Conrad Press logo was designed by Maria Priestley.

Printed and bound in Great Britain by Clays Ltd, Elcograf S.p.A.

Dedicated to my friends who made
publishing this book possible

PART 1
ERICK

1

An unexpected encounter

This morning's conditions had appeared promising for a successful hunt; no wind and a clear sky. Perched on top of the steep embankment, Erick had been lying for quite some time in his hiding place. The mist below in the valley hid a herd of caribou. Soon the sun would rise higher, burning the fog and forcing the animals to move.

Erick began to get impatient. He knew the warming sun would also stir up the mosquitoes and sand flies, descending mercilessly on every warm-blooded creature. Usually, the caribou would stay as long as possible under cover of the mist, giving them some protection from the roaming wolf packs. As soon as he spotted the first movements in the tops of the antlers through his binoculars, he got his hunting rifle ready.

Due to the climatic changes, the caribou had become rare in this tundra part. Year by year, it appeared to be more challenging to find enough game to hunt, undoubtedly one of the many side effects of the increase in temperature and the disappearing permafrost. It also allowed trees to grow, covering more and more of the grazing grounds that the animals relied on. The nature of the tundra was changing, forcing some animals to adapt—especially those that could not move further north. Bears and wolves had no difficulties in this regard. One of the less pleasant consequences of these multiple environmental changes was that large carnivores had discovered a new kind of prey; humans, more effortless to hunt and plenty in number!

The human stream into the north had increased year by year. Most of these people had no previous experiences with the northern winters harsh climate. These were desperate men and women, often unprepared for the extreme environment and without efficient hunting gear. In this unfamiliar terrain, it was easy to get lost and disorientated. Consequently, they often turned from hunters to the hunted. Many of them, already emaciated from the long trek on foot, died in the thousands. Lately, Erick had begun to come across their remains more often.

With his finger on the trigger, Erick was ready for the warming air to absorb the remaining mist. This was when he had to place his shot before the mass of bodies would move. The herd suddenly stirred and immediately began to stampede into the open. Erick failed to make sense of the unusual behaviour of the pack; he had lost his chance to aim at a specific animal. He swore to himself in frustration. He was just about to shoot into the mass of moving bodies, hopefully wounding one of the animals so that he could track it down afterwards, when he heard the sound of human voices and the whinnying of horses. Behind the herd of the running caribou, out of the rising mist, the heads of a few riders appeared.

Erick could make out five men on horseback, followed by two massive wagons. Each was pulled by four slowly ambling oxen, flanked by two men on foot on each side of the wagons guiding the beasts. Obviously, the appearing caravan had been the reason for the stampede and his lost opportunity of today's hunt.

Erick decided to pack up and abandon his position when he spied a long line of people, about fifty in his estimation, trudging behind the carts. Undoubtedly, they were slaves, tied to each other, most stumbling and occasionally falling and then repeatedly whipped to keep them moving. Erik did not like the look of it at all! He had heard of these slave traders, but he had never seen a caravan of that size and so far north. He usually only came across lost bands of desperados or, in some cases, hardened criminals. No one else dared to track so far inland towards the north, preferring the routes along the coast instead. Most of these people fled from the overcrowded and miserable conditions in the large cities to the south. Recent rumours also had it; the nations on the southern Baltic shores were turning equally inhospitable towards refugees. Unfortunately, survival was not the only reason for people to move. New tales of hidden wealth in the ground of the northern lands were attracting all sorts of unsavoury characters.

After observing the caravan and carefully assessing the situation, Erick decided to make contact. Traders always offered opportunities to barter and exchange valuable news, and Erick was also desperate for some vegetable oil. These newcomers might offer both. Whatever the information, it could influence his decision not to stay much longer in this area, forcing him to move further north. Before leaving his hideout, he prepared his usual ruse, positioning a well-camouflaged dummy fashioned out of grass and an old tracksuit behind a decommissioned World War II machine gun.

Erick sauntered down the hill towards the approaching caravan, carrying a sack containing goods to trade with. He walked with confidence, showing himself to be in complete control of the situation. With his height of six foot five, he made an imposing impression. A sawn-off shotgun in his holster and a semi-automatic gun casually placed over his shoulder added a particular aspect of menace. Without a doubt, here came a man you would not want to mess with.

How much did they know? Only one of his weapons held a cartridge! He also had fashioned a bulletproof vest stuffed with a thick layer of books, which was invisible under his coat. This gave him an even more massive stature. Experience had taught him arrows and crossbows, and even bullets could not penetrate books.

Erick stopped at the halfway mark and waited for the caravan to approach the spot where he stood calmly, trying to appear as harmless as possible, which was in direct contrast to the approaching traders. Three of them were already holding their crossbows at the ready. When the caravan moved closer, Erick could make out their faces, leaving him without doubt; these guys were trouble! Obviously, guns had become increasingly rare and desperately sought-after items.

Erick showing no signs of distrust, raised his hands in a friendly gesture of peace—the kind of greeting used by all men in the wild. To Erick's annoyance, one of the men still aimed his crossbow menacingly at him. He responded by sliding his semi-automatic quickly from his shoulder and casually holding it without aiming it at anyone in particular. The men immediately without apparant change got the message. They were only too aware of the firepower of Erick's gun and the futility of their crossbows in such a contest.

Before anyone could speak, Erick addressed the man closest to him with a friendly but decisive voice.

'If anyone of your men has the intention to act irrationally, I advise you to focus your binoculars on the top of that ridge behind me where my partner has aimed his machine gun on your caravan. We intend to cause you no trouble. I am just looking for some useful items you might want to trade.'

The men quickly stored their weapons away, realising under these circumstances that any aggressive action would be somewhat suicidal.

Both sides relaxed, as the possibility of conflict had been averted. The leader now raised his hand as a sign of peace, calling on his men to take it easy. As expected, such a situation would not pass without vile words and spitting on the ground.

Erick had so far not changed his demeanour and kept up his act. He calmly continued with his negotiations without taking his eyes off the slavers.

'So now that we have come to an agreement, are you interested in any kind of business deal? I am also interested in information; what is going on in the south of the continent and why are you travelling so far north with so many slaves in tow?'

They replied that in the east, along the Baltic seaboard between Poland and Russia, a low-level civil war had been ravaging for some years, and all public transport systems had broken down. Middle and southern Europa comprised a few large cities. The countryside was deserted because of the drying up of rivers, making it increasingly resemble a northern African landscape. The large metropolises along the routes towards the north of the continent had turned into traps for anyone who intended to go further. People who tried to leave those big cities did not make it very far. They either got robbed and then killed or were taken into slavery by the marauding bands because most of the citizens of these former technologically advanced societies had lost the necessary skills for survival in the present reality. Farming in the countryside had ceased, apart from a few well-defended valleys still watered by running rivers. Undoubtedly the chaos resulted from the unstoppable influences of climate change. The further one went south, the more extreme the observable effects.

Erick nodded and thanked the man. In general, most of it he had heard before, only with one slight difference—every time, the description of the situation sounded worse!

Without further questions, he went straight to business. He opened his sack, exposing six rabbits, several reindeer skins, a large bag of hazelnuts, and a jar of wild berry jam.

Erick asked if they had some cooking oil to trade in exchange.

The man in charge shook his head.

'Oil is costly, but what about a slave instead? Maybe you would like one of the slave women as a concubine?' he replied somewhat sarcastically.

At the mention of the slaves, Erick looked down the line of the emaciated wretched souls and then shook his head. He had no use for slaves, especially not for those pampered people from southern or middle Europe. Those individuals would not last through one winter in this part of the world. Judging them by their condition, Erick already expected them not to be alive by the time they reached their northern destination.

Then his eyes fell on a young girl trailing behind as the last one in the chain. She was pitiful, emaciated down to the bones and covered in tattered rags. She had stopped and was desperately urged by the man next to her to catch up while he pointed at the man with the whip. However, her posture made her stand out from the rest of the slaves, and, despite her condition, she appeared defiant.

Erick sensed a kind of stubborn intelligence. Well-proportioned in her physical appearance, although slightly stooped, she stood taller than the rest of the slaves.

Suddenly an inexplicable emotion stirred in Erick's mind that he had to rescue this girl even though he knew he would accuse himself later for the utter foolishness of his kindness.

Here in the tundra wilderness, pity would only endanger your own life! He was not quite sure about his motives either, but on the spur of the moment, he decided to save the girl from her inevitable death while his mind still tried to object to this sudden irrational rush of empathy. Had he been alone for too long, having lost his sense of reality, or was it a moment of insightfulness telling him that this girl needed saving and had come into his life for a reason?

So, he pointed at the girl and told them she would be part of the bargain.

Erick's sudden change of mind, having chosen the most pitiful of the slaves, left the traders for a moment speechless.

Then they started laughing, obviously thinking they had now got a lunatic at the hand of whom they could get the better of. Trying to make the most of their advantage, they began to haggle, obviously intending to push up the price.

'Oh no, you don't want that one, she is tonight's dinner for the rest of them,' they replied sarcastically.

'Just look at her, she is already half dead. She will be lucky if she makes it to the end of the day. Why don't you take one of the fatter and older ones; they keep you warm in bed.'

Erick felt a wave of anger building up in him. If his submachine gun had been fully loaded, he might have killed that bunch of cutthroats on the spot. However, for Erick, there was no such thing as losing himself in a violent encounter when there was still plenty of room for negotiations. A man who could not control himself had no chance of survival in this part of the world.

So, he calmly responded, insisting that he preferred the young girl. After all, the rabbits he offered were part of the bargain and could sustain the slaves another day.

'Well, six rabbits will not do; most of us will still go hungry. So you can see she is quite valuable to us. But let's say you throw in the gold ring on your finger and we have a deal,' the leader responded.

Erick played along, arguing that the exchange was now far too much to his disadvantage, especially when it came to the ring being his most precious memory of his deceased wife. In reality, this was a ruse he usually played with traders of such ilk. Erick secretly enjoyed the little game every time he had a chance, and the con never failed with such seedy characters.

Most people were quickly impressed by gold, especially newcomers from the south, where it was now the only currency. How little they understood. Here in this remote wilderness, gold had very little value. Whenever he needed to push a deal to his advantage, Erick flaunted a gold ring on his finger as ostentatiously as he could. After all, he had plenty of these cheap, run-of-the-mill, golden rings in store.

As these unexpected encounters were the only chance for entertainment in these remote parts of the world, he played them along, infusing his words with a touch of sentimentality, seeing those objectionable characters enjoying his apparent mental pain.

'Well, no ring, no deal,' the man in charge responded with a sneer, convinced of being in the winning position. Erick, stretching the farce a bit longer for his own pleasure, kept up his act of soul-searching decision-making. Once he had them where he wanted, he responded, sounding as if trying his best not to lose too much in the bargain, 'A bottle of oil would definitely make the deal.'

The man in charge nodded to one of the men on foot, who began to rummage in the cart, coming up with a greasy half-litre bottle of oil. Erick, uncorking it and recognising the scent of sunflower oil, nodded his approval. He pulled the ring off his finger and handed it over with his other trading goods.

Despite having succeeded with his ruse, in anyone's opinion, the deal could not be described as lucrative on his behalf. Now that the bargain was struck, the slavers laughed out loud, not withholding their contempt for this foolish man from the woods. Erick could not help but agree with them on that part! What was he going to do with the girl? Would she even survive until the end of the day?

They cut her loose and pushed her towards him; she collapsed instantly, supplying additional amusement for the traders, who responded with another barrage of hysterical laughs. Trying to outdo his companions with sarcasm, one of them shouted after Erick, 'Maybe you can use her bones for tonight's dinner.' Again a renewed volley of laughs followed.

Erick, without taking any notice of their ignorance, raised his hands before they could turn away.

'One more question,' he asked. 'Where are you heading to, and why are you using the more difficult land route, instead of sailing along the coast?'

The traders, already cracking their whips over the heads of the slaves, spurred on their horses, shook their heads in disbelief as if Erick had just asked a most stupid question and shouted back at him over their shoulders:

'We are heading for Hammerfest. Because the sea is swarming with pirates at this time of the year, the land route proved safer and there are also not enough boats for hire!'

Disconcerting information, Erick thought! This was the beginning of summer. It could only mean one thing—there would be even more people travelling along this route, and most of them would possibly perish on the way. As the law of the land still stood, only the toughest and most experienced human beings would survive in the northern wilderness.

While contemplating the news, Erick watched the caravan slowly moving out of sight.

The moaning girl at his feet brought him back to the present as she desperately begged him for water. Erick handed her his canister, which she could only hold with incredible difficulty.

Despite the distraction of the girl's terrible condition, Erick's mind was still focusing on the disappearing caravan. These kinds of men could not be trusted. They might have seen through his ruse by now. They might return and ambush him while he was carrying the girl up the hill and unable to defend himself readily. He decided to loiter for a while until he was convinced he would have enough time to reach his hideout without the risk of being ambushed. He picked the girl up gently in his arms and slowly walked towards the ridge.

His camp, made out of sticks and rocks, roofed over with reindeer skin, was only a temporary resting place—one of many similar locations he had established over time, sites he usually used on his long hunting excursions when it was too late for him to return home, or the weather had turned sour. In his mind, he nicknamed these places his summer hunting lodges.

These places stood in stark contrast to his home, located deep in the Tundra wilderness. The house, located in rough and unapproachable terrain, was rather large and very sumptuous, camouflaged by thick undergrowth and securely protected by spiked ditches and bear traps.

2
Erick's residence

The house had once belonged to a wealthy industrialist, who had made his break from the twentieth-century civilisation a long time ago after he became fed up with the inhuman direction the high-tech industrialised world was taking and having become aware of the unhealthy, destructive results of these so-called advanced technologies.

Nonetheless, escaping was one thing, but sustaining the dream proved, in the end, more difficult than he had imagined. The man, already in his fifties, softened up by life in luxury, was not prepared to live a life of utter simplicity.

While planning how to proceed with his way of disappearing without a trace, he dispersed most of his fortune among his extended family members without disclosing his reasons.

Due to the short summer months, it took him several years to build a comfortable retreat in the northern reaches of Finnmark. The place was without access to any roads. Instead, helicopters were used to bring in all the necessary building materials and workmen from the nearest port town.

The interior had been decorated in style and furnished luxuriously, complete with oriental carpets and valuable art pieces. Of course, by the time of Erick's arrival, after years of neglect, their former glory had faded, and many items had deteriorated beyond repair, which meant a plentiful supply of firewood.

Erick did not mind the run-down conditions, having no attachments to luxuries, but the place still provided a more-than-comfortable living situation. He kept items that still served their purpose and even sometimes repaired them amateurishly with his limited skills for the craft. However, there were many surprising discoveries. He found a safe in the basement, which contained a relatively large amount of gold bullion and jewellery. He wondered why the old man had bothered to bring treasures like these into his isolated existence. Maybe he kept it as insurance if he changed his mind; after all.

Erick did not care much about gold or jewellery. In this remote wilderness, such items were quite useless! Out here, it was necessary to be in good health, possess hunting skills and make the best out of any situation.

The house had been expertly built and was structured solidly, but it was far too extensive and opulent for what was necessary to survive in isolated comfort. The thick outside walls were built in natural stone and covered with timber logs on the inside. On top of that, they were rendered with clay for extra insulation and then lime-washed for appearance. At first, Erick wondered about all the effort that had been made but soon began to understand and appreciate the need for such solidness as winter approached.

The building consisted of two storeys. The ground level featured a large lounge room fitted out with two fireplaces, taking up one-half of the length of the building. To one side, a door led into a reading room, housing an extensive library and a fireplace. A well-equipped kitchen and dining area completed the ground level on the opposite side of the lounge room. Over time the library became Erick's preferred room to spend his evening hours, especially in winter when it was nearly impossible to heat up the entire house.

The old man had, without doubt, received a stream of regular visitors in the early days of his stay. The entrance hall, between the lounge room and dining area, featured a sweeping staircase leading to the upper level, containing four large, luxurious en suites. A covered balcony surrounded the upper floor completely, allowing access through French doors on both sides.

Below ground, the building included a cavernous basement dug into the permafrost. This consisted of a fully stocked pantry, a wine cellar, and a cold room for game, and also functioned as a bunker, including an arsenal for all kinds of weapons for hunting purposes. A tunnel had been dug out leading from the basement, maybe in anticipation of an invasion, into a nearby ravine.

Furthermore, there were two barns. One of them was holding two disintegrating snowmobiles, possibly becoming useless when petrol became increasingly hard to come by in the later years. Beside them stood a horse-drawn sledge, still reliable and ready to go.

The only problem was the missing horses.

After arriving at that place, Erick discovered to his horror, the two dismembered skeletons of the horses in the second barn! The barn door, unmistakably broken down violently, still showed a bear's claw marks.

Despite the awful discoveries and disappointment he encountered on his arrival, he appreciated the place from the first day of his stay.

The biggest challenge for Erick was posed from the beginning by the extensive whisky collection. He had to remind himself not to drink it all up in the first month after his arrival! Implementing a rigorous ritual, he was satisfied with himself by finding his equilibrium after a few weeks.

The story about his relationship with that place began far back in his early days as a young man in the army. Erick had befriended the industrialist, later turned recluse, at a party in Oslo.

Life had taken its turns, and unfortunately, he had never found an opportunity to follow up on the invitation the old man had extended. Only when Erick had decided it might be wise to move northwards did he understand how far the old man had foreseen the coming disintegration of Europe's civilised societies. He still possessed the coordinates that marked out that place on the map. This information had been given to him, and a few other selected individuals, and Erick had never betrayed that trust, knowing very well how much his choice of privacy had meant to the old man.

Unfortunately, despite having taken care of his paranoia, including his security precautions, it ended not too well for the escapee, who had died all alone and possibly starved to death—may be too incapacitated to look after himself—and it could be assumed that his servant had been killed while hunting for food, or had never returned from a trip to the nearby settlement.

Erick found the old man's frozen, dried-out body in an armchair in front of the snowed-in fireplace. He had planned to bury the body as soon as the ground was soft. But, after having stored the remains in the horse barn without much foresight, forgetting that the door did not lock properly, the body must have eventually become the meal for the roaming wolves.

It did not take long, and soon after his arrival, Erick's first bouts of excitement and enthusiasm were replaced with realism when he became aware of how much effort the estate's maintenance required. Erick soon found himself in a full-time job as a handyman and carpenter, and what had broken down could only be repaired with the available material on site. Unfortunately, the old man's dream had been built with the supply chain of civilisation in mind—a possibility long past.

In addition, to the already tricky situation, Erick had minimal talents as a handyman, and the place was too extensive for one man to keep in pristine condition. The plumbing had disintegrated long before Erick arrived. After some unsuccessful efforts to repair the leaking pipes leading to the upper level with what he could find as replacements, he gave up managing to improve only one bathroom. Eventually, he concentrated his efforts on the ground level as well as he could, which proved to be enough of a challenge.

In time, he had turned the lounge room into his sleeping area, resting on a sumptuous divan near the fireplace where he also cooked most of his meals or roasted game on the spit.

During wintertime, a bucket with warm water served all his hygienic needs, whereas, in the warmer months, the nearby creek supplied a more enjoyable alternative.

After bringing this place back into a functional order to serve his basic requirements, he secured the outside perimeter, installing an elaborate system of traps, ditches and spiky thorn bushes in the close vicinity of the house against possible intrusions by marauding bands of outlaws. Despite the remote location of his place, Erick expected that sooner or later, more and more groups of unsavoury characters migrating from the south would find their way even into this desolate pocket of wilderness.

In the ensuing years of his stay, while coming across an increasing number of tracks crisscrossing the landscape, he decided to convert the luxurious former lodge into a fortress by installing heavy shutters on the inside and outside and placing a loaded shotgun under every window.

During the short summer period, he dug ditches all around the house at a distance of approximately fifty meters, and wooden spikes were placed at the bottom. Covering those ditches with branches and dead leaves completed the design.

Of course, all his installations needed constant maintenance, keeping Erick busy all year round. But he enjoyed working on his elaborate creations, and the hard work kept him fit and distracted. Over the years, he became highly attached to his little empire, determined to defend it against any odds. A thick band of trees had been planted over the years around the estate, and the understories of the trees were increasingly stacked with dead branches and bushes. A hundred meters deep, this barrier had become a nearly impenetrable thicket. To add excitement to his work, he placed a few vicious bear traps in places where nature had been reluctant to take off, just in case someone tried to enter through the 'back door'.

In the last fifteen years, Erick had kept up the improvements and maintenance of his residence while also enjoying his solitude and simple existence without ever feeling the need for company. In the summer months, hiking along the creeks and riverbeds, he occasionally ventured out to one of the settlements further to the north. These excursions were necessary to procure essential items like salt, oil and candles in exchange for animal hides, wild berries or cured meat, with the possibility of some extras thrown in, as long as the wares were not too heavy to carry them on his back. On these occasions, he could seek information about how the rest of the European continent was faring. Along the way, he observed with great concern the slow melting of the permafrost and the results it had on the landscape. The creeks were often flooded in spring and turned bone dry for the rest of the summer. Trees were growing faster, and reindeer were becoming scarce.

However, today's encounter with the slavers' caravan shook his equilibrium more than all the negative signs of the disappearing permafrost! He knew now for sure; times were changing for the worse and not for the better. The increase in migrating people from the south meant competition for space and the troubles that would inevitably come with it. The rising influx stood in stark contrast to the trickle of the toughest survivors who had dared to penetrate the tundra that far during the last fifteen years of his residency.

However, the extensive slave caravan was entirely different from what he had seen before, causing him to expect the end of his tranquil existence sooner than he had anticipated.

3

The slave girl

Erick expected the slave traders to return by nightfall, trying to rob him and his imaginary mate of the valuable weapons. In these reaches of the continent, guns were now highly sought-after items and ammunition, even more so. He did not intend to stay longer than necessary at his hunting lodge.

He boiled up one of the bush hens he had caught that morning and used the brew to give the slave girl some strength for the arduous journey back to his house. Unfortunately, she was too frail to feed herself and had trouble swallowing the hot soup. Erick had no choice but to spoon-feed her slowly, using up valuable time by letting her rest at intervals before continuing.

Before they left, he hid away his defunct machine gun and the straw puppet, arranging the interior of the hut as if it was a real lived-in place featuring a dismountable bed, a self-made armchair, several cooking utensils, and even an old army coat hung on a pair of caribou antlers. To make the setup even more convincing, he placed a Bible on the large rock in the middle of the hut. Erick did not expect to see any items which could be of practical use again. Out here, anything, no matter how trivial, that could make life a tad more pleasant was worth its weight in gold.

He hoped his ruse would work, thereby intending to bluff anyone who, by accident or by intent, came across this little hut—a setup convincing enough to make anyone believe that this place was his sole residence and dissuade them from following his tracks further into the hills.

Soon after they had started to return, it became apparent the girl could not walk by herself for much longer. Despite the weight of everything else he was already carrying, he slung her over his shoulders like a dead animal. And at first, her emaciated, skeletal body seemed to weigh hardly anything. But after two hours of walking upright, tracking through dense undergrowth and up steep rocky inclines, even his powerfully built body began to ache under strain. He had no choice but to leave most of his gear behind, stored away high in a tree to be picked up later.

Once arrived at his home, Erick, ignoring his fatigue, went straight into the kitchen and began to prepare a soup from dried vegetables and herbs, which were the fruits from his small summer garden or collected from the wild, adding for extra strength a slab of fatty reindeer meat, chopped into small cubes.

Erick had, over the years, learned from experience; one could not maintain a healthy body in the harsh northern climates without these varieties of vegetables and green shoots that provided the necessary vitamins and minerals. His storeroom in the basement was filled with all kinds of preserves, mushrooms, edible roots, dried herbs, wild berries and a lot of cured meat.

While the broth was bubbling on the kitchen stove, he placed the girl on his divan in the lounge room, covering her body gently with blankets made of arctic wolf pelts.

Once ready, he set the soup aside to let it cool down and returned to the lounge room, where he found the girl fast asleep. Exhausted as he was himself, he saw no need to wake her. He sat next to her, taking a closer look at her features. In his estimation, she was possibly not older than eighteen. Her emaciated condition and years of brutal treatment made her appear older than she maybe was. Her face was finely structured, with high cheekbones, a wide full-lipped mouth, now all broken, dried and chipped, long, dark eyelashes, olive skin, dark hair and a defining nose. The Moorish-shaped eyes hinted at Spanish or Moroccan ancestry.

While lost in his musings, Erick did not notice the girl had opened her eyes. She looked at him questioningly and confused, uttering the incomprehensible words, 'Do you want sex now?'

Erick jolted upright, horrified at that remark! He could only imagine what kind of horror this girl must have experienced when, even in her condition, she felt obliged to be of such service. It must have been her survival instinct compelling her to offer her body, no matter the circumstances, even in this terrible condition of near death.

Erick could feel his anger rise against those slavers. Repulsion and sadness welled up all at once. Holding back his tears and unable to speak, he put his hands softly on her shoulders, shook his head, and, without uttering a word, put the steaming bowl of soup in front of her. After sitting her comfortably upright, he slowly spooned the broth into her mouth.

The girl, exhausted as she was, swallowed with great difficulty and fell back more than once during the process. For Erick, there was no question of letting up. She needed strength, and he fed her the whole bowl of soup with constant encouraging gestures, soothing words, and smiles.

He was hoping for a few words of clarification about her, only to find the girl fast asleep again after returning from the kitchen. For a moment, he stood there, unsure of what to do. Should he leave her in the lounge room or carry her into one of the upstairs bedrooms?

Suddenly aware of his fatigue, he poured himself a large glass of whisky and fell into his favourite armchair to contemplate the recent events. The whisky had become a rare pleasure these days. The once large store of the precious liquid had now withered down to a few bottles. However, today's events deserved some soothing elixirs.

Sipping his whisky slowly, Erick drifted in and out of his thoughts. For the first time in many years, this unexpected encounter was upsetting his tranquillity, troubling him with unease. Also, he was only forty-two, still vigorous enough in his body and flexible in his mind to move on and start again somewhere else. However, he felt today's events were heralding the end of his secluded, unassuming existence—his retreat from the outside world; he would have to move, forced on by the violent waves of desperation reaching up from the south.

He awoke, surprised to see that only a few embers were glowing in the fireplace and still sitting in his armchair since last night after getting lost in his musings. Erick shivered from the chilly morning air permeating the house, not to mention the slight inebriation he felt from one too many whiskies.

It now came back to him that he had intended to put the girl in one of the upstairs bedrooms to provide her with privacy. He went to inspect the upper-level en suites and was taken aback by the musty smell and the dust covering everything. His neglect of those rooms was only too apparent, and he now blamed himself for his laziness.

First, he decided to aerate the whole upper level and clean one of the rooms as best he could. Afterwards, he would cover the bed with fresh sheets and animal pelts. He chose the largest of the bedrooms with windows presenting a view of a sun-flooded vista in the morning. As it was early summer, the nights were still cold, so he lit on the en suite's fireplace too.

After a few hours of domestics, Erick looked around, pleased with his efforts, for it was all he could do for the moment.

The girl was still asleep, so he decided to carry her upstairs. But when he lifted her up, he was hit by the gut-retching stench that emanated from her tattered rags. He must have been too exhausted last night to notice those terrible conditions.

Before anything else, the girl needed to be washed and cleaned!

To begin with, he placed a large kettle filled with water to boil over the open fireplace and then cleaned the one still functioning upstairs baths. He swore again at himself for letting them deteriorate to such a state of disrepair and uselessness. He set about scrubbing the tub's surface and afterwards plugging the hole with a piece of shaped wood and filling it halfway with cold water.

He went downstairs, removed the tattered rags from her emaciated body and threw them into the newly stocked fireplace. Throughout the whole procedure of undressing, the girl gave off small murmurs and soft cries, her mind possibly dealing with nightmares of past experiences. Erick was glad she was still unconscious, which might otherwise have caused some embarrassment for both of them.

The boiling water was soon ready, but the hot kettle was somewhat difficult to carry. Afterwards, Erick carried the still sleeping girl upstairs and lowered her gently into the tub, intending to let her soak for a while in the warm water, when she suddenly awoke with panic in her eyes, trashing and kicking.

Erick used his hand by placing it in a calming gesture on her forehead while, with his other hand; he reached for a bar of soap, asking her if she was strong enough to wash. Tears were suddenly running down his face. It had been a long time ago since he had cried over a human being.

She looked questioningly at him before he realised he had spoken in Norwegian, but she nodded when he addressed her in English.

With nothing else to say and seeing she was enjoying her hot bath, Erick went downstairs to prepare breakfast but thought otherwise; the girl needed some dresses first. He looked her up once more to ensure she was managing on her own and searched for suitable clothing among the moth-eaten items left behind by the old man. Erick decided on a pair of silken pyjamas, which he had never found attractive enough to wear, finding their tightness far too uncomfortable for his athletic build. They would be a loose fit for the girl, who appeared pleased when he laid them next to her bathtub.

The early morning activity of caring for the young girl had been strangely invigorating; by now, Erick had forgotten entirely about his hangover. Even the aches and pains caused by the previous day's toil had magically disappeared.

Erick usually got up before sunrise and jogged down to the creek to take a cold bath. But today, the sun was already high in the sky, his rituals had lost their controlling power overnight, and his whole life had suddenly taken a different direction. Erick could not help but feel slightly disorientated by the turnaround of his previous existence, and it did not help the situation when he saw the empty bottle of whisky next to his armchair. It had been his monthly allocation, used up in one night.

Something else was stirring up his distracted mind—a clattering sound could be heard from the direction of the kitchen, so he jumped up, reaching for his revolver, only to remind himself seconds later that he now had a housemate!

Erick walked over to the kitchen entrance, feeling rather foolish with his revolver in his hand. Not knowing how to behave around the girl, he grunted noisily, shuffling around on the floor before asking her if she needed anything. It did not work! She flinched when she saw him holding the revolver and instantly retreated to the divan in the lounge room, muttering some unintelligible words that might have sounded like an apology in her native language.

Erick raised his hands in a gesture of calmness, realising they had not even introduced themselves to each other.

'I am Erick,' he offered, holding his hand out to her. 'You speak English?' he asked her slowly, assuming she had no knowledge of his native Norwegian.

'Elena, yes I speak English but not too well,' she responded shyly, 'and thank you rescuing me and preparing the bath for me yesterday.' she added weakly, not letting go of his hand as if to make sure her newfound freedom was not slipping away into a dream.

'Please tell me as much about yourself as you can and where you come from,' Erick continued.

While she began to tell her story, Erick set out the table with the most sumptuous breakfast his pantry allowed; he even sacrificed his last precious tin of coffee beans.

Despite his warnings to slow her food intake, she gulped down four cups of hot coffee in no time and was shyly asking for more. He admitted apologetically that it was all that he had. He had saved them for a special occasion like the one she was experiencing. At that, Elena suddenly burst into tears and apologised, her voice tempered with fear, claiming to be greedy and irresponsible, again offering him sex to make up for it. At first, Erick, confronted by such a humiliating reaction, was shocked and lost for words.

His eyes filled with tears, and all he could do was put his hand softly on her shoulder, shaking his head and assuring her that it had been his greatest pleasure to have been able to have brewed those precious beans just for her.

Using a more severe tone of voice, he promised her she would never have to prostitute herself to anyone else again. She was now free; he would help her with all his ability to restore her health and her former self.

However, Erick realised under current conditions; his promises might have been over-optimistic. He had no idea how deep the emotional scars had been edged into her psyche. And in cases like that, a person's psyche might never recover.

They sat at the table into the late afternoon, nibbling at nuts and dried berries, drinking cups of herbal tea, and she was grateful for his effort to re-brew the coffee beans again.

Yes, she was eighteen years of age from Spain and was named Elena as a child, but she had not been called by her name for many years. She and her father had left Madrid about four years ago. The city had been slowly descending into chaos after many years of social and political decline, despite desperate attempts by the city's administration and institutions to uphold law and order. Like most other citizens, they were hanging on to the spurious hope that the situation would return to normal again.

Alas, in the end, as had happened in all large cities in the southern part of Europa, once the administration had lost control, the disintegration of law and order became unstoppable! Fearing for their lives and livelihoods, most of the teaching staff from the university where her father held a professorship had fled the city.

Assuming the northern cities of Europa were still in control of their social institutions and could provide stability, her father decided they should make their way to Oxford, trusting his good connections at that institution and hoping for a new teaching position. Unfortunately, the events had already run ahead of them! Pushed to the brink of collapse by the massive influx of desperate people, the fabric of social cohesion had, like everywhere else, begun to deteriorate rapidly all over the south of England.

When they arrived, her father discovered some of his old friends had taken flight to Scotland—even to the islands further north or elsewhere, like the Scandinavian countries, or they had chosen to take a voyage to Iceland.

Iceland, overburdened with immigrants, had to all boat peoples' dismay, introduced a complete blockade for new arrivals. Vessels without special permits were being sent back to sea. Torpedoes were unscrupulously used against those boats that did not follow orders or dared to land on remote beaches in the dark of night.

Undeterred by so much bad news and trusting his good connections would serve him, her father had purchased a passage for both of them on a ship destined for Iceland. As it turned out, and to their horror, the ship operated as a slave trader. By the time they had reached the high seas, the guns had come out. All the passengers were stripped of their valuables and identity papers. Those who resisted and old were either killed or mercilessly thrown overboard. The valuable, healthy ones were locked into the hold and shipped to one of the many slave markets that had sprung up along the Baltic coast. After that, Elena never saw her father again!

At first, she was sold to a Swedish weapons merchant, becoming his favoured concubine for the following fifteen months. As long as her youth and beauty kept him enthralled, she lived a life of luxury. Once he had become bored of her and found a suitable replacement, he sold her to a high-class brothel in Stockholm. From there, she tried to escape several times, and for her obstinacy, she repeatedly received severe beatings. Finally, as a warning to others, she was sold off to a remote Nordic mining town known among all female slaves as 'the antechamber of Hell'.

Here, her existence as a prostitute under extremely harsh conditions of starvation and brutality took its toll. She soon became too unattractive even for those desperados slaving in the mines. Elena, now unprofitable, was sold off for a pittance to the slave traders Erick had bought her from two days before. She had simply been reduced to being a food supply for the other slaves on their long trek north.

Erick shuddered at that thought which left him speechless for a long time, his mind occupied with the wildest of imaginations. He had no doubt and knew from his own experiences that running away from chaos does not stop it from happening and eventually would arrive at his doorstep! Having chosen a life in this inhospitable tundra environment, his self-imposed isolation, of wanting nothing to do with the rest of humanity, had been irresponsible in some ways. For fifteen years, he had lived that illusion of being able to leave everything behind before the dreaded reality finally caught up with him.

However, for the moment, he refused to let his mind be taken over by the anguish of the approaching challenges and his own tragic memories.

With some effort, Erick switched his mind off those dark thoughts before he regained his usual optimistic nature. After cleaning the table, he suggested with a broad smile a walk around the estate. His good-natured attitude had an instant, positive influence on Elena, whose emaciated features lit up with a faint smile, giving Erick hope that her spirit had not been wholly extinguished. This open display of optimism, which Erick usually imparted to her in any given situation, would become one of the characteristics she loved most in her new friend. She did not know yet, but as long they were together, she would rely on it to supply her with emotional strength.

The beautiful surroundings of the house among the wooded hills left a positive impression on Elena. During the walk through the under grows, she stumbled several times. Erick had forgotten how frail she still was. He offered her his arm to lean on, which she accepted gratefully. Erick also made sure to point out all his security installations so she would not, by accident, get caught by one of those dangerous traps.

Even though the excursion had taken only half an hour, Erick noticed how much it had exhausted the young girl. He scooped her up and carried her the way back to the house.

On their return, Erick suggested that Elena take another bath with the infusion of some medicinal herbs. He placed her on the divan before he went to fetch the necessary firewood, inspired and carried away with surprising optimism. But before he stroked the match, he hesitated for a moment, asking himself when was the last time he had used that boiler. Would it still hold out against the pressure built up by the steam, not burst and flood the upper level before the girl could take her bath?

Erick himself preferred the cold waters of the nearby creek. Since he had joined the army, he perceived a hot bath as decadent. While the water began to heat up, he scraped the tub again and listened to the ominous gurgling sounds of the decrepit pipework. His luck held out, and finally, the water began to flow, somewhat rusty-coloured but steaming hot nonetheless.

He called out for Elena that the bath was ready, and on her arrival, without any hesitation or inhibition, she began to undress before he could leave the bathroom. How sad, Erick thought, how far degraded she was to feel just like an object.

Erick had no illusions about her recovery process. It would demand a lot of patience from both of them—physical and psychological. Was he really up to such a demanding task without having the skills and insights? But what choice did he have? How he saw it at this moment, it was up to him to focus all his energies on bringing about the optimal restoration of the young woman's former self.

Surprisingly, these thoughts about the unexpected challenge felt invigorating, and his face lit up with a broad smile. Maybe the girl coming into his life was the necessary step out of his isolation and back into society. Lately, he had felt an instinctive desire to reconnect with a form of community for quite some time. His sheltered existence had been an excuse not to deal with his issues and the unavoidable reality of challenges. His choice of not choosing at all led him into isolation instead of freedom, an escape into a lifestyle where choosing had become meaningless! The unexpected new situation was a jolt of intensified meaning!

It appeared that Elena decided to submerge herself for an eternity in the hot, soothing waters of the bathtub. So Erick took the opportunity of rummaging through all the wardrobes and dressers in search of a suitable feminine outfit. The closets were still filled with fancy clothing, and most did not make sense to wear out in the wilderness. The old man had brought with him his complete city attire—most of it badly moth-eaten by now. Only a few items, made of synthetic material, had survived the ravages of time and were still in an acceptable condition.

Apart from a few evening dresses left behind by the old man's illusive female visitors, he had no luck, especially regarding the right underwear style. Ultimately, he chose the most valuable items that would best serve the climatic conditions, expecting the girl to adjust them with a few snips and needlework.

Considering the circumstances, Erick was convinced that female outfits were Elena's most minor concern. The girl was tall and built with a strong frame, so she would quickly fill out the available clothing with a healthy diet.

Erick was surprised by being overcome with mundane thoughts such as the sudden need to fuss about domestic issues like clothing and dresses for a woman. Up here in the northern reaches, keeping warm was the only priority, and vanity could hardly count as a vital factor.

His rumbling stomach reminded him of more pressing issues—what to prepare for dinner. It was still too early in the year for some green salad leaves or whatever else he could grow in the short summer period. However, the range of choices was not great, and neither were his cooking skills. He thought of a hearty meal of fatty reindeer meat and some tinned vegetables.

Erick, feeling slightly disappointed after his foray into all the wardrobes, bundled up the somewhat suitable garments and was ready to leave the upper level when he became aware of the chaos he had left behind. Giving off a few grunts of displeasure, he stuck to his principle of never leaving unfinished business behind. Piling the chosen outfits on the bed first, he returned everything that had landed on the floor back into the wardrobes when he suddenly noticed the steam emanating from the bathroom, slowly penetrating the upper level of the house. Somewhat bemused and chuckling to himself, imagining the girl might have cooked herself into a stew, he carefully opened the door to enquire if she was still alive, upon which he received a pleasant murmuring sound. Smiling and satisfied with his progress, Erick continued with one of his many daily tasks; he went outside to chop for the night's required supply of firewood. Despite the still cool nights, Erick usually stopped heating his place as soon as the snow began to melt, but his new housemate possibly needed more warmth than he did!

Erick loved those simple physical tasks. They helped him clear his mind from nagging irritations.

The trees for firewood were usually cut in winter, enabling him to use a sledge to move the heavy logs. Unfortunately, over the years, it had become necessary to cut down the trees further and further from the house so as not to denude the protective shield they provided for his residence. The task did not stop there. These logs needed sawing into appropriately sized pieces so they could be chopped, reducing his physical labour in the winter month. In response, he devised a contraption by modifying a two-handed saw, which was operable by one man alone. This was just one of many solutions forced on him by his solitary life in the wilderness!

After working up enough sweat for the day, Erick looked forward to the hearty meal of reindeer stew. He had already placed the kettle over the fireplace before leaving the house. The casserole was now bubbling along in its pot, admitting its tantalising aroma throughout the house.

Alas, his task was not finished yet. The chopped pieces of wood needed to be carried into a small shed and stacked up. But, feeling unusually impatient, Erick shook his head. Enough for today, he told himself and left the pile lying in the open, hoping it would stay dry overnight.

When Erick entered the house, he saw Elena lounging on the couch dressed in her new attire. Wearing the old man's oversize shirts, jackets and trousers, it appeared as if she had shrunk. At that sight, he could not help but smile.

'Well, I guess I will have to make you handsomely fitting boots as well to go with your new hunting outfit,' was all he could utter into his beard.

After the meal, Elena needed to retire to her new room to rest, complaining about stomach cramps; she was obviously not yet used to eating a meal heavy on meat. Still, feeling more often than not shaky on her legs, all she could do the following days was eat, bathe and rest.

The process of gaining bodily strength turned out to be slower than both had expected. Elena had been carried along by the enthusiasm of her sudden freedom for the first few days after her rescue. Those energies began to dissipate, reminding her again of her fragility. However, there was no need to push anything. Erick was glad not to have to make any rash decision about how to proceed after her recovery.

So he went along with his usual routine, allowing him the time necessary to contemplate this new situation from every angle. First, he was glad the girl carried no permanent physical damage due to her time as a slave. Erick was convinced she would soon regain her natural physique and strength. However, the healing of her psyche would undoubtedly prove to be a challenge for both of them.

A few weeks later, out and about on his usual hunting trip, Erick came across his hideout on the ridge again. As he had expected, it had been wholly raided of every valuable item and, obviously with a vengeance in mind, also burned down because of the disappointing lack of real valuables!

While busy retrieving his dummy and the old machine gun from a little cave nearby, Erick heard the sound of whinnying horses and shouting humans drifting up from the valley. He was left without a doubt that the usual trickle of new arrivals had now, indeed, turned into a steady flow. The wheel ruts, snaking along the valley ground, appeared more profound and permanent, a sign impossible to ignore, confirming his assumption about the approaching end of his tranquil days in the wilderness.

4
On borrowed time

Erick was pleased with himself. His care and the high protein diet soon began to have a positive effect on the girl's physical constitution, a process supported by the impact of the increasingly warming summer temperature, the growth of wild berries, mushrooms and green shoots, collected and dried, to spice up their diet during the long winter period.

The tundra turned into a wildflower paradise in late summer, supplying Erick with medicinal herbs and some rare wild honey, invaluable to Erick's strict health regime.

By now, Elena had regained her full physical strength, in stark contrast to her psychological conditions, which would suddenly shroud her mind in darkness, forcing her to withdraw from all activities, insurmountable barriers blocking Erick's efforts to aid her.

Those were moments of emotionally demoralising intensity, straining the relationship to the maximum of endurance. It appeared nature intended to hold back Elena's emotional healing until her physical strength was restored. Nightmares were constantly occurring during that phase, forcing her repeatedly to curl up in a foetal position. But even though those moments tested Erick's coping capacities, he interpreted these repeated nightmares as the beginning of an opening-up process and so more or less welcomed them.

Challenging times for both, Erick had initially insisted she should sleep in her own bedroom, withstanding her persistent protest. However, he soon gave up on that arrangement as it happened more than once every night that he heard her screaming in her nightmares, forcing him to run upstairs and calm her down. After coming to terms with the unsustainable situation of missing out on vital sleep, he allowed her to share his bed with him. At first, it appeared as if this new arrangement was a sufficient antidote against Elena's nightly screams. On the other hand, having slept alone for fifteen years, this new arrangement was challenging, if not irritating, for Erick.

It was worse when Elena suddenly clung to him when experiencing one of her bad dreams. Erick, wanting nothing more than for her to heal, saw no choice but to endure the torture for the time being. He convinced himself that the quicker Elena's damaged psyche could be restored, the faster this unbearable arrangement would end!

On the other hand, Erick was careful not to probe into her past, fearing she might feel pressured, causing her to close up completely. He imagined that, under the circumstances, it would be no easy step for her when being asked to reveal her most degrading experiences.

Therefore, Erick made every possible effort to create the right atmosphere for Elena to open up, mainly during the evening when they were lounging comfortably in front of the crackling fire, by soft candlelight, a whisky by his side and entertained by the natural sounds on the outside.

He kept their conversation purposefully mundane, talking about the daily encounters in the wild or their need for future food supplies.

So, it was not surprising to him when she was able to reveal those incidences that had been the cause of her latest nightmare. Also, she could suddenly break off during those sessions and withdraw into herself, leaving him guessing.

To bridge the awkwardness of the moment, Erick would start to talk about his past experiences in the wilderness, his encounters with wolves, bears or the occasional marauding gangs, which mainly ended with some of them being killed and others left behind wounded and possibly soon to be killed by wild beasts. He realised on those occasions how reluctantly he himself was to talk about his life in the city.

Having observed her rapid recovery, Erick expected that Elena would also realise that this harsh and sometimes brutal climate was made for survivors only. Knowing from nightmarish experiences in his past, this extreme environment offered but one choice. She might perish unless her life force re-establish her former self and provides a path out of the darkness.

To support Elena's healing process, Erick used every opportunity to build her confidence, including physical challenges. He had begun to take her on hunting excursions so she could learn how to deal appropriately with the unpredictable and unforgiving wilderness. On those trips, he gave her no chance to ponder her dark past; instead, she had to be constantly alert, listening to the sounds and reading the signs of nature.

At first, Erick prioritised his efforts to establish Elena's hunting skills, repeatedly reminding her of the unforeseeable dangers she could face at any given moment. Skilful self-reliance was paramount, the only guarantee to survive in these lands.

With the slow improvement of her strength and abilities, his training program became more specific but also more confronting and dangerous. It included how to run down wounded deer or wild boar, the slaughter and butchery of the animal on the spot and how to store the meat up in a tree for later recovery, how to climb trees to collect fruits and nuts and also how to escape from roving bears and wolves. And on occasion, he forced her against her loud protests to wade through rivers or swim and hunt for fish in icy cold lakes.

Finnmark's summer periods were short, putting pressure on the few warm months to accomplish as much hunting and gathering and the necessary maintenance work on the house as possible. The midnight sun kept them busy for long hours; this was not the time for pussyfooting around! Hibernation could be left to the dark winter days.

Elena's physical abilities and hunting skills improved rapidly, much to Erick's delight. However, her inner healing appeared to stagnate. But for the moment, it was not on Erick's priority list. One thing after another was his usual motto. He knew the coming long winter nights would allow them plenty of time for soul-searching while they sat around the fireplace.

Erick had had enough experience not to underestimate the will to recover in the young. And on one of those late evenings in autumn, Erick got a surprise. They had curled up in front of the fireplace in their usual manner, resting their weary bones after a hard day of hunting, and were quietly staring into the flames.

Elena, having been in unusually high spirits all day, without a preamble, began to talk about the years she had lived through as a slave. This time her words came without tears or the sound of moodiness, as if she had broken through an invisible barrier.

Occasionally Erick's hair stood up on end on hearing the implicitly detailed descriptions of Elena's life as a prostitute and slave. More than once, he could not hold back his tears. Acting as an observer appeared to help her to lessen the pain. She told her story in the third person and used a different character to act out her narrative, avoiding seeing herself as the protagonist.

To protect her mental state during that storytelling, she created a fantasy world in her mind where she played the role of a princess enslaved by an evil lord or witch. In other situations, she took on the personality of Cinderella.

To avoid beatings and further degradations, she did whatever was necessary without complaint, never lost her will to survive and was constantly looking for opportunities to escape. Despite all her misery, deep down, she still believed that one day the saviour would free her from all her suffering, and all pain would be forgotten.

Unfortunately, in the last month before her rescue, her life as a slave took a turn for the worse and became unbearable. It was a time when her illusions began to evaporate, replaced by desperation and the fear that death was imminent. Elena came close to losing all her will to live!

Seeing Elena open up with such frankness and without suddenly falling back into her usual dark moodiness when she confronted her past, Erick felt a jolt of joy. It was a moment when he started to feel hopeful Elena was on the path to regaining her psychic health.

It was as if a heavy burden had lifted from his shoulders. How many months had he waited for this moment to arrive? So far, survival training and exercises have significantly stimulated her physical health and bodily conditioning. She had become a fast runner, swimmer and fairly good hunter in the four months since he had freed her. From the outside, she had begun to look impressive. Her beautiful feminine features were outstanding to look at. Her thick, black hair, now shiny, had grown long and full. But Erick reminded her again and again without a healthy psyche, she would not be able to deal with the demands of the harsh world out there.

Seeing the impressive physical improvements, Erick encouraged and pushed her to take on new challenges. It was time to take Elena's training up a few notches.

There were, of course, other more obvious reasons. Erick had become increasingly wary and was beginning to fear their hideout would sooner or later come under attack from one of the many marauding bands he encountered when he ventured beyond his usual hunting realm. He needed to condition Elena to be able to stand her own ground in case he was killed, and she needed to escape on her own. However, for now, Erick kept that detail to himself.

As he described it, Erick had been a lieutenant in a Norwegian special forces unit in his previous life. As much as he remembered and was able to, he intended to pass on his skills of martial arts techniques, expecting her to acquire these abilities as fast as possible. By the end of autumn, Erick introduced a gruelling exercise program, seeing she had recovered her full physical strength. He also insisted that in their practice, they used real weapons, which resulted in both of them coming away with bruises and cuts on many occasions.

At times Erick thought he was pushing her too hard, but, despite her fatigue and aching muscles, Elena did not complain once and instead thanked him every evening with a big smile for his relentless efforts to build up her self-esteem. Afterwards, she usually submerged herself in a hot bath and sometimes even dispensed with the evening meal, going straight to bed instead.

However, Erick also noticed specific behaviour changes in Elena, which began to irritate him. As far as he was concerned, their relationship was purely platonic; he was the mentor, and she was the apprentice, end of story! But lately, he noticed she was giving him these irritating looks and vibes that usually someone in love does impart.

Over the following weeks, the situation became increasingly uncomfortable for Erick; he would have preferred to wrestle with a bear or shed the blood of an enemy.

The temperature, still a balmy twenty degrees at noon, made it possible to go swimming every morning. It had never seemed necessary for either to wear anything but their bare skin. But, on one of these occasions, Elena suddenly wound her body around his own and pressed her lips to his mouth. Erick was well prepared, alert for quite some time and expecting the worst. He lifted her gently in his arms and carried her onto the shore, laying her down on the soft, sunbathed, warm grass. The girl, excitedly expecting their first sexual encounter, wiggled her body in anticipation. Seeing her expression of love and desire, Erick nearly burst out laughing. Trying to keep a straight face without giving away anything, he slowly spoke, displaying a slight discomfort in his voice and only too aware of the expected disappointment on her part.

'Dear Elena, I truly love you but I am not in love with you. To me you are like a daughter; you are my student and I am your teacher. Until now, I was only concerned with your recovery and wellbeing, but soon I will tell you my own story so you may understand me better. For now, hear one thing: I am a man who desires only men! I love women and I am a great admirer of their beauty. Putting my own personal preference to one side, I actually see them as the most beautiful creation nature has ever come up with, but I have no sexual desire for them. And I am truly sorry for disappointing you, my dear Elena.'

For a moment, she was quiet, staring out onto the lake's calm waters, then she suddenly threw her arms around him, sobbing heavily and clinging to him as if he could slip away at any moment. He sat there holding her gently, letting her have this soul-cleansing time.

Elena gazed at him with her beautiful dark eyes, now all teary, then began to kiss him all over his face, only stopping when a cold breeze blew towards them from across the water, returning them both to their physical presence.

Erick was glad that the issue of his homosexuality had finally been cleared up, and he now felt foolish for not having told her much earlier. Then again, he had seen no reason why he would need to explain himself to anyone about what he had been all his life.

Unfortunately, Erick's desire for a relaxed atmosphere between them in all matters sensual did not come to much. To the contrary! Elena now saw no reason to hold back with her 'sisterly love', as she called it. From that day on, she crawled into his bed every night, uninvited, for all kinds of reasons: being scared of the howling wolves, feeling cold, or having nightmares. In truth, she just wanted to cuddle up to him and feel safe.

Erick saw no alternative to dealing with the situation other than just giving in. After fifteen years of solitude, he would have to learn to share his bed again with another human being. Furthermore, until now, Erick had been cagey about his troubled past, avoiding opening old wounds. But she had begun to pester him to tell his story, claiming that, after having revealed herself, she had equally the right to know about his history. Yet he was surprised by how difficult it felt to warm to the idea.

Soon the short autumn came and went. For a few weeks, nature exploded overnight into all shades of red and orange before the first snowstorm swept the show away. The days shortened, and the sun struggled to stay above the horizon.

Lying in front of the warming fireplace became their preferred evening pleasure, accompanied by one or two glasses of his beloved single malt whisky. Erick, observing anxiously the rapidly dwindling stock of his comforting elixir, saw it as another sign that their time at the lodge might come soon to its end!

Before Elena's arrival, he had indulged in his nightly habit rather sparingly, but now in her company, he enjoyed drinking one or two glasses every night. Her presence had brought an end to his monkish existence, which also began to influence what had, until now, been his rather bland cuisine. Elena turned out to have a talent for a more refined style of food preparation than he had.

On one of those nights, when he had just finished the last two glasses of a twenty-five-year-old single malt Highland Scotch whisky, adding his fifteen years of residency to it, making it forty years of age, Erick felt suddenly somewhat sentimental.

He began to tell his story. This time he needed no probing from Elena.

He grew up in Oslo; his mother was a biochemist, and his father was a colonel in the Norwegian army. Despite his father's insistence, Erick had no intention of following in his footsteps to join the army. After his short military service, he began to study physics and mechanical engineering, specialising in robotics, but halfway through his third semester, he saw the writing on the wall. Europa was slowly sinking into chaos, brought on by the rapid climate changes, disrupting transport and infrastructure, resulting in a food supply shortage and riots. Civil societies' structures began to deteriorate, already undermined by many years of corruption, and the disappearing funds for social services hastened the collapse of governmental rule. Martial law was declared to hold the slide into anarchy. Still, with the disappearance of a functioning monetary system, the remaining security units soon abandoned their posts, allowing lawlessness to spread all over Europa and possibly throughout the planet.

Displaced, desperate people had forged their way towards the north for many years to escape civil war, famine, droughts and rampant plagues devastating Africa and the Middle East. But now the trickle had begun to turn into a flood, sweeping away what until now had been perceived as the tight border control against illegal immigration, usually reinforced with heavily armed military units, who were given the right to shoot until the news about the indiscriminate slaughter of civilians ended the mission. Consequently, the gates were thrown wide open, and following the mass invasions, the administrations of the European countries collapsed, one after the other.

Under those dire circumstances, Erick saw no hope in the continuum of his academic ambitions and decided it was time to pursue a more pragmatic career path. He re-joined the army, volunteering to train with a special forces unit, a sensible solution, as the demand for security personnel skyrocketed all over the continent.

Erick as a lieutenant, and his sergeant, were assigned to stop people-smuggling organisations. During those months in the military training camp, the sergeant became the love of his life, and soon after, they were posted together on the Norwegian south coast as a last attempt to hold off the human tide. Despite the overwhelming human wave, Erick and his partner, true to their principles and loyal to their vow, stayed in position for a few more months with a few faithful men on their side, soon after their commanding officers had left. They lost complete control over the border. Their defence lines slowly turned into a rear-guard battle. Erick tried to maintain the discipline to the end, but his company, depleted by desertion and lacking clear orders from above, fell apart and scattered. In the ensuing chaos, the governmental institutions began to falter.

From then on, it was every man for himself. Erick and his partner were able to acquire a military truck, stacking it with as many supplies from the barracks' stores as they could get their hands on. Of course, competition for any kind of hardware became intense. Fights over the spoils broke out regularly, especially among those soldiers who had planned to carve out their own security operations.

Erick and his partner decided to move as far north as possible, away from the chaos around the metropolitan area of Oslo. They hoped to settle among those people who were still applying themselves to reasonable levels of social order. But they soon discovered the disintegration had already spread like cancer while they had stood diligently on guard on the southern coastline. Contrary to their beliefs, the situation worsened further north they travelled. Here marauding bands became a constant threat. Being highly trained in all aspects of close combat and heavily armed, they managed to fight them off repeatedly until their luck ran out. About halfway towards their planned destination, at a tight bend in the coastal road, their truck was ambushed by a troop of twelve men. Despite the overwhelming odds of two against the many, they fought vigorously, killing or wounding most of their adversaries, with only a few managing to escape. Unfortunately, both of them got injured during the battle. Erick could pull the truck out of the melee, racing ahead desperately to find a hospital for his mortally wounded friend; it was all Erick could do. By the time he reached a still-functioning hospital, his partner was dead. Winter was approaching fast! There was no time to mourn. After he had had his wounds taken care of and his lover cremated, Erick continued his travels north, hoping to reach the previously marked-out place before it began snowing.

The trip became even more perilous when he ran out of diesel oil, and without a petrol station in sight, Erick was forced to trade his truck in for a couple of horses and a cart. Unfortunately, the wagon could only accommodate a fraction of his equipment and provisions. However, in the northern reaches, sought-after products like military hardware fetched the excellent price of five ounces of gold.

Not long after he had left the trading station, the first snow began to fall, and the wolf packs could be heard roaming along his trail, waiting for the weary travellers who might succumb to the cold or simply get lost in the unfamiliar terrain.

The snow layers began to thicken, and Erick had no choice but to trade his cart for a sledge. Again, he had to discard some of his stock, so the horses could pull through the still-wet layer of snow. This time the bargaining did not turn out in his favour. When the weather worsened, Erick was forced to take shelter from an approaching snowstorm at a remote farmhouse. The following morning, having woken up from an alcohol-induced stupor, Erick discovered that the farmer and his wife had taken off with his horses, his sledge and most of his equipment. The apparent friendly couple had plied him generously with vodka and listened hungrily to his news from the south the night before.

After so many mishaps, Erick was ready to accept reality in any kind of form. Having lost his mode of transport and feeling too inexperienced to track during winter through these northern parts of the country on foot, Erick decided to hunker down at the farmhouse until spring, expecting to fight off wolves and marauding criminals during his residency. As the farmers made off in a hurry, they had left plenty of grain and dried fruit, which Erick supplemented with the occasional game he managed to hunt down.

As spring arrived, Erick went on his way, the old man's hideout marked on a map. He had a rough idea of where he was going. But after the string of misfortunes behind him, Erick kept his optimism at bay; there was no assurance if the old man was still alive. After all, nearly ten years had passed since he had visited the hunting lodge with his father. Those had been orderly and comfortable days. They had arrived by helicopter. Erick knew no roads were leading to this remote place in one of the furthest reaches of Finnmark. Trusting in his excellent military maps, he had no doubt of finding his way to that place. Besides, he learned to navigate the landscape with or without maps during his military training.

However, nothing could have prepared him for the disappointment he encountered on his arrival!

5
Under siege

By now, it had been nearly two years since Elena's arrival. Her second spring was marked by the return of the wild geese. Here and there, green shoots were breaking through the crusty snow. These were dangerous times! They could not rely anymore on fresh snowfalls overnight to cover their previous tracks.

Erick was reluctant to go on extensive hunting trips while leaving Elena alone. Once again, it was time for newcomers to pass through the land. Those marauding groups could easily stumble across their footprints, leading them unwittingly to Erick's hidden residence.

Having gone on a hunting trip together, Erick and Elena had left the house as usual in the dark, just before dawn. Wrapped up in their fur coats, they were now lying in hiding overlooking a large clearing, boggy from the melting snow and featuring a large, ice-free pond in the middle—the watering hole for the resident wild beasts!

The day before, Erick had spotted the track of a moose nearby. He was hoping that the animal was still hanging around. The birch trees were heavy with fresh buds, and the patchy snowdrifts exposed the first shoots of groundcover, favourable conditions that could attract a grazing animal.

For smaller prey, they usually used their bows and arrows. Two arrows were generally sufficient to bring down smaller game, and Elena, having surpassed her teacher by now in marksmen ship, often managed to kill the target with her first shot. But for a large animal like a moose, Erick would have to use his high-powered rifle.

Erick was counting on the time of the day, expecting no one to hunt so early in the morning. Of course, a gunshot was a dangerous giveaway that could be heard for miles, alerting humans and wolves alike. Their excitement grew when, suddenly, a moose emerged from the thicket, a young bull attracted by nature's fresh offerings.

As usual, Erick felt a sense of reluctance before bringing down such a beautiful beast as he admired the animal's assuredness of being one with its environment. But his hunting instincts took over as the excitement of having such a rare opportunity arose. The creature appeared in a perfect position for a straight shot through the heart.

A sudden volley of gunshots broke the spell, hitting the beast in the chest and bringing it to its knees before another shot, shattering the head, finished it off.

A moment later, two men dressed in white padded jackets and hoods displaying Russian army insignias entered the clearing. One of them blew a whistle, and a third man on a dog sledge arrived shortly after. Erick was swearing quietly into his beard, not so much about the missed opportunity but expressing his relief of having escaped from being discovered.

How could he have missed those intruders? Where did they come from so suddenly? What was worse, there was the possibility that these men might have noticed their tracks, even though Erick and Elena had carefully circumvented all snowdrifts on their way. The only thing they could hope for was that this troop of soldiers was on the march towards a specific destination, and they had come across the moose's imprints by pure luck. However, hunting for such a large beast indicated they were possibly part of an extensive unit of soldiers. Otherwise, why would they want to burden themselves with so much meat while on the move?

Erick felt suddenly ill at ease by the unexpected turn of events. Usually, he could hide his anxiety from Elena, who had started to read him like an open book. But to his dismay, this time, the signs were written all over his face and were expressed in his rushed movements. Stepping into their earlier tracks, they retreated quietly, hoping for a sudden weather change, which would, with any luck, obliterate any imprints they left behind.

Never before had Erick seen Russian military units penetrating so far west since he resided in this part of the north—they usually went south along the Baltic coast for better spoils. The only thing that could explain their movements was that trouble was brewing across the border in the east, causing the troops to disperse in all directions. This encounter could possibly be the first of many to follow.

Unfortunately, it would be a dinner of dried reindeer meat again, and, as a precautionary measure, they would do without a fire for warmth or cooking. A smoking wood fire could easily be smelled for miles on these cold nights.

To their relief, it began to snow again—only lightly, but maybe enough to cover their tracks. Erick kept to himself all day, not saying much while his mind was busily mulling over concerns for their safety. Such moodiness irritated Elena to the hilt; after all, she was an adult and regarded him as her partner. But she had also learned not to pester him. In situations like this, Erick usually fell back into a kind of survival mode, which he had relied on for so long; tense, highly alert and ready to strike. This morning's encounter indicated it was time to make the necessary preparations so they were able to move in an instant.

Erick spent the rest of the day inspecting the traps around the house, repairing defective parts, loading all the guns and checking their functionality. He locked the shutters and bolted all the doors but one. When he asked Elena to accompany him on his inspection of the escape tunnel, she at first refused, claiming to be scared of its claustrophobic tightness, the spider webs and all the small scurrying animals that had taken shelter there over the wintertime. But when Erik told her with a stern face that her life would depend on it, she followed him without further words, closing her eyes and holding on to him.

Erick felt sure the need to run could come any day, but where would they go?

From now on, they avoided using firearms when hunting. Gunshots could be heard in this quiet and sparsely wooded terrain for miles. It was back to the old-fashioned mode of crossbow and bow and arrow.

In most cases, the chance of killing a sizeable animal outright with an arrow was unlikely. Usually, what followed was long-winded tracking along the trail of blood. However, the competition was not to be underestimated; wolves and bears could smell blood over long distances, and sometimes by the time they reached the carcass, the leftovers were not worth fighting for.

Having spent hours in wait, they finally managed to shoot down a young pig. They were lucky; shot at close range, the arrow had penetrated deep, the animal did not get very far before it collapsed, and a knife blade to its heart ended it. Tied to a pole, they carried it over their shoulders. When it came to larger animals, they would usually divide up the carcass, taking the most valuable pieces on their first trip home, and deposit the remainder high up in a tree to be picked up on the following day. This was not necessarily an absolutely secure location, lynx were excellent climbers, and crows could turn up in large numbers.

Their spirits ran high on their way home in anticipation of the meal of freshly roasted boar that night. When suddenly, about a mile from their home, a gunshot could be heard from the direction they were heading. Erick was sure that the sound had been triggered by one of his shotgun traps. Both fearing the worst, they increased their pace.

Now confronted with the unexpected, they left the boar hanging from a tree branch and fell into a fast trot. As they approached the lodge's vicinity, more traps were going off, followed by screams of agony. Orders were shouted in Russian, and barking dogs could be heard from different directions. Obviously, the traps had worked efficiently, but many had also managed to get past them.

Erick, had no doubt they were dealing with a sizeable troop of attackers. Nearing the house, they fell to the ground and began to crawl, carefully negotiating the traps and spiked ditches securely camouflaged by the undergrowth. Two more gun traps went off, accompanied by screams. Erick asked Elena to stay behind while he crawled towards the house. What he saw made his blood boil, but he had to remain calm. It was essential to think clearly now and to react with decisiveness. The visibility among the trees gradually lessened as the sun was slowly setting.

In the dim light, recognising friend or foe became difficult, giving Erick and Elena a chance to reach the secret tunnel entrance without being caught.

The soldiers had begun to use their rifle butts to break down the locks but were getting increasingly frustrated that their violent efforts were having no effect on the heavy wooden doors. It was now too late for Erick and Elena to defend their home, and it would be suicidal to attack such a large group of invaders equipped with superior firepower.

While they carefully circumvented the place until they reached the entrance to the tunnel, Erick felt a sudden bout of emotional pain over the loss and imminent destruction of his house. It increased his determination not to leave without making a stand, swearing to himself those men would pay for their invasion.

Elena refused to stay behind while he entered the house through the tunnel. She wanted to be part of the action. So Erick gave in without reply; there was no time for arguments. Footsteps could now be heard on the floorboards above; no doubt the ransacking of the place had begun.

Erick had calmed down somewhat. He needed a cool head to prepare a sufficient counteroffensive. Also, time was not on their side. It would not take long before the trapdoor, hidden under a carpet, was discovered. The most important thing now was getting supplies into their rucksacks and as many weapons and ammunition as they could carry.

The painful-sounding destruction upstairs was getting louder and more violent. While Elena packed the essentials, Erick searched for a special wooden box, labelled unmistakably 'dynamite'.

With a sudden smirk, he exclaimed excitedly, 'Oh, I'd completely forgotten that I had more than one of them. I used them in winter when I came across a wolf's pack on my way home carrying the game. One or two of these sticks would be enough to scatter them in all directions. They might be equally effective against a pack of marauding soldiers here and now.'

They finished filling their rucksacks with all the valuable items the basement could provide. To Erick's dismay, a bottle of whisky was not among them. He positioned the dynamite sticks in different locations so the resulting explosions would have the most damaging effect, placing a significant number below the trapdoor. Then, he began to roll the fuse out along the tunnel.

Outside they quickly crawled under a thick layer of branches to protect themselves from the danger of being hit by flying objects. Not far from their hiding place, they spotted the glimmer of a cigarette among the trees; possibly, a soldier posted to guard the dog sledges. With a last look at his beloved lodge, Erick ignited the fuse, then waited excitedly for the explosion to blow the house and the invaders into oblivion.

Four explosions, each following the other at short intervals, shook the ground. Obviously, the explosives store in that basement had been much more extensive than Erick had anticipated. 'And in all these years, I slept on top of that,' he mumbled to himself.

Large rocks and flaming debris rained down all around them. Their thick branch covering proved very valuable, softening the impact of the missiles. The explosion had flattened everything nearby that had previously stood upright. Torn trees were burning all around the ruined house. Flying splinters had wounded or killed everyone in the open near the lodge. The soldier on guard by the dog sledges came running towards the carnage when Erick shot him at point-blank range.

The explosions sent the dogs into a complete barking frenzy. In the darkness, deepened by the burning ruin, it was impossible to tell how many invaders were still alive. Erick and Elena did not waste any time rushing towards the sledges, where the demoralised animals had already begun to turn on each other, pulling the reins in all directions. There were more than twenty sledges. Erick cut all ropes holding the dogs, apart from the two they intended to use for themselves and watched the animals disappear instantly into the night.

There were many surprises. Conveniently using one of the burning branches for illumination, they quickly rummaged through the provisions the soldiers had brought along. They selected the most suitable items for their journey: top-grade weaponry, ammunition, food conserves and, to their surprise and delight, a considerable hoard of gold coins— possibly stolen from a Russian museum. This fortune would help them to acquire whatever would be needed on their travels and more than replace Erick's store of valuables, which had been lost in the explosion.

Whatever they had to leave behind, including the sledges, Erick piled up and set alight with the hope of slowing down any of the troops that might follow, but he also saw it as a kind of retribution for his losses.

While they loaded up their equipment, Erick heard sounds of agony coming from different locations surrounding the still-burning ruin. Without a doubt, a few of the attackers were still alive, now lying in their own blood, begging for help. He was sure they would not make it through the night because of their devastating wounds.

Despite his anger towards them, he wished for no one to be ripped apart by a pack of hungry wolves that would, without a doubt, very soon take up the scent of blood and the burned flesh of the dead. So he went back into the carnage. Here Erick came across five mortally wounded men, some missing limbs and others bleeding from numerous wounds. Their eyes were marked by terror and agony, and everyone was begging to be relieved from their misery. So, without hesitation, Erick shot every one of them in the head.

Soon they were on their way, collecting the wild boar from the tree, cracking their whips, spurring on the dogs, intending to put as much distance between the bloodbath and the painful memory of their lost paradise. The howling of wolves could already be heard in the distance.

6
Flight

It could be assumed that the unit of soldiers, which had ransacked their home, was only a scouting party, with a large troop most likely following behind.

They were now in a precarious situation as they traversed the wilderness; scouts could easily pick up their tracks. All they could hope for was a sudden cold spell and a lot of snowfall to obliterate their sledge ruts completely. On the other hand, sudden snowmelt would force them to continue on foot, slowing them down considerably. Whatever their chances, their survival depended on the mileage between them and their possible pursuers.

Standing on the back of his sledge and cracking the whip above the dogs, Erick thought through all the possible scenarios his pursuers might attempt to undertake, all depending on a still functioning chain of command, in which case the situation for both of them could become highly perilous.

Erick still did not understand why a sizeable military troop would move so far north into such inhospitable terrain where there was nothing to gain, food and other resources were hard to come by, insufficient to feed many soldiers. The only answer Erick had for himself was that the situation further south must have severely deteriorated. Those men might have been driven by the promises of opportunities in the north instead of competing with the many for the dwindling resources in the south. However, from here, it was not far from where the icy waters of the polar sea would wash around your ankles.

It had been well known for many years that northern Siberia had become the refuge for the nations from central Asia, which were escaping from desertification and driven on by the overwhelming push from the Indian subcontinent. During those migrations, only the European part of the Russian Federation managed to stem the tide from the east and south. But it could be assumed that the administration had succumbed to the same chaos that had already undermined all institutions everywhere else on the continent.

One could expect the moral standards held by these troops to be of the lowest kind. Undoubtedly their aspirations did not differ from those migrating fortune seekers travelling up the Norwegian coast; a flood of lawlessness heading northward eventually ending up at the North Cape with no further to go! Erick and Elena were under no illusions about what to expect ahead of them. The waves of migrants might have been moving towards the north for many years but had, until now, magically passed by Erick's idyllic residence.

These men and women had already gone through the culling processes in the big metropolises in the south during the previous twenty years. After coming to terms, like many others, with the fact that there were no prospects left for them to carve out a decent living, they went on their way into the unknown, driven by hope and unrealistic expectations. They were doubtless the toughest and most ruthless. Thousands perished, having to dodge pirates and highwaymen on the road. And when they finally reached the coast of the polar sea, they were stunned by their inhospitable destination! All those who made it that far were survivors, knowing they had nothing to lose!

What drew most of them to this place was that there was money to make! Now that the ice cap had disappeared, the sea was open for exploitation, offering plenty of fish stocks and other ocean creatures for the take. Every trawler in the northern hemisphere, who could still manage to find diesel oil, was now heading in this direction to cash in on the hoped-for bonanza.

Without a doubt, the Norwegian and Siberian harbour towns had become the new frontier, a situation not dissimilar to the lawlessness the gold rush in the Wild West of America had created in the nineteenth century.

Alas, there was one big difference in comparison to those golden eras of the past: the wild north might offer a new playground for the adventurous and the fittest. But this time, the stream of new arrivals would not cease, and when the toughest of the toughest had no further to go, what would happen when they were forced to pitch against each other?

Both had no illusions about the grim prospects offered by their path. They had lived a dream hidden from reality. Like everyone else without a place to hide, they were just about to be thrown into the chaos of the new world order.

However, their advantages over the newcomers included knowledge of the terrain and how to survive under harsh climatic conditions. In their current situation, possibly pursued by a large military host, Erick and Elena even considered at one point in their travel to escape towards the south instead of to the north and into middle Europa. Norway was small, and anything was possible with a bounty on their heads. But for now, that was all speculation and lots of maybes. As long they kept moving and covered their trails, they might be saved from their pursuers.

Erick was suddenly driven out of his contemplations when his sledge, jumping over a hump, was turned over, throwing him into the thick undergrowth. Luckily, besides a few scratches and bruises, he had no serious injuries. While swearing profusely because of his stupidity, he reloaded his sledge, and they pushed on. But it had been a sign that the ground was beginning to lose sufficient snow cover. After a few days, it would be near the end of April, the sledges finally lost their usefulness.

Dog sledges were sought-after items, fetching premium prices, even at the end of winter. They sold whatever they could not carry at a trading post. Paid for in gold and silver chunks, undoubtedly the new currency of the north! Soon they would reach the coast, where they could mingle with other travellers, which did not make their situation less troublesome.

Erick now regretted not having investigated the surrounding area of his residence more thoroughly after the explosion for survivors who could report about the two people who had taken off with the sledges and the gold. In hindsight, selling the dog sledges and their surplus might also have added to the precariousness of their situation. These items could easily be identified, linked to them and inform on the direction they had taken. Erick realised, to his dismay, he had for too long trusted in his luck and was entirely out of touch with his former military training. But now was no time for regrets; they had to find a secure hiding place as quickly as possible until they could find a boat to take them out of there!

To put his mind at ease, Elena assured him they had done everything possible to put as much mileage behind them as they could during the previous week. So far, nothing indicated they had been followed as they had acted to the best of their abilities, not to mention the inhospitable environment and all the drama that was going on around them! Elena gave him a big hug and a smothering kiss, knowing it would make him extremely uncomfortable and laughing at his protest in response. But Erick, under his thick skin, was grateful for her comforting gesture.

It was late afternoon; on the descent towards the coastal plains, navigating the thick low scrub, Erick's instincts went suddenly on high alert. He was sure they were being observed and followed for quite some time. He had felt ill at ease and the hair on his back rising up. Living for so long in solitary isolation, having only nature as his master, his senses had become remarkably fine-tuned over the years—an ability impossible to acquire through a technical training program.

Just seconds after he had told Elena to duck and keep low among the bushes, the hail of bullets went over their heads. Sounding out the guns, Erick counted five shooters. They had rushed in, sure of their victory without proper aim, as soon they had spotted their target. Erick and Elena could use these shortcomings on their enemy's part to their advantage. They were obviously impatient and under an incompetent command.

Erick left Elena in her position to cover for him while crawling through the thick undergrowth, intending to attack their pursuers from the rear. It was the first time Erick had to trust Elena completely to perform in battle. To his great pleasure, she had become an excellent marksman, never missing a target. She would never waste a bullet unless she was sure about the kill. The memory of her time as a slave had led her to develop a bloodlust towards anyone threatening her or her friend. At times, Erick thought his training might have been too efficient, seeing Elena showing no hesitation in making a kill when necessary!

He slowly crawled towards the enemies' positions while Elena tried to flush them out of their hiding with a few well-aimed bullets. The five men had begun to fan out while carelessly lifting their heads above the scrub, two targets for Elena's superb marksmanship. This time Erick wanted to make sure no one got away with sending a report about who they were or where they were going.

He intended to use his knife instead of his gun, silently cutting the throats of his victims one by one. His plan did not work out. Dismayed, he realised the labyrinth of thick tussocks provided an equal covering for his adversaries too. In the end, he saw no other possibility than to expose himself and trusting in the layers of books functioning as his bulletproof vest, he suddenly stood up, hoping that Elena would take a shot.

A volley of bullets hit Erick in the chest, where he was protected, but one hit the elbow of his right arm. Momentarily stunned, he went down and fell flat on his back. He could not feel his lower arm, and he was bleeding, but the books had saved his vital organs. The use of the knife was now out of the question, so he used his left hand to pull out his handgun instead. To his delight, Elena had taken advantage of their enemies' exposure and shot two more of them. Only one more to go, she called out to Erick when she noticed a movement in the top branches leading away from her. She waited, making sure he was escaping in a straight line before she aimed just below where the branches had moved. The man threw his arms up and disappeared. When she reached him, he was still alive, so all she could do was cut his throat.

Elena checked quickly that none of the other soldiers was still alive before she returned to Erick, who was not quite sure if he felt dizzy from the pain and blood loss or from Elena's impressive performance, asking himself had it been his teaching to fight with such ruthlessness or an inherited savage instinct? Seeing Erick in such a bad condition, Elena close to tears was now fussing over him.

The elbow was shattered entirely—not a clean shot through—destruction caused by one of those hollow bullets designed to cause maximum damage. Elena's considerable efforts to stop the bleeding were only partly successful, leaving her no choice but to tie a tourniquet around Erick's upper arm and support the arm in a comfortable sling. They both knew if the wound did not get medical attention soon, his lower right arm would have to be amputated.

It was still about ten miles from their position to the coastal town of Tana Bru, usually no big deal for a healthy person, but under the circumstances, it would become a challenge. Checking on their assailants' possessions, they collected all the ammunition. Before taking off, they rested their nerves and ate some of their provisions. Intending to lighten Erick's burden, Elena carried as much of his equipment as possible.

Dusk soon fell, and trekking through the thicket became even more arduous. Nonetheless, Elena pushed ahead relentlessly, being only too well aware of the precarious situation they were in. When Erick began to struggle, she lightened his burden even more and, in the end, carried all their equipment, feeling nothing but the urge to find medical help.

Erick had a rough idea of where they were going. He had once visited that place when it was still a tiny fishing village, but by now, it had grown into an extensive, overcrowded, squalid settlement. The ramshackle buildings lining the one-street town of the early days were now reaching far into the hills and sprawled across the river. The harbour was dotted with lights from numerous vessels of all sizes and nationalities. Even now, at dusk, the streets were busy, shops were open, and deals were being made. Everyone was going somewhere or had come from somewhere, but all were strangers to each other. In response to the increasingly squalid conditions, most of the former inhabitants had left in frustration, either moving further north or into the hinterland.

Unsavoury characters were loitering everywhere: drifters, outlaws and doubtlessly, many serious criminals. However, when they entered the town, people moved cautiously aside; people in fur coats coming in from the wild and heavily armed were better left alone. The wilderness people were known for their ruthless toughness. Those men and women knew how to fight against wolves and bears and endure starvation periods under unusually harsh climatic conditions. Messing with these characters usually leads to a fatal outcome for the aggressor.

By nightfall, they had reached the middle of town. Erick could now barely stand up and refused to walk any further. He sank down on a bench in front of one of the shops lining the street, selling and dealing with just about everything. Seeing no other option than finding a medical doctor, Elena went to the very next door. A big, Mediterranean-looking woman stood behind the counter with arms as thick as a sumo wrestler. Masses of long, black hair covered her shoulders and ample bosom. Elena was slightly repulsed by her extreme unattractiveness and mean appearance. After hesitating, she was ready to turn around and leave when the woman addressed her in a melodic voice in Spanish-accented English. Elena stopped in her tracks, smiled in response and addressed the woman in Spanish, receiving a broad, warm smile and a heartfelt, *'Buenas Noches.'*

'Señora Mendoza. ¿Cómo estás? ¿Puedo ayudar?' she introduced herself. However, for Elena, this was no time for niceties. She quickly explained her desperate situation in a few Spanish words and added she would love to return later for a lengthy conversation. Still, for now, she needed a doctor immediately for her wounded friend sitting outside the shop!

Señora Mendoza explained that there were two doctors in town; one for animals and one for people. Both could perform any necessary operation—which usually involved removing bullets, stitching up stab wounds or amputating limbs. Both were expensive and had long queues in front of their surgeries day and night. Also, the people's physician was the more expensive one.

Fortunately for Elena, he was a good acquaintance of Señora Mendoza and owed her big time. Without further words, she offered to take them there immediately while calling out to the back for her husband to attend the shop for a while. To Elena's surprise, a small, charming man appeared, greeting her warmly.

When the two women stepped out of the shop, Erick was lying nearly unconscious on the floor. Unable to stand up alone, he was helped along on each side by the two strong women, moaning in pain.

Two heavily armed men were guarding the front door of the surgery. Señora Mendoza explained that the guards were posted there for one reason: the physician, one of the most sought-after professionals in town, ran a very lucrative practice and consequently had become one of the wealthiest men in town.

They were asked to leave all their weaponry at the front desk. To Elena's surprise, the surgery was very well-staffed and professionally run. A fact that proved once again money could buy anything, even in this remote part of the continent.

When she noticed Elena's hesitation to leave her weapons and possessions, Señora Mendoza assured her she had nothing to worry about. She vouched for their safety before leading Elena and Erick up the stairs into the surgery. As one could expect in such a place, no regular hours were kept here. The steaming hot waiting room was filled with the injured and the wretched; some were drugged, semi-conscious or moaning in their pain, and others were wealthy looking and possibly after more than just a consultation.

Fortunately for Erick, Señora Mendoza, taking no notice of the protesting voices, pushed ahead in front of those who had possibly already waited for hours. Luckily, the doctor was still consulting—even at this late hour. At first, he was not willing to prioritise Erick's case over and above all the other patients, despite Erick's precarious condition. A few heated words were exchanged before Señora Mendoza called them to follow her into a second surgery room.

The doctor was a short, wiry man, similar in appearance to Mr Mendoza, with dark, piercing eyes behind gold-rimmed glasses. He offered no smile, no conciliatory gesture; he asked them straight away if they could pay in gold or precious stones. Otherwise, he would not proceed any further with his consultation.

Her new friend informed Elena about the kind of expected payment, so she presented the surgeon with a handful of Russian gold coins.

Nodding in agreement, the doctor examined Erick's arm and, after a few minutes, came up with the diagnosis, confirming Elena's worst fears, which she had harboured all along. The doctor made it clear there was nothing he could do to fix the splintered elbow and, to avoid the risk of gangrene and other complications, the lower arm needed to be amputated above the elbow straight away.

While preparing his tools and the anaesthetics, his assistant weighed the gold to ensure no disputes would occur afterwards. Only then did the doctor set about amputating the arm. Erick, by now delirious and oblivious to the whole situation, was given a dose of morphine. In these parts of the country, morphine was extremely expensive. A vial traded for half an ounce of gold. The drug would be available for the operation only. Afterwards, Erick would have to cope without it. Painkillers might be purchased on the open market for the right price until the healing process is complete, or they would have to find other means of dealing with the painful aftereffects. Already on the verge of a mental breakdown, Elena became utterly horrified at that prospect.

While Erick was slowly losing consciousness, both women were asked to return to the waiting room. At first, Elena insisted on staying by Erick's side throughout the procedure. Following the doctor's demand, Señora Mendoza convinced her that it might not be a good idea to be burdened with the memory of that operation right now. Elena began to cry. It became too much for her to comprehend that the man who meant everything to her, whom she loved more than she had ever loved someone, had now become a cripple. Señora Mendoza listened patiently to the young woman blaming herself for having failed to protect her friend. He was the man who had risked his life for her, who had brought her back from nothingness and restored her to her former self. How could she have let that happen to him?

Elena's mind was in turmoil. She was suddenly swamped by a wave of anger towards the doctor. How could this man, a professional who had vowed to save lives, act more or less like a mercenary! But, had she, not herself, experienced enough cruelty and debasement in the past to realise that this was the new normal? Then she cried again for judging this man harshly; after all, he was her only hope for Erick's recovery.

After the operation, Erick was rolled out and placed in a nursing room, and the doctor asked her to return the next day. Erick would have to spend the night at the surgery under his observation. Even so, Elena knew there was nothing she could do for her friend, she reluctantly left him behind. Again it was on behalf of Señora Mendoza's insistence that Elena finally agreed. Under the circumstances, the surgery was, for the moment, the best place for her friend to be, and she was somehow pleased that this service was part of the care procedure.

Elena had planned to find a place to stay nearby, but Señora Mendoza would have nothing of it and insisted that she should stay with her. She was highly excited to have the young woman as her guest. It had been quite a while since Señora had spoken Spanish; she also expected to hear some exciting news and interesting stories as a bonus.

After a sumptuous dinner cooked by Señora Mendoza's husband, both women retired to a comfortable lounge.

Wrapped in blankets, they sat in front of a large fireplace. The night was long, and Elena was in no condition to sleep. Much to Señora Mendoza's delight, there was much to talk about.

A precious bottle of wine had been opened, and Elena managed to forget the turmoil of the past few weeks—especially the previous day. But in the back of her mind, Elena could not help agonising all night about Erick's condition.

Both women returned to the surgery together in the early morning hours. Erick had now caught a high fever, which had been expected, and he was moving in and out of consciousness. Under the circumstances, Elena worried for good reasons that her friend's life might be in danger. She dared not imagine a life without Erick. Terrifying days passed, and Elena knew she would have broken down without Señora Mendoza's emotional support.

Every morning they went to the markets together, searching for fresh meat, fish and vegetables. Afterwards, they would cook a strengthening brew and spoon it slowly into the bedridden Erick. But they were not always so lucky. Demand outstripped supply on most days, occasionally forcing Elena to hunt in the hills behind the town on her own. Such an undertaking was not without danger. Not only did she have to contest with the roaming wolves but also with other hunters supplying the markets.

These were not wilderness people who lived by a specific code of conduct. They were townspeople who did not apply any fairness in their hunt for game. Especially when it came to a female competitor, all bets were off! Without Erick at her side, Elena felt suddenly alone and exposed during those excursions. Erick always knew what to do when on the hunt. While usually brooding and appearing absent-minded, his senses were sharp and on high alert. He never panicked nor let fear get in the way of critical decisions. Now for the first time out there all by herself, feeling also the pressure to perform, she was scared, not so much for herself, but what would happen to him if she should lose her life? The moment had arrived when she would have to prove to herself if she had become the hunter she believed to be.

Elena usually took a handgun, a knife for self-defence, and her very efficient crossbow to hunt for snow hares or geese. On these forays, silence was paramount to not alert the competition. Elena did not fear dealing with the danger posed by the wilderness. She had become a versatile hunter, mastered the art of camouflage, and knew how to deal with wolves and bears. But, when it came to those unpredictable townspeople who did not play by the rules of fairness, Elena still felt insecure and vulnerable. Her life in isolation had left its mark, but she was young, and adjustment would not take too long.

During the second week of their stay, Erick showed signs of improvement; Elena, with two rabbits and a goose slung over her shoulders, returned in the late afternoon. The weather had been warming up considerably, so she had exchanged her heavy fur coat for a leather jacket and tight reindeer slacks. She was oblivious to how provocative and feminine her figure must have appeared to the townsfolk. Most of these hardboiled frontier men were not shy in coming forward when it came to the acquisition of a woman.

Elena, her mind occupied with preparing the meat for Erick, wanted to get home quickly. She was only two blocks from Señora Mendoza's shop when three drunken sailors stepped into her path, displaying unmistakable intent. It was too late for her to avert the dangerous situation when she suddenly found herself encircled by these three burly men, salivating with the excitement caused by imagining the most colourful sexual derogations, obviously thinking they had just come across the highlight of their evening's entertainment. Elena decided to run. Dropping the carcasses, she was just about to turn when a fourth man blocked her path. That was the moment when the drunken sailors sealed their fate. Changing from the hunted into the hunter, her knife slashed the face of the man in front of her, and she followed up with a brutal kick to his groin. When the second man behind her tried to pin her arms down, she shoved the knife deep into his upper thigh while head-butting his nose. Seeing their companions lying on the ground, the two other men made only a feeble attempt to fight. But, before one of them could raise his pistol, he suddenly went down, having been shot through the chest an instant earlier.

When Elena looked around, confused and surprised, she saw Señora Mendoza standing in the middle of the street, lowering her rifle. She now stepped closer and hit the two sailors lying on the ground with the butt of her rifle for good measure until they stopped moving. Senora Mendoza had started to worry as the afternoon drew into dusk, and there was still no sign of Elena. She had gone instantly to look for the girl, knowing that bad things could happen unexpectedly in this place.

A crowd of onlookers had gathered when the trouble started. Most of them cheered on the fight but were disappointed about the outcome. On approach, Señora Mendoza only had to raise her rifle menacingly, and the crowd dispersed quickly. Unfortunately, the game lying unattended on the ground had disappeared during the fight and would be feeding someone else's hungry intestines that night. Nonetheless, Elena had come away uninjured, which was more than she could have hoped for under such circumstances.

7
Recovery

The healing process took its time; however, owing to both of the women's care, it went without complications. So far, Erick and Elena had made no specific plan on what to do next or where to go after his recovery. Two months later, as Erick regained his strength and they did not want to outstay their welcome at Señora Mendoza's home, they rented a shack for an exorbitant price. On hearing of her new friend's plan to move out, Señora Mendoza protested vigorously. Despite their increasingly cramped living conditions, Señora Mendoza had come to perceive them as a family unit. But secretly, Erick and Elena had begun to yearn for their privacy more than anything else.

As the weather in these latitudes was highly unpredictable, winter could start overnight, and autumn usually lasted only a few weeks. Rain could turn to sleet, and the night temperature could fall below zero without warning. For Erick, it was time to start a rigorous training program to regain his bodily strength before the beginning of winter. So far, the weather was holding, and the days were still warm, allowing him his daily runs through the hills without much hindrance. Building up his stamina again was one thing, but improving his left arm's strength and dexterity proved far more challenging. How to draw his gun with his left hand posed not such a problem, but throwing and using the knife needed hours of training every day.

His doctor, who had developed somewhat of a liking for both of them, appreciated having found an equally sophisticated man in Erick, who shared an understanding of the finer things in life. Over time he found he had been looking forward to every consultation with Erick. The visits developed into a long-drawn-out conversation, often lasting into the night and were usually accompanied by a good bottle of whisky.

At the final consultation, the doctor came up with a suggestion. Of course, he apologised beforehand that the idea might be far-fetched and even insulting to Erick's current state of mind.

He, like so many others, had also come up from the south of the continent many years ago. He was once a professor at the Sorbonne and a consultant lecturer in London and Berlin. At that time, a high-tech company existed that had previously engaged in developing bionic prosthetic limbs for badly injured soldiers and later became involved in a classified military cyborg project. As much as he knew, all NATO signatories had sponsored the project in those days. It was perceived as the ultimate weapon to stem the tides from the south, the last hope to prevent the collapse of civil society.

Much could have happened over the years, and the doctor could not say if the project was still continuing, considering the breakdown of the general fabric of middle Europa societies. In his opinion, it was more likely that all scientific research on an industrial scale had ceased to exist by now. If Erick ever desired a bionic forearm, his travels into the heart of Europa in search of that elusive high-tech company would only have to rely on hope. Besides, who would willingly return to the chaos of middle Europa after escaping it? For now, to lift Erick's spirits, the doctor had a more straightforward solution that was far cheaper and could be good enough to save him the arduous journey.

He knew of an excellent blacksmith, a man of many talents and skills who might be able, with the help of the doctor, to fashion a sufficiently functioning prosthetic arm. The device might be crude and less sophisticated in comparison, but it could assist in most practical tasks. Of course, knowing Erick, he might also prefer an extension, like a retractable blade. If Erick was ever interested, he could arrange a meeting with the blacksmith to discuss the design.

Slightly surprised and somewhat confused about having to walk around with a metal arm, Erick went home with his mind in turmoil. So far, he had not thought further than regaining his physical strength, but the doctor's suggestion had touched a nerve. Erick had to be honest with himself. Over the last two months, he had avoided acknowledging that he had lost his right forearm. But the discussion with his doctor had caused the reality of not being a fully functioning man to suddenly come crashing down on him.

Under the circumstances, the doctor's suggestion had been well intended and the best possible solution for Erick's complete recovery, but he did not foresee the devastating effect it would have on Erick's psyche. Erick struggled for days with depression. He went in and out of darkness, reached for the bottle and became inebriated on more than one occasion, to the extent of passing out.

During this time, Elena did not let him out of her sight; she knew him only too well. Erick would eventually come around and accept reality as he always did. So, she let him be, made sure he could not injure himself during these dark moments and cared for him in any possible way.

The prospect of having something artificial attached to his body felt disturbing for Erick. He had always relied on his natural abilities and was convinced that a person should be able to manage with whatever they had.

But, as the saying goes, time heals all wounds, and eventually, when Erick emerged from the darkness, he listened to the doctor explain his ideas about constructing the prosthetics.

A mild form of optimism began to replace Erick's depressive mood, to everyone's relief. The doctor also realised it might be wise to drop the subject of the bionic arm, which could have partly contributed to Erick's confusion. But, after having conversed with Elena, who agreed with the doctor's suggestions, Erick did not waste any more time, as it appeared, all that he had needed was her confirmation and moral support. So, together they visited the blacksmith to have the necessary measurements taken.

The blacksmith initially from Ireland, Patrick was a character in his own right, a former engineer now marketer of opportunities, a blacksmith by necessity and a late-blooming philosopher. To Erick's delight, he was also gay, and much to Erick's excitement, he produced a bottle of twenty-year-old single-malt Irish whisky at their first encounter. Erick was not surprised about the cunning of his doctor, who understood the fostering of friendships among like-minded people as his calling. Erick was delighted and saw himself very lucky to be introduced to a sympathetic soul in this backwater of civilisation.

The complication of how to proceed arose at the outset. Everyone was silent at first, not knowing where to begin the discussion of such a delicate subject. It turned out all involved were highly disappointed when realising things would not go as smoothly as they had expected. To start with, Erick came up with somewhat unrealistic ideas about the design of his new 'attachment', differing considerably from the concept the doctor or even the blacksmith had brought to the table at their first meeting.

Ultimately, everyone agreed Erick's new attachment would not be a simple run-of-the-mill metal arm. The smith offered to produce some preliminary sketches for their next meeting, which eventually led to highly detailed drawings, all followed by lengthy discussions.

The smith argued that he had to take care of other clients, not to mention the time and costs of such a complicated undertaking. The doctor remarked that a simple device would do for the time being, reminding everyone that the prospect of a bionic arm was an issue to be considered for some time in the future. In contrast, Elena insisted that only the best would do for Erick. While the arguments flared, Erick quietly poured himself a large glass of single malt whisky.

After the first meeting, those bottles reappeared miraculously every time the little group came together. Erick sipped contently whilst waiting for the arguments to run their course.

When the heat subsided, everyone held a glass, and the discussion began earnestly. Ultimately all agreed to Erick's demands as long the costs could be met. The smith was not yet willing to commit to an exact timeline; by his rough estimation, it would take at least three to four months, if not longer, before the first fitting could be tried, to be followed each time by subtle adjustments until the prosthesis felt comfortable to use. They had better be prepared to stay over winter.

In the ensuing weeks, Erick and Patrick spent nearly every evening and some nights together, discussing, drawing and playing with new ideas. In addition, Erick felt very comfortable and understood in the presence of his newfound friend. Surfing on a wave of positivism, Erick was utterly oblivious to the jealous looks he received on occasion from Elena. It was not about Erick's enjoyment of sexual pleasures—she was happy for him—but she had felt suddenly left out and sometimes even ignored since Erick and his new friend Patrick worked so intensely together on Erick's prosthetic arm. She wanted to be involved as she always had been. Had they not shared everything since they had met? Luckily, Señora Mendoza seemed to understand everything about men in particular.

It was past midnight. The whisky glasses were nearly empty when Erick and Patrick heard a knock at the door. There stood Elena, all flustered, teary and speechless, staring at them both. Erick stood up and immediately put his one-and-a-half arms around her. Elena began to sob. After she had calmed down, her mood changed suddenly, verbalising her bottled-up frustration loudly and angrily. Both men were taken aback, now looking meekly and somewhat guiltily at one other. Without a word, Patrick procured another bottle of his excellent whisky and filled three new glasses.

From then on, it was agreed that they would include Elena in the discussions about the work in progress, and Patrick, a natural charmer, was delighted to have a beautiful young Spanish girl around. Helped by the whisky, the clouds were soon dispersed. The conversation was overtaken by sentimental tales about the old times when Europa was the centre of the universe, with its abundance of art and cultural beauty. Elena opened up and contributed her share of good memories of her long-gone childhood world passionately.

8

The journey south

While the prosthetic arm took shape and its final adjustments were in progress, winter had settled in with generous layers of snow and icy winds from the north. The friends were now even talking about a Christmas party. This was an odd suggestion in Erick's mind with the world in such turmoil. Despite his disinterest, he decided not to throw a spanner in the works and agreed to join in as long no one asked him to bake cookies or sing Christmas carols.

For quite a while, the issue regarding what they would do once spring had returned was nagging in the back of Erick's mind. As much as they liked their new friends, they both agreed that staying forever in this godforsaken town had never been an option for them.

This was the end of the road; it was a place for people who had resigned themselves to their disappointments and settled for what they had found. Despite Erick and Elena's apparent decision to leave, their friends tried to persuade them to stay for good. Did they not understand this was the new normal? Where else could one turn while the world became more chaotic?

On the other hand, going back towards the south was a gamble of high stakes and many unknowns. Moving away from these northern reaches was the most daunting of all prospects for Erick, who had difficulty imagining how to live in any other climate.

However, there had been the doctor's suggestion and the prospect of getting a completely new arm which would function as if it was real. Of course, that could also turn out to be a fairy tale. The place for such futuristic engineering might have once existed but had possibly fallen into ruin by now. Too many questions to consider and no certainties!

Christmas had come and gone, during which Señora Mendoza's efforts had created a splendid feast! All seven friends had come together, including the doctor's wife and Señora Mendoza's husband. They had managed to keep it up for three days until all drink and wild boar had been completely devoured.

By the end of January, Erick clamped on his new forearm for the first time. The event was celebrated with a little party where he showed off his new device. The smith used as many alloys as possible for the forearm to make it light but without compromising the structural strength. The fingers of the hand were assembled from small metal rings to give it some flexibility but could only be closed to a fist if pushed against. The forearm featured a long flick knife submerged in the underside. It could glide into the hand when triggered by a shoulder movement, and a single spike could also be ejected from the upper side—a suggestion from Patrick, an idea Erick had taken up with great enthusiasm. Because of the development of this intricate mechanism, the construction process was prolonged and needed numerous trials before they were finally working to Erick's satisfaction.

As a finishing touch, Patrick had given it a fine burnished finish. The smith had aimed for maximum mobility and comfort. In repeated trials of strapping the metal forearm to the upper, adjustments were made so that, in the end, Erick could hardly feel the weight of his prosthetics after the final steps had been completed. All in all, the work had taken six months to be finished—twice as long as they had anticipated and three times as costly.

The snow began to melt, and in some sun-drenched spots, snow flowers had broken through overnight. The smell of spring was suddenly in the air! During their prolonged stay, the subject matter of travelling south into the unknown, searching for that mysterious engineering plant, had come up more than once. Also, so far, the issue had not been spoken about in earnest. This changed once the forearm had been finalised and properly adjusted. Both knew a decision had to be made soon!

If Erick was under the illusion that Elena might shy away from taking on that dangerous journey, he was utterly mistaken. On the contrary, when the discussion started in all seriousness, she was not hesitant nor frightened to take on the challenge but expressed remarkable enthusiasm. The extended stay in that drab environment of the coastal town had made her even more determined. She was excited about the chance for a new adventure, new challenges, and even the experiences of danger. She did not think about the possibility of misfortunes. Nothing mattered as long as she went with Erick! During those conversations, Erick sensed, with slight irritation, that Elena was full of youthful illusionism when she proclaimed to welcome a challenge of her fighting skills. She hoped she might even get a chance to dish out some form of retribution to her archenemies, the hated slave traders! For a while, Erick was at a loss. How was he to deal with Elena's newfound élan?

Being occupied with his own problems during their prolonged stay in the last few months, he had obviously missed out on Elena's transformation. Without question, she had become more assertive in mind and body. There was not much left of that shy girl she had been on their arrival a year ago! Erick could not help positively apportioning blame on Señora Mendoza. He began to understand that Elena saw herself more and more as his equal, especially regarding decision-making. In most instances, Elena did not hesitate and confidently verbalised her point of view.

Quietly Erick was taking great delight in the development of Elena's self-confidence; at the same time, he didn't feel any less protective of her. She still had all her life in front of her. So why risk it on some unpredictable adventure, which would be extremely dangerous as far as he knew?

Elena's point of view took a somewhat different angle to the question. He soon discovered that she had more than one reason to travel south. She finally confided in him that she longed to see her homeland again! How could he argue with that? In the end, Erick withdrew. These newly arising aspects of their intended travel plans became too much for him to process all at once.

At least one subject did not demand consideration: their stock of gold coins was still plentiful—enough to see them off on an extended adventure into the unknown.

By spring, the trading vessels were ready to go on their journeys south while having to dodge the occasional ice floats on route. Those were minor troubles in comparison to the increasing threats of piracy. To minimise the risks of attacks, the ships would travel together in convoys, protected by two gunboats, manned by former army personnel now turned mercenary.

The service did not come cheap for the owners of the ships. The costs were then mercilessly offloaded onto the freight and the few passengers. The alternative, to travel along the coastal road, was known to be arduous, unpredictable and, above all, dangerous. Not only would the journey take much longer, but also, at times, you also travelled on your own—a high-stake gamble when considering the prying bandits and outlaws lying in wait along the way all year around.

Under these circumstances, the journey by boat was perceived as the less dangerous option.

Despite the pricey fare, getting onto the vessels for want of limited berths was still challenging. To secure their passage, they had to book in advance, even with the risk that the ship could leave without notifying them owing to overbookings, simple dishonesty or a forbidding weather situation.

While the departure time was still a month ahead, it allowed Erick more time to train how to use his new right forearm. The prosthetics' skilful and effective operation in all possible situations depended entirely on Erick's determination to achieve mastery. His goal was to turn his disadvantage into a deadly weapon, and it could also function as an effective shield.

They both trained relentlessly, so by their departure, he felt he was ready and confident that he had regained his former fitness. The workouts had also given a significant boost to Elena's own self-esteem. Above all else, she was delighted that Erick had overcome his depressive mood.

Of course, Señora Mendoza was not at all pleased about their departure. She felt a fondness for Elena that went beyond friendship, treating her like the daughter she never had, lavishly investing her love and hoping secretly that she might convince the girl to stay. Elena, in turn, was highly appreciative of the woman's good intentions but was overwhelmed on more than one occasion. Elena was no longer suited for homeliness. She had been through too much to settle for the mundane, the mediocre and the uneventful. Elena felt she would instead take on the world and embrace whatever awaited them 'out there'.

The day of their departure was near. Señora Mendoza, true to her Mediterranean nature, cried and lamented endlessly. Over the previous days and nights, she had spent her time in the kitchen cooking up a storm making sure that both of them had enough to eat for the rest of their lives! Her kind efforts were highly appreciated, as they had been informed of the ship's unsavoury and costly provisions.

The flotilla would pass on a specific day and time. Three vessels from their harbour would take them to a waiting position at sea. These were crucial moments; the unpredictable weather might turn into a storm at any moment. The convoy would not wait for them; to miss their connection would mean sailing on their own and without the protection of the gunboats. The radio transmissions by satellite were now subjects of the past. Communication was once again conducted in an old-fashioned way using light signals.

Diesel oil, now a rare commodity, had forced most shipping to revert back to sails or steam engines and, if possible, preferring to use both options. Coal was also difficult to source, so ships often ran out of fuel before reaching their destination. All captains and their crews knew any vessels that failed to join the convoy or fell behind would offer easy pickings for pirates. In addition to these known calamities, weather patterns had become unpredictable due to climate change, causing unexpected storms in times of usual calmness.

Despite the threat of pirates, unusual weather patterns and horrendous increases in travel expenses, the north stood now for hope and new beginnings! Most people still resided in the south, eking out an existence under increasingly desperate conditions, so the chance of getting on one of those boats became more difficult as time went by. The north presented itself as the last frontier, where food and resources were still plenty and the population density still low, where precious metals could be mined without permits and restrictions. As time went by those precious metals had become the preferred currency in most places of the south.

The factories in the south, now disconnected from their usual supply chains, had ceased all mass production. Consequently, the artisan trades had gained ground again, adding to the demand for high-priced natural products from the continent's north.

The artisans of the south were not the only ones looking forward to the deliveries of raw materials. Pirates, highwaymen, and petty criminals were all waiting to get their share of the bounty.

Once the ships had reached the open sea, the icy winds made it nearly impossible to stay on deck. After having experienced the alternative below for a few hours, crammed with cargo, shady characters, and in addition, extremely hot and smelly, Erick and Elena decided to huddle together on the deck. Wrapped in their fur coats, they managed to endure the icy winds, and helped by the occasional sip from their bottle of whisky.

Their ship, an old freight steamer, had added three extra masts onto its foredeck to increase its speed and save some fuel.

Their luck was holding for the last three days as the winds had blown steadily from the north.

As far as they could see, the convoy consisted of twenty-five vessels of all kinds and sizes, protected by a team of mercenary forces with two Russian gunboats, which patrolled alongside the fleet, menacingly displaying their heavy guns. Erick wondered if these boats were well stocked with the necessary ammunition and how these small gunboats, usually used for coastal surveillance, would hold up in heavy seas? Erick knew from experience these boats could not stay on course in high seas under gale-force winds.

Unfortunately, on the fifth day of their journey, the wind turned westerly, and the waves started buffeting the boats, pushing the convoy closer to the dangerous coastal waters. One after the other, the ships in convoy began to scatter, and by nightfall, the strong winds turned into a storm.

The captains knew it was wise to stay on the high seas as long as possible, no matter the conditions, and to hold on to their planned navigation route south. They were aware of the many dangers they would face in case of trying to seek shelter in one of the numerous fiords along the coast. The cliffs were the least they worried about. This was now a pirate territory, former fishermen who had lost their livelihoods and turned scavengers.

Their boat began to roll in the heavy sea, and down in the hold, everything turned into chaos. Bales of fur, dried meat, salted fish and everything else, including the passengers, were thrown all over the place.

Captain and crew knew what awaited them should the weather not improve soon. To their dismay, the storm lasted for another three days, battering the ship relentlessly. When the winds began to drop off and the sky finally cleared, all that could be seen were two other southwardly heading steamships. They had lost their protection in numbers and that of the gunboats!

This new situation took its toll on the morale of the crew. Agitation became apparent, and the anxiety worsened when the captain ordered to issue weapons to every sailor and asking the passengers to do the same, as far as they could.

The now failing wind slowed their progress considerably. What made matters worse was that their southbound vessel was overloaded. Their provisional sails only added a bit of extra speed and would not be efficient enough to hold them on their course should the weather turn violent again. As their ship ran low on fuel, it began to fall behind the two other vessels, which were still running on steam.

It was on day twelve of their journey, somewhere near the coast of Alesund. The shipping traffic had increased, but without being part of a larger convoy and without the protection of the gunboats, the chance of being attacked, especially at night, was now a constant threat—all in all, very dire circumstances!

Despite their slow speed, staying on the high seas was their best option and the only chance of avoiding trouble until they reached the Danish coast. To seek out an unknown port so they could take on fuel would most likely risk their journey's end.

Then the weather turned nasty again, with massive waves battering the ship. As expected, the inefficient sails could not hold them on the course, and slowly the wind pushed them towards the unpredictable dangers of the coast. Crew and passengers alike began to lose all hope, believing their faith had been decided for them. In this situation, the captain had no choice but to steer towards calmer waters! All they could hope for now was a port sympathetic to their plight and willing to supply them with fuel.

9
Pirates

Despite the unfavourable weather conditions and the increasing panic, which had overtaken most of the crew and passengers, Elena and Erick reacted indifferently to the situation. Instead, they choose to indulge in Señora Mendoza's food supplies.

Past experiences had taught them to take any situation as presented, and they had not expected the journey to be without difficulties. Their motto was to be prepared for any kind of event—difficult or dangerous—to deal with whatever was thrown at them and fight to survive at any cost. Having no property to defend made the situation more manageable. If necessary, jumping overboard at any given moment was considered one of their options.

By evening, the vessel was drifting dangerously close to the shores. Running out of options, the captain decided to steer the ship towards the small port of Sovik. At least that harbour was not located inside a narrow bay or a deep fjord, where they could be easily trapped and assailed.

While the vessel slowly entered the calmer waters of the bay, powered only by its small sails, the captain instantly became dismayed when he saw the bay was dotted with many small islets. Without a doubt, this was a perfect place for an ambush!

The assailants did not waste any time and appeared suddenly behind one of those small islands. Through the fading light of dusk, a large tugboat and two smaller vessels could be seen steering in their direction. To everyone's horror, the aft deck of the tug displayed a 22 mm two-barrelled flak gun and a rocket launcher. As menacing as they might have appeared, Erick had doubts whether these weapons were still in proper working order or even had the necessary supply of ammunition.

A voice bellowed through a bullhorn across the water, ordering them to cut the sails and throw over two ropes once the tugboat was side by side.

Even before the order had been given, Erick understood the situation clearly and instantly made his way to the bridge. He knew that escape or counteractions would be impossible once the pirates had pulled them onto the docks. As long as they stayed afloat and away from the shore, they might still have a chance to fight back or turn the situation to their advantage.

Erick opened the door to the wheelhouse with a plan forming in his head. Irritated by his uninvited entry, the captain ordered his men to throw Erick out immediately. Erick, having no interest in a time-wasting brawl, pointed the flick knife from his prosthetic at the throat of the man who had come closest. With a commanding voice, Erick told everyone to shut up and listen, laying out his plan without preliminaries. He asked for four able men to perform in close combat, willing to kill without hesitation, and the captain to give immediate orders to lower two rescue boats on both sides of the aft deck. This action aimed to create a diversion that hopefully would force the two smaller pirate ships to take after them. On the approach of the tugboat, a few bales of fur would be thrown down, intending to irritate and engage the tugboat crew for a few seconds, which consisted, as Erick had made out, of no more than six men. In that instance, they would throw down two hook lines for Erick's team to lower themselves quickly onto the tugboat.

Their success would depend entirely on how swiftly and ruthlessly they could act. After that, it would be close combat with knives only. Erick also demanded that he position two men with rifles at the bow with the instruction to shoot at any man trying to attack them whilst lowering themselves down.

As vital moments passed in indecision, the captain, obviously no friend of violent confrontations, initially considered Erick a madman. But when he heard his crew siding with Erick's suggestions, he changed his mind and agreed that Erick's plan was the best they could hope for. Without further comment, he nodded to his men to follow Erick.

Vital minutes had passed to put the plan into action. Now, beginning to panic and without much else to do, the captain took charge of the rescue boats on the aft deck. Erick, Elena, and their team of volunteer fighters positioned themselves at the bow as planned, where the tug was already close. The ropes were lowered, and one of the sailors immediately began to throw several bales of fur overboard. Having not expected such a reaction, the pirates protested angrily. While the men on the tug distracted with moving the bales aside, Erick, Elena, and the four sailors glided quickly down the cables. As it turned out, the pirates were no match for Erick and his team. After all, they were only fishermen and had no experience in close combat. When the knives came out, it was too late for them to reach for their guns.

Despite the danger, Erick and Elena were both excited by the challenge of the threat. For the first time, they had a chance as a team to experience actual combat. When slicing off the arm of one of the pirates and disembowelling another opponent seconds later, Erick felt a strange elation. At the same time, he was surprised about his ability to dispense such brutality and how wasting a human life felt so easy.

Satisfied with the performance of his combatants, Erick recognised three men in his team must have had some military training. He later found out they had been members of the Russian Special Forces. That kind of news left Erick in a state of uneasiness; mercenaries as they were, these people could not be trusted!

Erick could still not help but keep a close eye on Elena during the short battle. When assuming with some trepidation that she might be in danger, he saw she was just playing with her opponent. A hulk of a man but clumsily moving, she finished him off by slicing his throat without much effort.

The man positioned at the bow of their vessel had taken out the man in the tug's wheelhouse when trying to aid his comrades using a handgun. One of their own had now taken charge of the flak gun and was blasting away at the two smaller pirate vessels. The first went up in flames immediately, receiving a shot into the engine room. The other sank slowly, forcing the pirates to jump into the freezing waters and call out desperately for help. All was over in a few minutes, to everyone's satisfaction and relief. The pirates were taken as valuable prisoners to be traded for fuel.

Unfortunately, one of Erick's team members had received a fatal knife wound above the groin, where his innards began to slip out. Knowing his death would come slowly with extreme agony, the man begged to be shoot in the head without delay.

These were hard men, so the pain of losing one of their mates passed quickly. After a minute of silence, his body was thrown into the sea. With only one man lost on their side, the danger had passed surprisingly quickly. Now shouts of triumph broke out as everyone on board was relieved by the outcome.

While the tensions began to subside, passengers and crew fell into each other's arms. Scruffy, unsavoury characters, having quarrelled amongst each other during the journey, were now generously sharing their last bottles of vodka.

To everyone's delight, not least the captain's, the inspection of the tugboat revealed some pleasant surprises. It was a comparatively large vessel, purpose-built to pull oil tankers on the high seas. Its holds were filled with enough diesel oil to get them into Oslo harbour and maybe even to Copenhagen.

Immediately after the event, the captain, who was not a man of many words, shook Elena's and Erick's hands generously and ordered his cabin to be cleaned and made suitable for the two of them to stay in for the rest of the journey. Erick accepted graciously for Elena's sake, not caring much about such comfort for himself.

The captured pirates were exchanged for new supplies and extra fuel. Captain and crew rejoiced that having the tugboat pull them all the way might enable them to reach their destination in a fraction of the previously anticipated time.

At the port of Göteborg, they offloaded some of their goods, some passengers disembarked, and a few new ones joined the ship.

Of course, the primary purpose for docking there was the sale of the tugboat! Boats like these, which were still in good working order, of exceptional size and had additional equipment such as a functioning flak gun, were highly sought after by all mercenary companies.

The captain, aware of the value of his merchandise, drove a hard bargain and received an equally high price. The exchange bought them all the diesel oil they needed to reach Copenhagen, including enough for the return trip to the polar circle.

The profit was fairly divided among the crew. The team also agreed anonymously that Elena and Erick should receive an extra bonus on top of their share in the form of a small purse of gold nuggets. Such a gesture instantly earned the captain respect and increased popularity. After all, without their initiative and vigour, the crew and their ship might now be sitting at the bottom of the sea.

A week later, they lowered anchor in Copenhagen.

Before Erick and Elena could step off the gangway, the captain held out his hand, thanking them with a few kind words for their valuable contribution, adding he was in their debt. A cabin on his ship would always be available, no matter the circumstances.

Moved by the captain's emotional responses, they gracefully parted as friends. And Elena, in a moment of affection, surprised him with a heartfelt hug, causing the usually scruffy man to shed a few tears.

10

Arriving in the chaos of the altered state of Europa

Erick sometimes became highly emotional during their walks through the city he loved and had fond memories of. What they now experienced was a chaotic, debilitated Nordic Venice. The coastal suburbs had partly succumbed to flooding or were permanently submerged by the rising tides. So-called 'Swampies' now occupied most of the upper storeys of those dwellins that were still standing. These people used small rowing boats to navigate among the buildings and were living on the proceeds, left behind by the tide after it had receded.

During the last ten years, the city had developed into the exchange hub towards the wild north and the unforgivable south. Endless streams of newcomers from the south arrived daily at the city. These ever-increasing numbers of the disappointed and disillusioned provided the gangs around town with new members. And many of them had gotten stuck there in the past on the way north, having run out of funds and energy to move on.

Four main routes of transmigration had established themselves over time: two land routes—one that led along the Baltic seaboard and the other, a more dangerous one that led through Sweden and Norway. The quicker routes, the third and fourth, could be taken along the Norwegian coastline or the Baltic Sea.

Erick also noticed the uncommon warmth for this time of the year, causing the once lush green Danish landscape, usually drenched by constant rainfall, to appear somewhat parched. This was possibly one of the main reasons why it was now more difficult to buy the Danish cheese he loved so much, for which this country was once famous. Unmistakably, the world had changed during Erick's life in isolation and tranquil illusion, and he still struggled to adjust to the changes. It was time to familiarise himself with the new reality, and quickly at that.

Despite the undeniable overall regression in technologies, Erick was surprised that some of the engineering achievements of the twentieth century were still in use and seemingly unaffected by any disintegration! For example, the trains showed no signs of debilitation, rather the opposite. They were high-tech, super-fast, massive, and bulletproof. These trains were two kilometres long and protected at both ends by heavily fortified carriages, which displayed machine gun turrets, reminding Erick of those nineteenth-century military trains used by the Turks in the Middle East. Obviously, money was to be made from goods transportation to and from the south. Material collected from dissembled, defunct factories, desperate immigrants who had lost everything looking for new opportunities, or the adventurous types destined for the 'promised lands' of the north! The return shipments towards the south contained various food items, mainly fish, wild game, vegetables and precious metals.

On observation, the train appeared to be a secure and relatively reliable mode of transport, supplying the obviously still-thriving but increasingly debilitated metropolises of middle and southern Europa with all necessary goods.

Because of the lack of demand, the southward trains offered only two—but simultaneously very luxurious—passenger carriages. Not surprisingly, only a few people could afford the exorbitant fares in these desperate times. However, on their return trip to Copenhagen, the wagons, devoid of merchandise, were converted into passenger carriages with three levels for accommodation to the maximum of their capacity. Those were the lucky ones, people desperate to get out of the south, having paid for the expensive fare with their last precious possessions, in contrast to those who were unable to secure a ride or were without funds, had to track along the land routes under life-threatening conditions.

The trips down south were usually only undertaken by daredevils, criminals, mercenaries or people who had to conduct some lucrative business. As far Erick had understood, the only lucrative employment offered in the south were positions as bodyguards for some of the mega-rich—those still holding out in some Mediterranean resort towns. This was a desirable proposition for any able-bodied former army member who valued payment over life expectancy. So, under these circumstances, it was no surprise that most of the train passengers to the south were former military personnel of any shade or colour, be they Russian, Swedish or Danish special-forces members. These men knew their own value and the places where to find lucrative employment for their particular skills.

Despite the discomforting information about their fellow travellers, Elena and Erick discovered to their dismay, that ticket prices were increasing day by day, and seats had to be booked in advance for the routes to Paris, Madrid or Lisbon. The credits they had to buy for every custom stop on the way brought their blood finally to a boil. All in all, twelve stopes to Paris and paid in advance with the overinflated price of two ounces of gold!

When purchasing their fare at the station, the freelance dealer shook his head in disbelief every time he sold a ticket. For him, finding a passage towards the north, out of the increasingly unsustainable situation in Copenhagen, was already an issue! But why anyone would want to travel to these shitholes in the south was beyond his comprehension when everyone down there was trying to escape in the opposite direction?

While Erick busied himself with the formalities and payments, Elena overheard a man speaking of a horrendous experience on his last trip to the south. The man had witnessed the savage slaughter of passengers during an ambush, causing Elena a sudden bout of anxiety and doubt. Had they made the right decision? After all, this journey was merely the search for that elusive bionic arm and not an attempt at a suicide mission. What if they lost their lives or ended up in slavery? Was the trouble they were going through worth the possible life-threatening consequences? After a moment of soul searching, Elena decided to keep her doubts to herself.

It seemed the purchase of the tickets had been the easy part of their travel arrangements, as they were forced to find suitable accommodation for the next two months before they could embark on their journey to the south. The trip could take ten to fifteen days before reaching Paris, their final destination. They had been advised to bring their own supplies because the food was often scarce to come by, and if available, the prices were astronomical.

From the very first day after arriving in Copenhagen, they noticed the scarcity of food. Not only proved the acquisition difficult, but the competition for quality items was fierce. Shops and markets could only be located through word of mouth. Eventually, they were pointed in the right direction. Fortunately for them, as long as they had precious metals to trade with, it was possible to buy the desired goods. Their search concentrated on anything that did not deteriorate too quickly and was especially suitable for a long journey. They preferred such specialities as cured meats, nuts and cheeses, all that were highly priced and sought after. For Erick, two loaves of dark Russian bread stood at the top of their list, high in nutritional value and durable. Elena suggested that a few bottles of vodka might be handy as bargaining goods.

They moved into one of the costly small hotels, many of which had sprung up everywhere in the city, catering mainly for the waves of newcomers and offering the same services.

During their stay, Erick derived as much information as possible about their travel destination from their fellow hotel residents. He was told that the European states had fragmented into small jurisdictions and fiefdoms over the last twenty years, similar to those perilous times in the middle Ages. Every single one of these little independent counties was trying to extort their customs duties from any passing traveller and goods merchants.

And this was the good news! On some occasions, forced on by a scarcity of all kinds, payments were not even enough. Then everything would be confiscated, and the captured people would be sold into slavery or killed.

Of course, all these extra custom duties contributed to the cost of any kind of merchandise, and by the time they reached their final destinations in the south, prices might have risen tenfold. Also, despite the heavy protection of its mercenaries, the immense length of the train made it vulnerable. It could unexpectedly come under attack by the local warlords and their bands of renegades. So, if they had harboured any illusions about a smooth ride into the south, they had better let go of it.

As soon they both had settled into their accommodation, Erick went about to try and track down some of his past military contacts. He hoped to purchase a few quality weapons and other valuable items necessary for their survival. Of course, all the locations Erick remembered had changed or simply disappeared. At first, he could not find any trace of his former friend and comrade Karl Hendricks, as there was not much left of the city's communal administration. All he came across were emergency intervention facilities, concentrating on rioting prevention, medical duties and fire alarms. And those services only applied to the inner-city circle; the vast suburbs had to take care of themselves.

However, not all institutions seemed to have disappeared. The old admin building was still standing, now deserted of staff, but it still housed many documents from the past. After having bribed the janitor, Erick managed to get access and began his search for the former residence of Karl Hendricks. On the fifth day of reading through the files, he found his name connected to a daughter's birth certificate. The address was located in a former well-to-do outer northern suburb of the city, favourably situated on higher ground.

On arrival, they found the district had been turned into a gated community and was patrolled by a heavily armed local militia. When asked to leave all weapons behind, Elena decided to stay at the entrance and wait for Erick to return.

The place stood in stark contrast to most other parts of the city they had previously passed through. The streets appeared exceptionally peaceful, populated by only a few people, who obviously went after their usual day-to-day business. The still tree-lined streets were devoid of debris apart from a few rusting cars on the curbside. Children were playing football in small parks, and here and there, Erick saw people pushing handcarts or bicycles overladen with goods—possibly purchased on a black market nearby. Here, one could nearly fall for the illusion the good old days were still in place.

He found a solid stone building at the address, a three-storey structure surrounded by a high brick wall and topped with military-grade razor wire. This gave Erick the indication he must have arrived at the right place. When moving the door hammer on the heavily metal-sheeted gate, he first received as answer a large dog's growl before he heard a female voice asking in a not-too-unfriendly tone what kind of business he had, knocking on her door.

It took Erick nearly five minutes to describe the common military history of his former friend and himself before the woman was convinced and opened the gate a fraction. Observing him through the gap, she was obviously slightly taken aback by his outlandish appearance and size while still holding the growling ridgeback by its collar, ready to let it go if Erick intended to make the wrong move. His voice must have made a convincing impression, gaining her approval to be the real deal. She stretched out her hand and introduced herself as Elizabeth Hendricks but preferred to be called just Liz. Shooing the dog away to his kennel, she invited him in.

She was a tall, slim woman, probably similar in age to Erick, holding herself with dignity and sophisticated mannerisms, all this in contrast to her face, displaying the strain of sadness.

Over tea, while apologising for the stale biscuits she had kept for such an occasion but for far too long Erick found out that her husband had left for a small, fortified island in the Samsoe Belt about two months earlier with a small troop of fellow soldiers. She assumed they had intended to retrieve some military merchandise. One could make a fortune overnight on the well-established and free-for-all weapons market, with all kinds of military arsenal leftovers.

Elizabeth had heard nothing of him since and assumed the operation must have gone badly. Erick was slightly taken aback by her rational manner towards the situation she had found herself in, expecting that Karl and his man had not survived a possible attack from a competing agent. Then again, she must have been aware that she was married to a military man. Those were uncertain times; tears were better saved for the appropriate moments.

After Erick was satisfied he had received all the information he needed to track down his friend, their conversation became more personal. When Elizabeth heard he had a friend waiting for him at the gates, she immediately got up and brought Elena back to the house. Because of her husband's military rank and standing in the community, she was still regarded as a person of authority. So Elena was allowed to bring their gear and weaponry along.

On the way back, Elizabeth suggested they stay at her house if they would like until their departure. Before they left to fetch their equipment, she told them they might bring some provisions, considering the general scarcity of food supplies even in these better parts of the city.

They returned the next afternoon with their meagre belongings. After having comfortably rested for a few days in comparatively luxury, enjoying each other's company, they searched for any clues that could tell them about Karl's whereabouts.

Maps and military logistic information dating back a few decades, were spread all about his office. Elizabeth gave them free rein to look for clues about her husband's disappearance. They assumed that the maps and logbooks hinting at the location of the weapons depot might still be displayed on his desk, as it possibly was the last thing he must have done before he left.

In the meantime, Liz managed to organise transportation and insisted on joining them as far as the small fishing port near the location of the expected island.

11
The fortress island

To approach a fortified island, used once as a weapon depository, was even in peaceful times a hazardous venture. With civil unrest brewing all over the place, weapon storages were highly sought after, being as lucrative as goldmines and possibly guarded accordingly.

A fisherman was hired to drop them off near the island. At first, the man was not interested and refused to go near the specific destination. It needed some convincing with the show of some shiny 'metal' before greed replaced his fear. They offered him double the amount if he returned the next day, and he agreed that he would wait for them a mile or so offshore.

The challenging part would be that they had to row their small dinghy to shore in the darkness of the early morning. Both would be dressed in the worn-out wetsuits provided by the fisherman. They also managed to acquire a waterproof bag for their handguns. Having to face such an array of difficulties and with the rising stakes of uncertainties for success, they felt wary about the mission. However, they felt duty-bound to help Elizabeth find her missing husband.

They had to row against a chilly wind for a mile before reaching the island.

In the dim morning light, they made out the shape of a 'state-of-the-art' Russian gunboat at the jetty, appearing somewhat tattered and in desperate need of a new coat of paint.

The fortification was a squat nineteenth-century concrete structure, surrounded by a thick growth of scrub and partly overgrown with brambles. They lay in hiding until dawn, starting to get cold even in their wetsuits.

No sentries or movements could be seen. An unnerving eerie stillness was lying over the fortress. Forced on more by the cold than by curiosity, they crawled forward, keeping low on the ground, while circling the fort in search of the entry gate. The metal doors were wide open, twisted and shredded; someone had obviously used explosives to gain entry instead of searching for the key. The real story began to unfold when they stepped inside the bunker.

Two badly decomposed bodies, dried out from the salty air, were leaning against the inside wall. Being spooked by the dead, Elena refused to go any further at first. For Erick, this presented just another warfare situation. They found more bodies on their way deeper into the fortress. Some wore Danish uniforms, and others displayed Russian insignias. The state of decomposition made any identification impossible. Elena stood back, trying to keep up appearances, while Erick began to search the uniform pockets of all the dead Danish soldiers until he came across Hendricks' ID papers. He gazed at his old friend's remains for a moment, trying to imagine him alive.

Of course, they would have to bring the corpse back so his wife could give him a proper burial. Erick looked around until he found a large enough sheet of canvas to wrap the body in. Once the body was secured and carried outside, they searched the gunboat. Here again, they found several dead bodies, but some must have survived the carnage as they showed remnants of bloodied bandages. Without outside help coming forward, they possibly had bled to death or died of gangrene.

Their initial plan had been to pile all the bodies up and burn them outside the compound, but only when they discovered an enormous amount of explosives inside the fortress did their plan simplify. They would blow up the structure and bury the dead under the rubble, including the immense store of weapons and ammunition.

Erick had no intention of flooding the market with state-of-the-art military hardware, which would only create more hardship for a population already under siege from too many threats. After having satisfied their needs for weaponry and ammunition, not to mention valuable items like canned food-stuff and all sorts of helpful hardware, they prepared the place for the destruction.

There was one challenge to overcome before they could leave the island: Erick set to the task of getting the gunboat engine running. However, the machine had been lying dormant for a few months and might not so easily start up again. Also, he was pleased that the tanks were well stocked. With his limited knowledge, Erick set to work. The engine resisted stoically! After hours of trying, he finally gave up in frustration.

Erick emerged from the engine room, his body covered in grease and on the verge of throwing a tantrum. So out of character for the usually level-headed Erick, Elena thought. One alternative was left to them. Using the signal gun, they would try to lure the fisherman to the island.

Six signal bullets had to be fired before the trawler captain approached the jetty hesitantly. With a few words, all was explained; no fisherman would refuse to show off his expertise with a dysfunctional engine. His compliance grew after they encouraged him to help himself to some of the valuable items from the military depot.

By the following day, the fuses were laid out, and the gunboat pushed off the jetty at full speed. Despite the reasonable distance between their ship and the island, their boat was showered with small concrete blocks by the massive explosion.

Elizabeth received them with a stoic demeanour at the wharf. She had not expected her husband to return alive but was grateful that she could put his body to rest.

Because the gunboat had no claimant to it, they made a handsome profit from its sale—not to mention the equipment and the hardware. The sum was shared between them and Elizabeth Hendricks. The conserves, weighing several hundred kilos, were transported back to her home, securing some of her needs for a few years to come. The remaining time before the departure was, to everyone's delight, spent peacefully relaxing at Liz's home.

The city was in flux; nothing was as it used to be, and a new train station was under construction far from the old centre due to the rising sea level. Consequently, all train travellers had to make their way to the city fringes. On their way, they had to pass through many unsavoury neighbourhoods, usually run by gangs and criminals waiting to pick off the single, unaware travellers.

Having been informed of the threats, Erick and Elena joined a group protected by a troop of highly paid mercenaries. On arrival at the station, its construction still undergoing, they were greeted by absolute chaos. Because of the lack of available completed platforms, goods and passengers were continuously being unloaded at the same terminal while merchants with their wares tried to get on.

People, trucks of all sizes and horse-drawn carts mingled without supervision, creating an environment ideally suited for thieves, conmen and ruthless opportunists. For Elena and Erick, both visibly armed to their teeth, with their belongings consisting only of their rucksacks and handbags, the situation did not pose any real problem.

No one stood in their way or tried any funny business. Voicing their dismay about the chaos to one of their fellow travellers, they received a hearty laugh. It was pointed out to them that this was nothing compared to what was waiting for them further south in the continent's heart.

Despite these first and unsettling impressions at the station, they were both overwhelmed when they saw the vast, massive train standing on the platform. It was over two kilometres long, three storeys high and pulled and pushed by two colossal engines at the front and two at the back.

At first, they wondered how the track could support such wide and high carriages until Erick looked over to the other side of the platform and, with surprise, discovered the railway tracks had a broader span than he could remember. Someone must profit considerably by willingly broadening the entire track system. Erick found out later that there was only one single rail line leading from Copenhagen to Paris beside the old, unused tracks still in existence.

When Erick enquired how the railroad company was managing the fuel supply for the engines considering the worldwide shortage of diesel oil, the man shook his head, displaying a condescending look on his face and saying, 'You must be from out of town.'

The company had acquired several nuclear engines from defunct Russian submarines. With so much unused uranium, there was no fuel shortage ever.

Erick, somewhat dumbfounded, felt unsure if he could entrust his life to such a situation.

PART 2
ELENA

12

Journey into savaged lands

They had booked a private compartment, which demanded an extra fee on top of the already exorbitant price, to ensure they could stretch out in comfort and sleep whenever they felt like it. Both had no inclination to mingle with their fellow travellers. Just in case the train would come under attack, they wanted to be in control and not have to deal with someone being overcome by panic.

The peace and quiet were welcome, a pleasant change after the crowded conditions they had endured at the station. Erick indulged himself with great fascination in studying old army maps of middle Europe, also bought for a considerable amount of silver coins. Elena rolled herself into a ball, slowly being put to sleep by the rhythmic movements of the carriages.

Erick planned to memorise as much as possible about the towns and cities on the route, including the layout of roads, rivers and topography. Considering what they had been through in the past few months, he did not expect everything to go to plan. Surviving in unknown terrain and culture would be highly challenging in case another disaster strikes.

The train had just begun to pull out of the Hamburg terminal when they got their first taste of minor irritation.

Without a knock, the door was suddenly and abruptly opened. Three bulky, bearded men entered, ordering them harshly and without apologies to vacate the compartment.

They spoke first in German and then in English. Elena told them simply to get lost, not in the mood to open her eyes. Erick, slightly irritated by the interruption, asked the man kindly to close the door while he gave them a dismissive glance. Expecting more trouble when his demand received no response, he slowly folded his precious maps, readying himself for action.

While contemplating the most efficient tactics to remove these individuals from the passenger suit, he politely pointed out that it had only been booked for two people. However, if they were desperate and there was no space elsewhere to be found, he would consider letting them occupy the four vacant seats.

The three men, undeterred by Erick's friendly remarks, pushed forward with four black-veiled women in tow, replying harshly, 'We are not sharing our space with non-believers.' All the while, the frontman was reaching out for Erick's collar.

Elena, without further warning, having by now reached the limit of her patience, knocked out the man standing behind the speaker with a precise kick in the groin. A few seconds later, even before the man in front of him could tighten his grip, Erick had broken his hand and hit him squarely on the jaw with his metal fist, sending him into the third man and the women still standing outside. All seven were now tumbling backwards out of the compartment into a heap. Unfortunately for the man who was last out of the door, having pulled a knife out on Erick, he suddenly found it had been quickly turned around and thrust deep into his chest.

In anticipation of possible future trouble, Erick gave them no time to regain the upper hand. He opened one of the carriage doors and forcefully threw the group out, one by one, including their belongings. Luckily for them, the train was still in slow motion. Before closing the door, he shouted after them that they could count themselves lucky for having suffered only a knife wound and a few broken ribs.

Elena and Erick both took this sudden disturbance as a warning that there might be more to come, reminding them to be on alert and keep the compartment door locked at all times! Elena came up with the idea of putting a sign up outside the door with a warning about smallpox infection.

While passing through Northern Germany, Erick remembered these endless plains as rain-drenched green pastures dotted with overfed Friesian cows. What he saw now was an appearance similar to the parched autumn landscapes of northern Spain. More disturbingly, signs of country life could hardly be seen. They observed a continuum of abandoned, grumbling and sometimes burned-out villages and small towns. Most highways appeared to be in disrepair; here and there, they were littered with broken cars and lorries.

The larger towns and cities still occupied had been turned into fortresses now featuring watchtowers and palisades. Small herds still grazed in the fields nearby, all surrounded by barbed wire and patrolled by teams of armed men. Sporadically they saw dust clouds on the horizon, possibly bands of marauders on the move whose aim was to trap caravans of travellers or raid unprotected villages, so they had been told. In the daytime, these bands tried to stay as far away as possible from the train line to avoid getting too close to the devastating firepower of the flak guns on top of the engines! However, like lions prowling the water holes at night, they usually waited until darkness fell to mount an attack.

The protection of the train was in the hands of a relatively large troop of mercenaries—about 150 in number. However, to Erick, this number still appeared deficient when considering the train length and the time it would take to rush through all the wagons filled with goods and people. Additionally, at every interval of ten kilometres, heavily fortified watchtowers provided security along the tracks, but Erick observed not all of them were in operation, and some required urgent repair.

Occasionally, they saw burned-out train carriages beside the railway line, telling their story to the passengers passing. Those images only added to the anxieties and doubts about the invincibility of the train and its security apparatus.

Their second custom stop was Hanover, once a medium-sized northern German city; it was now surrounded by enormous suburban slums, overcrowded with people in transit from the south. A troop of heavily armed inspectors entered the train, going from carriage to carriage, performing the occasional spot checks before the train was allowed to pass through the fortified gates and barbed wire fences. These had obviously been installed to protect the inner-city core from the slum dwellers, known for illegally using the train to get into the city. With its working infrastructure and secure food supplies, Hanover appeared obviously still highly attractive for some.

Suddenly shouts and gunshots could be heard, followed by loud protests from the carriages in front. Immediately after, a small group of people was mercilessly evicted from the train and left standing beside it to join the disadvantaged in the slums.

Warnings had been issued before their departure that anyone boarding the train without legal travelling documents and efficient credit chips would have to pay exorbitant extra fees or simply be thrown off the train. Their compartment door was suddenly rattled but not forced open; obviously, people feared infections even in these perilous times. And those fears applied even to the most ruthless of characters! They were asked to show their documents and credit chips under the door, so they could be stamped.

During their stopover, two goods carriages on the back were disconnected, and fresh water was taken on before their train pulled out of the station by nightfall. Their next stop would be Cologne and then Liège inside the Belgian border, hopefully giving them plenty of quiet resting time.

It must have been after midnight; they had just crossed the border into Belgium when they were suddenly woken up by the sound of gunfire. The train had come to a stop. Following the direction of the sound, the attack must have occurred at the back of the train—without doubt, the most convenient place to disconnect a few containers. Erick could not imagine how the attackers would overcome the flak gun on top of the two backward locomotives unless they had superior firepower, which was rather unlikely these days. The only explanation he could come up with was that they must have damaged the tracks. As could be expected, this ambush had been planned well in advance, possibly even conducted with some inside help. In Erick's opinion, the attackers were reckless and foolish simultaneously, and what about those nuclear reactors?

The sound of the battle increased. They heard orders being shouted all around, and heavily armed men were now rushing from the front of the train towards the raging battle. Erick, curious as always, decided to find out what had stopped the train, raising Elena's instant protest. She knew Erick only too well; his curiosity always got the better of him, but unfortunately, her protest fell on deaf ears. In her opinion, there was no need to risk possible dangers on the outside. Erick remembered before the train came to a halt, he had been woken up by a cacophony of bumps; now, he needed answers.

Of course, outside, it was pitch dark. The soft light from the curtain-covered carriage windows supplied some illumination to move alongside the tracks. It was a few hundred meters to the front of the train, and from where he stood, all seemed quiet; only the sound of the mechanical workings of the engines could be heard. At some distance, the searchlights from one of the watchtowers glided over the landscape. It appeared the ambush had taken place just between the ten-kilometre zones—obviously all well calculated to give the raiders enough time to get in and out.

He heard an explosion, and the barrages of gunfire suddenly stopped. Erick assumed the assailants must have overcome the defenders as more explosions could now be heard. Someone was possibly blowing open some of the goods containers rather impatiently. Not taking too much notice of the unfolding event at the back of the train and driven by curiosity, Erick moved cautiously towards the head engine. Above the locomotives, no light could be seen from the gun tower or from the engine room, both now obviously abandoned, maybe following a panic reaction by the train driver or precautious measures when under siege. It did not make any sense to Erick. However, he had the uncomfortable feeling that something was not right.

Now, with his eyes adjusted to the darkness, he came across many twisted steel purlins piled up in front of the locomotive. It would have derailed the train if they had been dumped all at once, but this had obviously not been in the interest of the raiding party. The obstacles must have been cleverly positioned at a certain distance from each other. As the pile in front of the train would increase, the train would slow down and eventually come to a halt without derailing it. Leaving the tracks damaged for weeks would hold up the train traffic and reduce the raider's profit margin.

The blow to Erick's head came swift and brutal.

13

Looking for the needle in the haystack

Not having approved of Erick's reckless adventure from the beginning, Elena suddenly felt anxious that something must have gone wrong. Leaving her no choice but to search for him despite possible dangers! Too much time had passed since Erick walked towards the front of the train for a simple inspection of what kind of obstacle had brought the train to a halt.

Erick might have stumbled into a dangerous situation or had a horrible accident, so in her mind, she decided it would be foolish to take the same route as he did. Instead, she let herself out of the back door of the carriage, slid underneath the wagon and began to crawl towards the front of the train. There was not much light around, but moving in the blackness between the tracks made the outside appear somewhat less dark. When she finally reached the front of the locomotive, lightly illuminated by the headlights, she saw a massive pile of twisted metal blocking the tracks. As far as she could see in the dim light, there was no sign of Erick and calling out for him might only cause unwanted attention. Staying low, crawling on her limbs, she circled around the pile, but still, she could not find any trace of Erick. All she could do was lie quietly and listen for any unusual sounds. There was nothing else to hear but the rhythmic hum of the engines.

Elena could only speculate; maybe a second team of the raiding party had been positioned at the blockade in case reinforcements came from the watchtower ahead. Erick must have accidentally bumped into them when they were about to leave after completing their mission. Suddenly Elena was simultaneously overcome by desperation and dread—emotions she experienced when being separated from Erick without knowing his whereabouts.

Despite aching to take action immediately, she realised that her only choice was to return to her compartment, wait in frustration and patiently until dawn. To distract her agony, she joined a group of security guards and some passengers to remove the obstacles throughout the night. At the first light of dawn, they had finally finished their task.

It was time for Elena to disembark. While hurriedly collecting their possessions, she was suddenly overwhelmed by the daunting question, where would she go from here? She had no idea of her current location, where she was in relation to towns or borders.

Stepping off the train, she asked one of the officials about her whereabouts, who roughly defined her location as being somewhere in 'no man's land' between Germany and Belgian. When Elena further enquired about the possible safekeeping of her belongings on the train, the man shook his head. The company did not offer any safety lockers. Any item left behind was regarded as booty and shared among the security personnel. Therefore, Elena left without options and shouldered her two rucksacks and the heavy guns.

In a bout of sympathy for the young woman, one of the train attendants advised strictly against the disembarkation, no matter the circumstances. She must understand that once she had left the train, she had no way of getting on again, and her ticket would become invalid. And after hearing her story about Erick's mysterious disappearance, he made it brutally clear that, whatever might have happened to her partner, he was more likely than not already dead, or if not, he would be possible by nightfall.

Elena thanked him for his honesty, turned and walked in the opposite direction of the now slow-moving train. Burdened with trepidation, she could not help but cry while watching the train disappear into the distance. The last two carriages were devoid of containers, and the last of the two backward locomotives was also missing—possibly damaged by the night's explosion to the extent of being badly damaged and already taken to some nearby workshop.

The stream of tears began to flow freely. Elena let it all out before she realised now was not the time for sentiments. Despite her feelings of sadness and vulnerability, she knew for the task ahead, she needed all her resolve to stay focused and pick up and follow the trails left behind by the marauders.

What drove her on was the awareness that she was Erick's only hope. She could not afford to give into any kind of weakness. This was her first test for handling a life-and-death situation alone—her most significant challenge since she had met Erick! Now she would have to prove how much she had learned, testing her abilities since she had gained her freedom from slavery: how to be strong and decisive in action, how to be vigilant and cunning and above all, ready to kill! The outcome of the situation was now entirely up to her. Somewhere out there, Erick counted on her, waiting and knowing she was coming for him.

Elena arrived where the ambush had taken place and had no difficulties locating the tracks in the ground that the raiding party had left behind, making it easy for Elena to follow. After walking for about two miles, she became aware her belongings and provisions proved too heavy a burden and needed to be taken care of! They would slow down her progress—especially the considerable weight of their gold! So, for now, the priority would be to find a secure hiding place for most of her stuff—a place she could easily find again on their possible return.

Not far off, the silhouette of a small town in ruins was beginning to unveil itself through the rising morning mist. Elena saw a church tower surrounded by a dense grouping of houses, some without roofs and most showing gaping holes. As long as the place was deserted, it could offer the right opportunity to hide her belongings. By the time she reached the outskirts of the settlement, the sun had risen high enough to diminish the ghostly appearance of the scene. Apart from a few stray dogs, Elena did not notice any signs of life. The street names were in French, which indicated they must have crossed over the border from Germany into the French-speaking part of Belgian during the night, not that national borders had any meaning in these times. But the fact helped her to orientate herself.

The streets were overgrown with small trees, bushes and dry grass sods, giving evidence that this place must have been abandoned for quite a few years. On getting closer to the centre, Elena was surprised by the size and dominance of the church building compared to the relatively small town. Then again, she thought, this *was* catholic Belgian and not the puritan North. The structure and its roof showed no signs of deterioration apart from a few broken windows. The doors were still on their hinges and appeared in good working order, and the front gates stood open like an invitation to Sunday mass—signs that began to unnerve Elena. After all, this place might not be as deserted as she had thought.

Elena, despite her suspicion, felt the urge to enter the building. She had not been inside a church since her Spanish days. Hesitantly, she stepped over the threshold, holding her handgun. At that moment, she was overcome by a feeling of reverence; possibly a trace of piousness left from her early childhood, despite having been brought up as a staunch atheist. The older she had become, the more she had begun to despise any kind of organised religion, not to mention their sinister and violent histories.

While she stood in the middle of that ample, quiet space, she experienced with surprise how her spirits began to rise. This unusual feeling was supported by the comfortably calm and cooling atmosphere inside, all in contrast to the rising temperature outside. She kept moving forward cautiously. Despite being utterly devoid of pews, the space was kept purposely clean as if still in regular use. The most striking evidence was the altar, decked with white linen and a few lit candles! Opportunities make thieves, she told herself while stepping forward.

Suddenly a man dressed in a black cassock, like in the days of old, appeared out of nowhere. Not at all surprised at seeing her, he smiled gently while stretching out his hand and bowing slightly. Then he introduced himself in French, 'I am father Eugene.'

Still stunned by this sudden appearance, Elena dropped her two heavy rucksacks and instinctively took up a fighting position.

'Of course, you must be surprised to find a house of God still attended by a priest in these chaotic times, I assume?' he continued, not at all fazed by her aggressive stance. 'Fortunately, this is 'no man's land', a refuge for all the troubled souls who now roam among the abandoned ruins of a once-great civilisation.'

For the first few seconds, unable to respond, she tried to come to terms with the unexpected, sudden presence of the priest. Elena had no doubt that he was genuine. He was a man in his fifties, tall and lean, with a firm but kind face framed by a grey beard and short-cropped hair. After studying his face and controlling her breath to make it slow down, Elena began to relax. If the man had harboured any ill will, he could have killed her without difficulties long before.

'My name is Elena,' she was finally able to utter, 'and yes,' she responded in her broken French, 'I am surprised. The town seemed deserted like most towns along the train line as I have observed during my journey...' But before she could continue, he begged her to follow him into the antechamber where they could talk in a more comfortable setting.

Elena could smell the freshly brewed coffee as soon as she entered the room. The aroma created a soothing atmosphere, a welcome distraction after the terrible experiences of the past few hours. It seemed that the priest had just been preparing his breakfast. When he noticed her reaction, he immediately poured a fresh cup of coffee and placed it in front of her. This was followed up by a thick slice of dark bread with cheese. He could not help but smile when he saw how her face lit up.

Still, under the influence of her slowly subsiding tension, Elena did not say anything, quietly savouring the rare brew, letting it calm her nerves. She had no doubt that he would be curious to hear why a young, attractive woman walked all alone into his church which was located in one of the most dangerous wastelands in Europa.

Once she had finished the offerings, feeling her spirits rise, she hesitantly began to describe the painful experience of the last few hours and her reason for walking into his church. After that, she gave him a short version of their travels, starting the narrative with the boarding of the train in Copenhagen, all enhanced with some background information for their reasons for the journey to Paris, whilst keeping information about her history and her life with Erick and their travels in the North to a minimum.

The priest was emotionally touched the longer he listened to Elena's story. At the end of her summary, she knew, by reading the priest's serious expressions, things were not looking too well regarding her rescue mission.

The priest had also heard of the fighting and the explosions. He was used to such frequent events along the train line—especially in the so-called no man's land between the two countries. Such raids appeared to happen more often, all pointing to the fact that people were becoming increasingly desperate around here.

He knew of the dominant raiding parties operating in the area and others across the border. Sometimes they might band together to increase their firepower when attacking larger targets, whilst, at other times, they would fight each other afterwards over the shares of the spoils!

By his calculation of the strength of the detonations and the gunfire, this raid must have been conducted by the raiders from across the borders, which were amongst the best equipped and most powerful in the area. All in all, it was as much as Eugene could speculate on the situation for the time being. Just to lift her spirits, he remarked that the tracks made by their heavy vehicles would be easy to follow. At the same time, thinking he had said too much, Eugene strongly advised against any attempt to go after them alone. A single person, and a woman to boot, was most likely to end up as a slave out there; or worse, he concluded!

Elena shook her head, stating stubbornly that even if it cost her life, she would never abandon her friend to his fate. However, despite her brave posturing, she knew he was right. What chance did she have of taking on a raiding party of ruthless cutthroats?

In this new world order, lawlessness was ruling supreme. It was no longer the centre of the civilised world where you might approach some authorities for help.

To make things worse, Elena lacked Erick's investigative skills and guerrilla warfare tactics. She had not yet acquired his ability to read and memorise maps, which allowed him to know his position in the context of the surrounding topography. Despite all her early confidence, Eugene's description of the harsh reality awaiting her out there slowly melted away all of her valour and replaced it with a sense of hopelessness. She could see now the chances of succeeding on her own were less than zero.

Troubled by his inability to help, Eugene noticed the desperation on Elena's face. His few meagre words of consolation only increased his own sense of hopelessness. After brooding for a while and slowly accepting the depressing impossibility of her task, Elena stood up suddenly, telling Eugene that despite all odds, she had no choice but to continue her quest. To travel fast, she needed to travel light! There was one more favour she was asking of him—could he take care of her possessions until her return?

After another feeble attempt to stop her, Eugene was only too willing to do whatever was necessary to ease her predicament. Nodding in agreement, he asked her to follow him into his bedroom. Here Eugene touched a hidden lever, which caused a large wardrobe to slide aside, exposing a dark opening. He lit a candle before they stepped into the darkness and down a stairwell leading into a crypt.

In the crypt, Eugene lit a few more candles illuminating a space filled with several stone sarcophaguses. They were massive and somewhat crude, displaying no ornaments and covered with thick granite slabs, far too heavy to move by hand. Eugene pointed to the last one at the far end of the room. Again, the priest operated a hidden mechanism, and the enormous stone slab moved silently aside. Elena was now staring at the church's precious reliquaries: ornate chalices and crosses, some fashioned of gold or silver, all decorated with precious stones.

'Well, I guess your own treasures will be in good company,' Eugene smiled encouragingly. Elena began to unpack what she intended to leave behind. On seeing the array of guns, knives, and gold bullions, Eugene shook his head but preferred not to say anything. Again and again, Elena checked the weight of her rucksack, discarding more and more of her equipment until she was sure it would be light enough that she could run without difficulty. After seeing Eugene's secret hiding place, Elena was convinced he trusted her and that her stuff was secure with him.

14
Reluctantly accepting God's help

Elena, having enough provisions but not wanting to offend Eugene's kindness, graciously accepted his offers of dried meats and fruits. She was just about to depart when he held her back once more. He appeared to grapple with the duties he had committed himself to as a priest. Were they religious in nature, or was it his duty to help the needy? Elena could not tell.

'I can offer you a ride,' he muttered reluctantly, 'as long as you never tell anyone later, because I am the stalwart of the neutral ground. I am not allowed to take sides for any party, otherwise my position as a mediator will become tenuous.'

Surprised, Elena thought, he was, after all, not just a priest restricted by his dogmas to fulfil his allocated quota of goodness according to the Good Book. He is a man who understands the need for pragmatism when necessary.

'How?' she asked, appearing somewhat impatient. Eugene, in his typical, non-verbal way, indicated that she should follow him through a large archway into the courtyard adjacent to the church. There, somewhat surprised, Elena saw a heavy motorbike. Its shiny chrome parts were gleaming in the sun. It left her with no doubt the machine was well-used and taken care of. A few helmets were hanging on a rack above. Pointing at them, Eugene asked her to choose the right fit.

He had decided to take her to the ambush site and then along the track the escaping party might have taken until they reached the border crossing. Also, now arbitrary and without official meaning, it was still accepted as a line in the sand by the marauding bands on both sides.

Unfortunately, he had very little influence and standing across the border, even though he was called up occasionally to function as an arbiter in their disputes. Not to endanger his neutral status, Eugene avoided compromising his impartiality or engaging in any conduct that could mark him as a traitor.

Elena, touched by the man's kindness, gave him a long hug.

While casually trying on several helmets, she told him that this would be the first time in her life that she was riding on the back of a motorbike. To this, he simply replied, 'Just hold tight!'

Elena wondered, at first, where he would find the necessary petrol for his motorbike, a vintage BMW. The question answered itself as soon he had started the motor. She smiled on sniffing the alcohol.

Eugene explained during their ride that alcohol was the most obvious and commonly used a substitute for petrol during these times. Driving along while surrounded by the smell of cognac was not to be sniffed at, Elena thought! The mention of cognac instantly brought Erick back into her mind and filled her eyes with tears. How much Erick would have loved to be surrounded by that smell.

Once they had searched the ambush site for clues, they followed the wheel tracks on the ground, deeply imprinted by vehicles loaded with heavy containers. By late afternoon they reached a wide road—obviously once a significant highway, still partly sealed but now sprouting dense patches of grass sods everywhere. Again, the recent imprints of a heavy vehicle were still visible on the vegetation. Here Eugene slowed to a halt, pointing at a sign displaying a German town's name at a crossroad, marking the limit of his sphere of influence.

Eugene appeared torn between his duties to his flock and being the Good Samaritan. Because of the dire conditions of the road, he preferred daylight for his travels and would need the rest of the afternoon for his ride back to his church. Elena became aware of his reluctance to let her continue on her own. His voice gave witness to the pain he felt about the situation.

'I know it is impossible to stop you on your warpath, so if your situation becomes dramatic and you are captured not far from here, mention my name. It might save your life!' Make up some convincing stories: that you are my sister or that I needed some medical supplies urgently. I will certify anything you say.'

He also warned her about the traffic on the road, not to trust anyone, and, if possible, to hide when she saw a larger group of men approaching. They embraced without further words and departed with a deep understanding and shared appreciation for each other.

Elena had walked on and already disappeared around the next bend, but Eugene had not moved, paralysed by his doubts and torments. Could he not have done more for this impressively determined young woman? Was it sensible to let the girl continue on her own?

Alas, the way things stood even in these godless times, his flock of brigands, thieves, desperadoes, and ordinary people all looked up to him. They were no less in need of his kindness than this young Amazon! Without these deeply felt responsibilities, he might have thrown away his cassock without hesitation and followed her into hell.

Observing the trail of imprints on the grass stalks closely held down from the tyres' impact, Elena concluded she could be only a few hours behind the marauders. Also, her desperation surfaced again now that she was on her own, to be the sole decision-maker still felt like an immense challenge to her. The answer to the most difficult question was now lying ahead: How would she proceed once she had discovered Erick's whereabouts? Elena decided it was better to put those thoughts aside and keep her mind clear for the immediate task. One decision at a time, as Erick used to say.

The sun was now close to the horizon, and in the distance, wooded hills began to replace the open fields.

Just after she came down a slight rise, she saw a hilltop castle across a broad valley. Surrounding it on its slopes below extended a small, fortified settlement. This was an inhabited settlement, judging by the smoke rising from different places behind its walls. Elena's instincts told her this was where she would find Erick. The road she had followed led straight into the medieval town.

What was the best thing to do for now? If the gates were going to be closed by nightfall, should she try and get into the town before? Would they let her pass without too much trouble? After all, she was a single young woman, easy prey in any man's eyes. Should she investigate the walls in the security of darkness, look for a way to enter secretly, risking capture or even being shot at? Her thoughts were suddenly interrupted when she heard the sound of a motorbike heading in her direction.

Looking around for a spot to hide, Elena realised, to her dismay, that the road led through open fields and no ditches on either side deep enough to conceal herself. She removed her sawn-off shotgun from its holster, holding it loosely by her side, and waited.

To her surprise, Eugene was coming to a halt beside her.

'On second thoughts, I apologise,' he muttered. 'You looked so lost and scared when I left you behind, I could not let you go on alone. You are too young to be wasted in these savaged lands,' he added with a wry smile.

Elena had no trouble showing how relieved she felt about seeing Eugene again.

'Something else we need to clear up before we continue,' he added somehow ironically. 'In case we are ambushed and I do not survive, Elena, you will need to be able to get away on the motorbike!'

Even though she saw Eugene was serious with his remark, Elena could not help but laugh. 'How do you imagine I could ride the motorbike?' she responded, smirking, her tone full of sarcasm.

'I am sorry but there is no way around that problem,' he concluded.

They drove on for a while until Eugene turned into a small track leading off the main road; surrounded by thick bushes, they were invisible from any road traffic. It took them an hour's crash course before Elena could manage to hold onto the handlebars without falling from the bike. In a wobbly style, she could finally drive in a reasonably straight line. For the rest of the way, the priest insisted on her taking the front seat instead pillion. She held her legs out for safety most of the time while they drove along slowly.

Dusk was already approaching when they spotted the ruin of a barn not far off from the road. A small grove of trees surrounded the building. Eugene suggested it might be a good idea to spend the night there and wait until morning before deciding further actions.

They arranged themselves as comfortably as they could for the night while Eugene told her everything he knew about the town. He confirmed her assumption that this small city was fortified and guarded at night. Only experienced thieves with enough insider knowledge of the place would dare to enter. The citizens of such settlements had become unforgiving and intolerant of outsiders who did not obey their rules. Harsh times demanded harsh responses! That was more or less the usual treatment of strangers who broke the rules in all these last surviving settlements.

The re-establishment of the old fortifications had been a slow process over many years, forced on by the increasing lawlessness all around. The people who had stayed behind on the surrounding lands had found it too challenging to protect themselves in villages and outlying farmhouses. Also, with their flimsy thin walls and light constructions, modern houses gave hardly any protection against invading gangs and the blasts of guns and rams. They abandoned their homes for more suitable places and moved into historic towns wherever they could find them. So, in time, not unlike in the middle Ages, hill castles and the town fortifications appeared to have been repurposed and reinforced. Owing to the swelling population, the building density of dwellings behind the walls increased. As anachronistic as it might sound, it had become the new reality all over Europa!

The night began to turn cold, so they curled up in each other's arms without inhibitions.

15

The town

They woke up before daybreak and shared some provisions Elena had brought along. The first traffic leaving the town before dawn consisted of old military trucks—possibly on the way to one of their 'business ventures.' This simply meant fulfilling their daily quota of raiding less protected places or ambushing unwary travelling parties who would be robbed and enslaved.

By the time the sun was up, an increasing stream of people had started to travel to and from the town by all possible means. The smell of the alcohol-driven engines began to drift as far as their shelter. Elena was amused and astonished by the variety of transportation methods. There were bicycles, steam-driven tractors, and horse-drawn carts, among many others. However, most people travelled on foot, weighed down by their heavy burden of tradable goods.

By mid-morning, the road was only travelled by ordinary people. The outflowing groups were possibly on their way to attend to their fields, and the incoming flow was made up of those who intended to buy or trade their wares in town. They did not recognise any more units of mercenaries or single-armed men.

Nonetheless, Eugene cautioned that they waited until they were sure the active members of the mercenary force had left. After midday, by the time most of the peddlers were starting to leave town again, the road would likely be less busy, and the townspeople would have their siestas. In Eugene's opinion, the early afternoon offered the best opportunity to enter the town without causing too much of a sensation.

Midday had passed; it was time to make a move! Soon after sunrise, it had turned sticky and hot inside the barn, luring Elena into a slumber. Having been cocooned in a world of her dreams for quite some time, she felt disorientated when Eugene shook her awake.

In the morning, they worked out a simple plan on how to proceed. Eugene did not dare to enter the town with her in the backseat of his motorbike. She also appeared too conspicuous as a woman in a rough leather outfit with knife belts and guns—a giveaway that she was not from around here! Such an attractive woman accompanying a priest would attract much attention even now.

So it was decided that Eugene would walk up the road to look for a peddler on the way out of town, from whom he would purchase some tattered dresses for Elena. Elena would have to store all her weapons in his motorcycle compartments because, as a priest, it was unlikely he would be searched for weaponry. However, she did insist on keeping a small flick knife hidden in her boots. Once she was dressed out convincingly as a local farm woman, she would wait for a group of similar-looking people who were on their way into town. Eugene would follow soon after on his bike.

As soon he returned with a long, tattered dress, plus a heavy thick, grimy-looking coat, Elena wrapped herself in the garments with great trepidation. As expected, she could soon feel the welcome bites from the many small critters inhabiting these items. To make it all the more convincing, she had to smear her hair and face with dried cow dung and let it hang dishevelled. The transformation was completed by adding a large, grey, floppy hat.

The afternoon traffic had thinned out by now, making it more challenging to find the right group of people to join. When Elena spotted an old couple pulling a small cart piled up with potato sacks struggling visibly to pull it along, she entered the stream of people just after them. She slowly passed the couple, only to turn around after a few meters, offering her help kindly. As it might be expected around here, the old couple refused point-blank at first, fearing some kind of ruse to separate them from their goods. Elena, giving them one of her winning smiles, continued unperturbed with her light-hearted conversation about the weather in her foreign accent. She must have hit the right note, and the couple took a closer look at her. Seeing her face was without malice, they accepted her helping hand with great relief.

Eugene had been right about the guards' conditions at the gate. Having washed their lunch down with a portion of wine, they now appeared sluggish and smelled of alcohol. The sentries were instructed to search everyone for concealed weaponry, 'especially' young women. However, the cow dung's strong smell and the signs of possible lice infestation in her hair gave them little encouragement, so they let her pass without much ado.

As soon she had traversed the gate, Elena was overcome with astonishment. If one excluded the power poles, solar panels, small windmills, and the few parked cars, what she saw completely resembled a medieval townscape. The streets were lined with stalls, covered with tattered awnings, trading everything from food and live animals to obsolete technological parts. People were dressed as if they had fashioned their own outfits from whatever material they could obtain. Unmistakably, knife belts were part of the established dress code, contributing to the palatable tension and anxiety. Obviously, no one felt safe despite the guards on the fortified walls. This picture presented, without a doubt, at least domestically, a return to the distant past.

It was not the only hint at less fortunate times. Many of these people were unhealthy-looking, crippled or displayed poorly healed injuries. One could only assume that medicine had become a rare commodity and that a healthcare system was not in existence. She remembered how surprised Erick had been when he pointed out that fact on their arrival in Copenhagen. But here, you did not have to look closely as it was everywhere. What made the whole situation even worse was that the place stank like a pigsty, a sign that things were far worse underground!

They had agreed to meet at a small church higher up the slope, the most unlikely place to be noticed as intruders. Eugene knew he could trust the parish's priest, who might also have some information about last night's raid.

Saying goodbye to the old couple, Elena trundled past the shops and stalls when she came across a smithy with some wares in front. She could hardly hold back her outrage when she saw Erick's metal arm dangling on one of the hooks. Its careless unassuming display made her blood boil. She felt as if Erick himself had been on display! It was all she needed as proof that her friend had been brought to this place. Unfortunately, it also could mean that he was already dead.

Elena struggled with the outpouring of her tears and simmering rage for a few moments, while coolness and composure were now the highest priority in dealing with the situation. She took a deep breath before calling out to the smith in a calm voice. A squat, broad-shouldered man with hands as big as shovels appeared from the darkness in the back. A cunning face and a pair of small, close-set eyes—not a person to mess with or to try to overcome in a wrestling match. She would have to be equally cunning and deceptive to get the vital information regarding Erick's where about.

It occurred to Elena too late that she had obviously shown a too keen interest in the prosthetic arm instead of first browsing aimlessly as if she was looking for any valuable item or even spending some time haggling over other wares. The smith immediately noticed it and pushed the price to the outrageous amount of two ounces of gold.

He knew his game and also understood the quality of the arm; he described it as a rare piece of craftsmanship and, judging her by her looks, beyond her means.

Elena stayed calm even though she would have liked to cut the man's throat instantly. Again, she swallowed hard and told the man with a big smile that she wanted to leave a down payment on it and would return by evening to pay the total sum.

Now the smith smelled blood and was trying to increase the price even more when Elena began to lose her patience. Unfortunately, her anger rose again and was now barely controllable. First, she needed to squeeze out of him Erick's whereabouts and slit the man's throat afterwards. But without striking the deal and any further words, she walked away. At least she knew Erick had been taken to this place, and hopefully, he was still alive.

Eugene had made his own inquiries. His friend reluctantly confirmed a raid had occurred the night before, but the vicar did not apologise to Elena. His town needed the supplies to sustain its community. Being left behind after the collapse of the central government and without outside help, they were entirely relying on themselves. The occasional raids were the only means to continue their existence. He also pointed out how often they came under attack by the corporation's mercenary army.

On the other hand, he was willing to help because he deeply disapproved of people being taken for enslavement. He had only a vague idea of where the prisoners might be held as he was purposely kept out of the information stream. His guess would be that they were most likely locked up in the castle before being transported to the slave market. Usually, the transport would go to a big city such as Cologne, Frankfurt or even Paris when enough of them had been captured.

Alarmed by this information, Elena decided there was no time to waste. Now that she knew that Erick was locked up somewhere in this place, she felt invigorated and determined to free her friend as soon as possible.

However, first, she would return to the blacksmith and interrogate him more severely. Eugene strongly advised against her taking this kind of action, but she ignored him outright and refused his offer to accompany her. He then feebly suggested that she wait for the transportation to the slave market and intercept the trucks somewhere en route and try to buy Erick out.

Elena could not help but laugh at such an inconceivable proposition. Under no circumstances did she want her friend to suffer more than necessary. So after a prolonged scrub of her body, using a lot of precious water, Elena indulged in a hearty supper at the priory. As soon as darkness fell, she borrowed a hooded mantle and armed herself.

She had been warned that guards patrolled the streets after dark, so she carefully avoided the few patches of streetlights on the way to the smithy. If anything went wrong, and in case of an emergency, Eugene had posted himself on his bike near the gate to take her as quickly as possible out of town. However, in Elena's mind, nothing could go wrong. She was now determined and would not hesitate to kill anyone who dared to stand in her way.

16

Mayhem

To Elena's great satisfaction, the smith was still at work, hammering away at his anvil. Yet, she realised she needed to lure him away from the fire and let him drop his massive hammer, a dangerous weapon when she had to try and overwhelm him. At first, the smith felt intimidated by her beauty and athletic build. Now that she was washed and her long hair was neatly tied at the back, he did not recognise her—even after she had taken the hood off her head whilst keeping her sawn-off shotgun well concealed under her cape. He even blushed and, for a moment, was lost for words but then quickly regained his scruffy brutish self again once he recognised Elena as the woman who had previously intended to buy the prosthetic arm.

'Well, the price has risen,' he stated bluntly, staring at her seductive figure, salivating and imagining new ways to strike the deal. She was, after all, not the poor peasant she previously appeared to be. He saw a chance to make some real profit and have extra fun here.

'I would not mind dropping the price if you can supply me with some exceptional sexual favours,' he said smiling, emphasising the term *exceptional*.

At that moment, Elena saw her opportunity to get close to the man, so she agreed, giving him a lusty smile. Out of curiosity, she asked how much the favour was worth to him.

'That depends,' he replied in a sugary tone, already seeing himself in seventh heaven.

Elena, still smiling, asked, 'Depends on what?' using her voice as demurely as possible and slowly moving closer. Now she could smell his repulsive body odour, and suddenly, she kicked him in the groin with her right ironclad boot with all her might. The man collapsed in a heap, only to receive a second blow to the head from the butt of her gun.

The guy was heavy, and she needed to drag him out of sight as quickly as possible. She realised she should have waited until they entered the back room. On the other hand, the opportunity had been too tempting. Who knew what kind of game he would have played later on? She turned off the lights in the front and closed the door behind her. Then she tied him up with whatever ropes were available, taking extra care so they would be tight and cutting off his blood supply as much as possible. Under these circumstances, there would be no need for torture afterwards.

As soon as the smith came round, he began to experience agony in his limbs. His eyes were bulging and full of fear, and he began to shake uncontrollably. Elena kicked him a second time in his groin, less severely, but enough to convince him there was no way out until he played along. In anticipation, he would scream down the neighbourhood she had gagged him.

She held her knife to his throat, telling him if he as much as opened his mouth after she removed the gag, it would be his last time!

He spilt the beans without much probing as soon as Elena began to ask her questions. First, she wanted to know where the metal arm was. Experiencing extreme agony, the man's only reply was a nod towards a locked cupboard in the back of the room. Not bothering to ask for the key, Elena took a hammer to the lock. It appeared that in the few hours since her first visit to the shop, the arm had become one of the smith's prized possessions! Once the prosthetic arm had been securely stored away in her bag, Elena asked the decisive questions about the prisoners of last night's raid that had been taken. Threatening the smith that she would cut off his fingers one by one for every unsatisfactory answer if she believed he was not telling the truth. The smith might have appeared large and robust, but he was no hero.

Yes, he had taken part in the raid the night before, yes, they had captured a few of the men who worked for the train company, and yes, one of them had a metal prosthetic arm, which he had taken as part of his share of the spoils. As a smith, he had recognised its value and intended to copy it, knowing very well that there was a market out there for such nifty devices and was especially impressed by the built-in flick knife. And yes, the one-armed man had been taken to the slave cages in the castle, which was holding many others who were waiting to be shipped off to the slave markets as soon as they had reached their quota and managed to organise enough trucks. Now assuming the danger of torture had passed, he remarked carelessly that he believed the cripple might already have been killed because he was not worth the trouble of being transported. Elena kicked him in the ribs without hesitation for that callous remark, cracking a few and not caring for his agony.

She continued her interrogation, abstracting details of the prison's location, the outlay of the castle, information about the positions and the number of men guarding the prisoners. Alas, the smith being only an auxiliary member of the raiding party, lacked a comprehensive knowledge of the all-over manpower at the fortress.

By now, the man could barely talk nor sit up, was bleeding from his head wound, having difficulty breathing and had lost all feeling in his limbs, not that Elena cared. Finished with her interrogation, she put the gag, despite his protests, back into his mouth. Then she began to construct a very elaborate mechanism, positioning him so that, if he fell forward, a noose would slowly tighten around his neck and eventually suffocate him. He started to twitch and shake with fear, expecting to die in this position if not released soon. To improve her contraption, Elena tightened a second rope to the chair he was standing on and connected it to the outward swinging door. She had to make sure he could not inform anyone about her interrogation. She told the terrified man that if she was captured, unable to return that night and release him from his bondage, he would be killed by the first person that unwittingly opened the door! His chair would be pulled from under him, and the tight rope would break his neck instantly.

Before sliding out of the back window, she told him that if he needed to change or add anything to his statements before she left for the castle, now would be a good time. If his information failed to be accurate, she would not return to release him from his bondage.

She went on her way, determined to free Erick, no matter the cost, swearing to herself to bring death to anyone who dared to oppose her. Before Elena turned towards the castle, she passed by Eugene's hiding place near the gate, instructing him to return to the church and be ready. His offer to come along, which did not sound very convincing, she denied without comment.

The town's dark alleys only lit sparsely here and there, making it easy for Elena to reach the fortress without being detected. The midlevel structure was looming menacingly above the town. Surprisingly, the fort was still equipped with a functioning drawbridge, and the gate was fronted with small watchtowers on both sides. There would be no guards at present, the smith had assured her.

Just as she approached the bridge, she heard a massive explosion from the direction of one of the town gates. She stopped and listened to the sound of heavy machine gunfire and exploding grenades from all directions. A second explosion at the opposite town gate lit the night sky with glowing embers and flying debris.

Suddenly Elena heard shouts and running footsteps from inside the fortress coming towards the open gate while she was still standing in the middle of the drawbridge.

In that instant, she saw no other option but to swing herself over the edge and hang there, hoping not to be discovered. A pickup truck with a flak gun mounted on the back rattled over the bridge a moment later. More small troops of armed men followed, carrying all sorts of weaponry, from crossbows to submachine guns. All seemed somewhat chaotic and disorganised, giving the impression of panic.

Clearly, they had been taken by surprise by the attackers. Fairly soon, the sound of footsteps subsided. Elena swung herself back onto the bridge, feeling the painful strain in her arms and now moved slowly towards the dark opening of the gate, her sawn-off shotgun held at the ready. More explosions and sporadic machine gunfire mingled with shouts and screams of the panicking townspeople. Elena had no doubt that these attacks were a measure of retaliation conducted by the corporation.

This new event brought on a dramatic change to her situation. She had to move fast! Sooner or later, she and Erick could be caught in the crossfire between the enemy factions.

The prisoners' cages were supposed to be located in one of the old stable buildings at the back of the keep. Unfortunately, inside the keep, surrounded by those high walls, it was even darker than outside. Elena could make out the openings of a few large doors. However, nothing indicated which one was holding the prisoners. Calling out for Erick was too risky, but finding her way without a torch appeared impossible.

Turning a corner, she saw a faint illumination from a small window slightly below ground. Carefully peering into the hole, she spotted an old man sitting at a table, slowly sipping from a cup, a shotgun leaning next to him. Elena took advantage of the door being slightly ajar and the man's position sitting with his back to it.

She moved next to him and knocked him out without delay before he could drop his cup. There was no time to waste! Judging by the intensity of the explosions, the fighting was drawing nearer. Grabbing the shotgun and a kerosene lamp hanging next to the door, she rushed towards the stables.

The first two stables displayed only empty cells, but when she opened the door to the third stable, she could hear muffled sounds and dark shadows moving behind bars. Elena did not hesitate to call out for Erick this time and instantly got her friend's humorous reply in return, 'What took you so long, darling?' On hearing his voice, her heart leapt. Once again, she realised how much he meant to her.

She was told to use the keys hanging next to the door to unlock the cages. After their embrace was over, Erick's cellmates from the train security team were quite surprised to see a single woman coming to their rescue. Erick was surprised she had brought his prosthetics along and strapped the device on without delay.

Elena quickly informed the released men about their situation and the danger they would soon face when the forces, doubtlessly sent by the train corporation, would storm the fortress. The bad news was that friends and foes could hardly be distinguished in this darkness! The good news was their guards had left and were now fighting the attackers.

Elena suggested that the captives' best chance of survival might be to stay behind the castle walls and raise the drawbridge, thereby cutting off the possible retreat of the marauders. Elena and Erick, wishing the men good luck, now standing there somewhat witless and demoralise, disappeared into the night before the men could ask further questions.

On the way to the church, Elena explained in a few words what kind of situation they were in. She told him of having organised an escape route with the help of a priest and the local vicar, receiving some looks of surprise and astonishment from Erick. Unfortunately, because of the unexpected attack, the circumstances had changed dramatically. A chaotic situation presented itself outside the fortress, making it necessary to use force to gain a path towards the church as quickly as possible before the enemy's troops could interfere with their escape plan.

People were screaming and shouting and panicky, running in all directions. Some carried weapons to join the defenders, and others were hauling carts, hoping to get away with their skin and possessions. No one took any notice of Erick and Elena! At least the mayhem worked in that way to their advantage.

In contrast to the streets, the churchyard was still deserted. However, people were streaming into the churches' front gate, hoping for a safe sanctuary. Elena had been told to knock three times on the small side door of the sacristy. There they were let in without delay.

With a few words, she described the last few hours' events to Eugene but knowingly avoided mentioning the treatment of the smith, who, in her opinion, was possibly dead by now anyway. The vicar led them down a hidden staircase into the crypt. Here they could hold out until the fighting was over because, in his estimation, all escape routes were out of bounds. He was hoping that the house of God would be spared when a sudden explosion shook the crypt's walls, nullifying the vicar's assumption and forcing him to rush back into the church to survey the damage and look after his flock.

The devastated vicar returned soon afterwards, completely covered in dust. He urged them to follow him into a smaller antechamber filled with one enormous wooden sarcophagus. Pushing at a hidden lever, the box slowly ground sideways and revealed an opening in the floor.

'Does every one of you priest people have this kind of escape route under your chapel around here?' Elena asked amusedly when a second explosion drowned out the vicar's reply.

The vicar, handing them his precious torch, told them to follow the downward spiral staircase into an underground passageway. It would lead them into a cave and finally to a steep ravine outside the town walls. Then he bade them goodbye, rushing back to care for the injured and possibly many dead.

Having not been used for many years, the ravine was now overgrown with brambles. Here the long flick knife on Erick's prosthetic arm proved, if not efficient, practical enough to cut through it.

They arrived at an elevated position overlooking the valley below. From here, they could observe the corporation's overwhelming force attacking the town from several directions, cutting off all possible escape routes, undoubtedly with one purpose—to eradicate the marauding troops once and for all! Fires had flared up all over own, and the screams of the desperate could be heard even where they stood. The total destruction of the town and the slaughter of its citizens were in full swing. Elena did not hold much hope for the released prisoners up in the fortress unless they had been able to establish some kind of contact with their apparent 'liberators'.

Aside from their friend Eugene, who took without question the side of the local populists, Erick and Elena had difficulty deciding on which side they stood. In reality, everyone here was fighting for survival in this increasingly harsh environment, all embroiled in the experience of impotence in the face of the hopeless environmental situation!

The group descended silently into the valley, their passage illuminated by the flames of the burning town. All they could do for the time being was hide in the thicket of the forest edge until daybreak. After that, Eugene planned to make his way alone to the barn, hoping to retrieve his motorbike unscathed, which he had hidden there hours before in anticipation of the unexpected.

To their amazement and elation, he succeeded without interference. He had approached the ring of the besieging troops from outside the town, claiming to be needed for the dying and deceased. As he had hoped, the mercenary forces did not expect any ill will from an unarmed priest. Eugene offered his motorbike to Erick and Elena on his return, so they may have a better chance of reaching Paris!

Both of them refused vehemently at first, and it was only after Eugene had assured them that he would soon be able to find a replacement they accepted his gift with gratitude.

There was no need for them to worry about him or the vicar. They both belonged here, in their place of spiritual guidance. People were still in need of the sacraments or for the burials of their dead. Soon their dispersed flock of brigands would regroup, and the community would find ways to start again.

Before leaving, Eugene gave Elena detailed instructions on how to retrieve their belongings at his church. Their goodbye was short, heartfelt, and truthful. They left behind two priests who felt satisfied at having saved two good people.

PART 3
MADAME

17

Innocents under the spell of evil

Under normal circumstances, the journey to Eugene's church would have taken them no more than twelve hours. The alternative route, taken as a precautionary measure because of the corporation's military intervention, led them in a wide circle. They drove north into German territory for more than twenty miles to avoid any possible spillover from the fighting. Another difficulty was the necessary acquisition of fuel on the way. Because only locals knew where to look, outsiders needed to enquire, pay several middlemen, and then be charged exorbitant prices. That was if they could locate those sellers at all.

Having completed the half circle, the distance of nearly two hundred miles of extra travel time, they crossed back into Belgian before reaching their destination. Both were exhausted and looking forward to a good night's sleep before heading toward Paris. Eugene's sacristy was more than a comfortable place to do so. They helped themselves generously from Eugene's food store, as he had told them to do, not that there was too much storage space available on the motorbike. All they knew from now on was the uncertainty ahead!

Following Eugene's advice not to drive along the old highway, now predominantly used by raiders and other unsavoury elements, they marked their route along the old country roads. Although those winding roads prolonged their travel time, they appeared less dangerous and possibly offered a better chance to find food and petrol. However, there was no time and space for complacency and no guarantee for a safe passage anywhere, as that former tranquil French countryside had turned into a savaged land.

In the following days, it was not so much the possible threats of danger that caused them to despair. It was the sight of the utter devastation of towns and villages, the denuded parched soil and withered forests, which more or less resembled a southern European landscape in autumn.

After four days of travelling along snaking roads, and despite the help of kind people on their route, their food supply began to dwindle fast. Also, the price of fuel and food began to increase the closer they came to their destination. According to their map, they still had another two days of travel before reaching Paris's outskirts.

They saw that most of the villages they passed through had become quarries for the fortifications of the few towns still holding out against the tide of their unavoidable demise. While driving cautiously through these ruined remnants of civilisation, they were more than once approached by people looking like scarecrows, emerging suddenly from nowhere, having heard the roar of the motorbike. When Erick and Elena tried to circumvent the blocked roads, the beggars became aggressive, even threatening. At times firing their shotguns worked as a deterrent.

Food acquisition had become impossible, no matter how much they offered, and gold was of no value to hungry people. What was even more difficult was the location of fresh water. Creeks and rivers were now often reduced to a trickle, foul smelling, and covered with oily brown sludge. Undoubtedly it was the result of disintegrating industrial plants and leaking chemicals of all types and varieties—a stark reminder that humanity's destructive legacies would prevail long after they had left the planet.

Over the last two days of their journey, they had gone hungry. Sometimes around the middle of the day, they arrived at the small but heavily fortified town of Montmirail, surrounded by low undulating hills, still pleasantly covered in green, approximately eighty miles from Paris's outskirts, according to Erick's maps. By now, hungry, exhausted, and low on fuel, they were willing to trade anything for a decent meal and clean water. But, because they refused to hand over their weapons, the gatekeeper declined them entry outright. While standing there, lost in their contemplation of how to deal with the situation at hand—under no circumstances would they pass by the opportunity this town might have to offer— a vintage Rolls Royce limousine pulled up beside them.

Elena noticed how the attractive woman in the back seat was observing their motorbike with some interest through the wound-down window. It appeared this woman had some kind of clout around here. As she exited the car, the guards at the gate stood instantly to attention.

She came over, smiling generously, and reached out her gloved hand, introducing herself as Madame de Bois. Madame enquired with great interest about their reason for travelling and their intended direction, contributing even more to Erick's discomfort about the situation. Elena told her their names in her broken French while Erick nodded reservedly, hiding his scepticism. Realising the two were strangers and unfamiliar with her native tongue, Madame instantly switched to English—the continent's universally used language. She presented herself with a regal composer, nearly as tall as Elena, with long, wavy red hair and a curvaceous figure, deceptive for most but not for Erick. Her predatory dark eyes, sharp nose, and slightly twisted mouth spoke of her real character, no matter how honeyed her voice and how sugary the smile was.

So far, Madame had hardly given Erick a second look, but she seemed to be quite taken in by Elena's beauty. However, Erick reluctantly admitted that this might be their opportunity to get into town without leaving their weapons behind. So he changed his demeanour from a dull, passive giant to a broad smiling charmer, dishing out compliments, which earned him a strange look from his friend.

Elena, in contrast, displayed an extraordinary gullibility. She obviously had been completely taken in by Madame de Bois' charm. Replying to the enquiries without hesitation, she quickly summarised their travel history and intention to go to Paris but left out most of the dangerous encounters. On hearing that, Madame, who was obviously impressed, replied with a generous invitation to be her guest's. While nonchalantly waving away the guards, she offered Elena a ride in her limousine. Erick, carefully composing himself, not giving away his suspicion about the all-too-generous gesture, agreed with a wry smile to follow on the motorcycle. He had to drive by himself now; starting the bike and holding onto the handlebar with his clawed hand was not without some difficulties.

Erick followed the car up a slow ascent through the town's narrow winding streets. He took notice of the well-preserved buildings surrounded by substantial fortifications. This unusual place might be explained by its close proximity to Paris and was possibly functioning as a kind of country retreat for the well-to-do of the city. While driving behind the limousine, he wondered how this woman got hold of a vintage car model from the twentieth century still in such pristine condition. The only explanation he could come up with was that it must have once belonged to a car museum in Paris.

They stopped in front of a cast-iron gate. Three armed men guarded the entrance, swiftly following Madam's order to open it. Erick could see a long tree-lined driveway behind it leading up to a large manor house in the middle of a beautifully maintained park. The limousine drove past the manor house until they stopped in front of a small villa at the rear of the gardens.

The feature of a helipad nearby with two small copters present somehow affirmed Erick's previous assumption. Only the absolutely wealthy could afford such items in this day and age of technological decline! Or maybe he had got it all wrong, and progress was still maintained in well-protected places for a selected elite.

Several servants rushed towards them as soon as he dismounted from his bike. Erick took their rucksacks off the back before their motorcycle was wheeled into an adjacent shed. At the top of the steps leading up to the entrance, two maids dressed in the traditional garb of the early twentieth century greeted them demurely. Erick could not help but feel highly agitated at that sight.

Before they were let to their rooms to freshen up, Madame informed them, looking particularly at Elena, she was giving a dinner party that evening and she would be most delighted if both of them could attend. Elena was just about to object when Madame added, 'Oh, don't worry about dressing up. I will send the appropriate evening garb for both of you.'

Erick noticed the sly smile crossing Madam's face when she walked away.

Elena could hardly remember when she had last seen a room like the one she was entering now. The elegance and style were overwhelming her senses. She stood there for quite a while, speechless, taking it all in, whereas Erick took no notice of the opulence. He had no time for such vulgarities in desperate times like this, regarding all luxuries as superfluous but, more significantly, as a waste of rare natural resources.

A gentle knock at the door stirred Elena out of her trance. Two elderly lady servants entered, one holding several garments; a suit for Erick and three dresses for Elena. The other servant was bearing a large tray with cold meats, cheeses, white bread, a bottle of red wine, and two crystal glasses. Things are getting worse, Erick thought! But seeing Elena's exuberant reaction, oblivious to the unnaturalness of the situation and enjoying herself, he kept his suspicions and cynical remarks to himself, just for now. After all, they had a difficult time behind them, so Elena deserved a bit of frivolity.

They stuffed themselves, disregarding all manners and etiquette. When satisfied, Elena started to inspect their suite more thoroughly, giving cries of excitement whenever she touched or sat on one of the many luxurious items which filled their suite. The interior of the bathroom simply took her breath away. She instantly stripped off, opened the taps, lowered herself into the colossal tub, and called for Erick to join her. As he stepped into the steam-filled room, he jokingly commented that having a bath before joining tonight's dinner party was probably advisable. After all, making the right impression could open doors. There might be a chance of meeting someone who could tell them where to find that mysterious high-tech plant. Erick had no idea how close that remark would prove to be true. Both did not want to leave the tub for a very long time, topping it up as soon it began to cool and staying in there all afternoon, dreaming along, not saying a word, and giving their minds a chance to roam free.

Only afterwards did Elena feel a jolt of guilt as she hesitated to pull the plug out. So much clean water was being wasted just for one bath.

Finding all the necessary items on display, Elena began her make-up procedure for the first time since celebrating Christmas at Señora Mendoza's. Throwing a sideways glance at Erick, she suggested that it might enhance his standing at the party if he shaved his beard so everyone could see what a handsome man he was. Grudgingly, he took up the shaving blade, giving off the occasional grunt of displeasure while Elena smiled gleefully.

The fact that there was nothing amiss in their luxurious apartment only fed Erick's suspicions that this was all a big honey trap. He decided to go along with it for now while agonisingly slowly cutting away at his facial hair. When he had finished, he left the bathroom, giving Elena the necessary privacy for more intimate procedures.

He had to admit that Madame's ability to measure him by sight was admirable. The suit fitted perfectly, and seeing himself in the mirror dressed in such style, long-gone memories appeared in his mind. He was again twenty-two, the best-looking gay man in the navy, seduced by many but in love with only one.

While enjoying his little twitch of vanity, Erick heard a quiet giggle behind him. Having been caught and feeling embarrassed, he turned around and was confronted by a being from some mysterious fairy tale. Gazing at Elena, now dressed in a tight black gown, the abundance of her black hair, beautifully tied in a long plait, left him speechless. When she asked him how she looked in a rather flirtatious manner, his throat was too dry to reply.

'Oh, go on; it can't be that bad,' she laughed.

After he had swallowed his paralysis, he just managed to say that it might be too dangerous to let her go to the dinner party. He received a generous smile for his compliment, kissing him softly on his lips, telling him, 'Erick, I am all yours if you ever want to change your preference, you know how much I love you!'

Both of them, overcome by a sudden awkwardness, began to laugh while falling in each other's arms, knowing very well nothing between them would ever change.

Then it was Elena's turn to pass judgment. Stepping back, telling him to turn several times, straightening his bow tie, pulling his cuffs and some creases here and there, and with a broad grin, she told him, he still looked like a yeti from the Himalayas! At the same time, she quietly thought that Erick would always be the most attractive man she had ever met, and she let a few tears run freely down her face.

It was getting dark. Both had just finished the 'dress rehearsals' when they heard a knock on the door. A maid entered, waiting patiently, asking if they were ready for the pre-dinner soirée.

Before leaving the room, Erick warned Elena to only drink modestly and touch nothing that someone else had not eaten or drunk. She laughed at his overly suspicious mind and told him to loosen up. Did they not experience enough dread during their travels? In contrast to Erick, Elena was undoubtedly in high spirits. This would be the first time since Erick had shared the bottle of whisky with his friend the smith, how they had danced drunkenly to the tunes of his guitar. Elena did not want to miss this chance to party. She did not even have the slightest suspicion that Erick might be jealous. But he was not finished yet. Again, he reiterated his concerns and held her back once more, alerting her with some of his observations:

'Elena, did you not notice all the curtains at the manor house were drawn and not a soul could be seen up there. Does it not make you suspicious?'

She smiled back at him, now telling him to let go of his distrust for once, promise not to spoil her fun, and be his charming self—at least, for that one evening.

18

Meeting the new crème de la crème

As soon as they entered the dining room, all eyes focused on Elena. Some of the males visibly held their breath, and others put down whatever they had just been holding. Erick could not help but assume that Madame had previously told them that a new, beautiful member might soon join their elite circle.

Madame was trying to make the most out of the moment by showing off her new acquisition and greeted Elena with an extra-special surplus of sweetness. She introduced her to everybody as if she were the latest creation of a famous designer, while Erick just got a simple nod.

After that first moment of surprise had passed, the two of them were thronged by all present, having only just minutes before being engaged in quiet, animated conversations. Cocktail glasses were pushed into their hands, and everyone wanted to be the first to 'interrogate' the outlanders from the wild north. Elena felt undeniably exhilarated and used all her youthful grace and Spanish charm, without inhibition, to impress the audience. Every man in the room, disregarding age and looks, seemed overwhelmed by her feminine beauty. They were staring at her as if observing a rare Renaissance masterpiece.

Erick recognised with astonishment; that the etiquette of the times had undeniably changed! Such behaviour of unrestrained staring would have been described as vulgar in the early twenty-first century during the high water of women's rights.

In contrast to Elena's charming performance, Erick was playing along at the fringes, acting out the part of the simple-minded, muscle-packed giant from the wild, who is willing to reply to all inquirers whilst laughing charmingly about the often silly question put to him by the few middle-aged matrons present, seemingly agitated that they had lost the stage to this extraordinarily impressive young girl.

Erick discovered he had misjudged his abilities to draw in the crowds. Having at first no genuine interest in being the centre of attention, his stories relating the gory details about wild beasts, the danger of all kinds, Russian raiding parties, slavers and pirates had soon turned the tide of the assembly's interest towards him. He actually began to enjoy himself the longer he was spinning the yarn. Erick made sure his account of the events made his audience shiver, not sparing the loss of his arm and the heroic stand Elena had made to rescue him.

Whilst playing his listeners, he secretly studied every one of these characters in front of him, all of whom seemed to regard these occasions as an opportunity to let go and get drunk on the abundance of high-quality champagne, spirits, and cocktails—everyone except for Madame.

However, Erick hid his contempt for these people even though, after a while, he began to feel his agitation rise at having to play along with the charade. He had to make a decision; without the dulling effect of alcohol, he might not be able to last through to the end of the evening. Erick had been eyeing the extensive display of the single malt whiskies but so far had resisted. Realising that, for the moment, it might be the best solution, as there was nothing else he could do. Waving at the waiter, he asked for a bottle, helping himself generously.

Having been plied with champagne, Elena was letting it all out, smiling and laughing with great delight, holding sway in the manner of a movie star. Glancing secretly at her, Erick asked himself if it was just jealousy that made him so uneasy about the attention she received. Considering what she had endured in her short life, why could he not let her have some fun for once without judging?

Despite the unusual character of the situation, the first of its kind since they had been together, he knew his concerns were valid. The whole setup smelled of deception to him.

Seeing no alternative but to loosen up so he could play along, Erick poured himself a few more glasses of that exquisite whisky. He had to admit, also grudgingly, that his mood was improving, and he was watching with delight how Elena played the floor. This event allowed her to express herself for the first time as a grown woman, something she had never had the chance to experience before.

Erick, on the other hand, now starting to feel the warmth of the spirit softening his mind, had to make sure he would stay in control. As practice had taught him, if handled sensibly, his consumption of high-quality whisky would hardly affect his judgment and responses as long as he drank water regularly.

Finally, having reached his equilibrium, Erick played the audience instinctively, with less interference from his mind, surprising himself with his irresistible charming abilities and noticing Madame's curious gaze directed at him.

His suspicions returned immediately; Erick had no doubt she was up to something and that something was unmistakably not of a sexual nature! While he kept spinning his tales, increasingly bloodcurdling and gory, which came easy now that he was mildly intoxicated, he observed Madams' every move. His audience was captivated and simply could not get enough! Cheers followed whenever he described how bodies were ripped apart; his knife sank into the flesh of a boar or an adversary.

After a while, having repeated the same story once too often, he introduced new varieties and spun a bit of fantasy, as no one seemed to mind. During the sumptuous dinner that followed, demands for more of his tales of carnage and destruction kept coming.

As the evening progressed, Elena and Erick held absolute sway over the table. As most of the guests, having by now reached high levels of inebriation and unable to resist answering the most intimate of questions, Erick turned the table and began to squeeze at some of the guest's minds.

He played one after the other, making the rounds, sounding them out one by one about the real purpose of these regular get-togethers and their position in Parisian society

During his existence in the wild for nearly twenty years, Erick's senses of observation had sharpened beyond the average abilities of these members of an over-refined society, their minds soaked with decadence, their achievements reduced to the squandering of their estates or inheritances, their intellectual prowess long gone, exchanged for empty pride.

What he saw above all were weak faceless yes-men and women who knew how to stay afloat; nouveau riche scammers, insensitive, cunning, ruthless, but also careful not to jeopardise their precarious position. To sum it up, these were the usual arse holes at any war-profiteering gathering! And not forgetting, there was also the dessert; the obligatory set of dolls, pretty and laughing shrilly at every pompous remark made by some male clientele, hoping one of them would provide the following week's meal tickets.

Erick was glad none of these people had any idea how naked they appeared to him, apart from Madame, who obviously played her own game of deception and manipulation. Erick became increasingly intrigued about whom she was deceiving here, everyone present, or just Elena and him?

Fortunately, late in the evening and to Erick's great delight, he realised that not all guests were vulgar, sinister, or evil. Some were actually likeable or even humble under their deceptive veneer. Despite their ostentatious outfits, one or two appeared to play a game equal to Erick's.

There was Charles Lecurbuyet, a former professor of history at the Sorbonne, kind and understanding but an absolute bore, who enjoyed his whisky even more than Erick did. He was a typical leftover from a dying civilisation—that large section of the overeducated conservative now lingering without real purpose, believing in a possible resurrection of the past, pathetically superfluous, and unable to grow their own potatoes. It appeared the only option left for them was to become spittle-likers of the new, overly ruthless Machiavellian breed.

One man managed to stand out from the crowd, the liberal-minded, provocative and unmistakably gay personality of Monseigneur Moulray—a staunch atheist without apology, who freely admitted that the catholic church was a corporation of privilege and still the most lucrative enterprise invented by the late Roman aristocracy to keep the ignorant masses in check and in their place. During their honest, intimate conversation, he invited Erick earnestly to look him up as soon as he arrived in Paris.

The moment Madame saw how these two men openly displayed an understanding of each other, she choked on her Chateau de Poways (or whatever brand it was). Much to Erick's delight, Madame's agitation increased considerably during the evening as she observed how easily most guests had taken a liking to Erick and that her previous evaluation of him as a giant simpleton had been wrong.

By the time late-night coffee and dessert were served, Erick had reached the limit of his endurance. All that he could fantasise about by now was when and how he could cut the throats of half the people present. Without a doubt, he had been let into in a human snake pit. Erick could only guess what might be lying ahead at their final destination in Paris. Despite its harshness, relentless violence and lack of sophistication, he knew the northern wilderness was more appealing than this cauldron of pretence and vulgarity. Erick's suspicions about the imminent danger they would face sooner or later in this place had only increased during the evening. Still, he saw no option but to act as if he expected nothing sinister. This challenging feat could only be managed by consuming more high-quality whisky.

Towards the end of the event, Erick was forced to put aside his contempt for Madame, marshalling his last charming reserves, buttering her up with sweet talk, asking about her ability to set up lavish dinners in such harsh times and her impressive qualities as a host? His unmistakable charm and drunkenness must have done their work. He might not have overcome Madame's suspicions. Still, Madame enjoyed his attention after he had avoided her all evening, and she explained in detail how she managed her estate.

Apparently, the area was still well watered by underground springs, which enabled them to build intricate water supply and preservation systems. All their foods and animal husbandry were taken care of in well-hidden greenhouses and underground stables, positioned and heavily guarded in the hills behind the town. This was the reason for their prosperity and attractiveness: supplying the well of citizens with healthy food and some vulgar, decadent attractions!

His state of inebriation helped Erick to keep up his joviality and charm. He had given up on his paranoia long before and also the determination to water down his alcohol consumption. If Madam had planned to kill him now, he would be unable to resist.

Elena, in contrast, had also ultimately let go of inhibitions but had kept control of her alcohol consumption! For her, it was intoxicating enough to have all men's eyes on her. Her radiance sustained; she only had the occasional sip of champagne. Erick had to admit he was impressed with her self-control.

They finally reached their rooms at late hours. Elena, still fully self-aware, managed, with the help of one of the servants, to get Erick up the stairs and straight into bed. It was left to her to undress him and tuck him in. Lying next to him, listening to his rhythmical breathing, she let her elation simmer, mulling over every phase of the evening she had enjoyed so much.

Sometime in the early morning, Erick awoke with a splitting headache. Besides his miserable conditions, he was again tortured by that nagging suspicion they had been caught in a trap, convinced that Madame was hedging a sinister plan for both of them. Without question, the dinner invitation had intended to confuse and provide a false sense of security for both of them. That plan had not worked in Erick's case, but how far she had influenced Elena, he did not know.

Erick got up and, under his renewed paranoia, made sure they could not be surprised in their sleep, wedged a chair under the door handle and checked all windows were securely locked. The heavy curtain created the impression that it was still early morning, causing Erick to fall asleep again.

19
The plot thickens

Erick struggled with his hangover but was saved by a sumptuous late breakfast that had just arrived in time.

Shortly before midday, a servant knocked on the door, presenting Elena with a riding outfit and an invitation to a women's only hunting party. Erick could not hold back his disapproval and frustration about Elena's blindness to the apparent charade, again verbalising his distrust for Madame with derogatory words and arguments. Elena ignored him. She was still in a party mood and became excited about the invitation.

As soon she had left, Erick regretted his outburst and reminded himself again that she was still young and her life had just begun, and all he had left about life was his cynicism. At her age, her hunger for experiences had no limits. Without further comment, he let it go and busied himself with cleaning his guns. All that he could do for now was to stay alert!

Once finished with his task, he decided to stroll through the town to observe its defences and, of course, its weaknesses, just in case they would have to leave in a hurry. Then he remembered he had intended to find out where their motorbike had been stored. He had seen it rolled into the shed behind the villa, and as expected, it was locked up, again confirming his suspicions and distrust.

The primary purpose of his excursion was to find a printed map of Paris. He considered it vital for them to know where they would be going. Unfortunately, as a result of that brief period of the invention of cyber maps, most printed items had become unfashionable and consequently had gone out of print. Times had changed. Under the new world order, maps had regained a value far beyond their original price, especially for overland travellers like them. With this in mind, Erick did not have much hope of finding such specific items.

Not long after he had left the manor house parklands, Erick sensed that he was being followed. When he stopped at a bric-a-brac store which sold a range of wares such as books to cooking pots, clothing, and now obsolete technology items, he found her suddenly standing next to him. It was the girl with a shopping basket, which had strolled all the way behind, and was not at all concerned about him noticing her.

Erick, now all curious, pretended to be absorbed entirely in searching through the box of books in front of him. He heard her whisper, whilst hardly moving her lips, that she wished to speak to him in a more isolated place. In about half an hour, she would be at the graveyard near the little chapel on the hill. It was urgent, and he must not miss the meeting if he cared for his and his girlfriend's life. The face of the shopkeeper appeared suddenly behind the window, inquisitively looking at both of them standing next to each other.

She was gone before Erick could turn his head. Wondering what that was all about, he decided to hold out at the store for a while to avoid any unnecessary suspicion.

He then entered the shop to enquire about books and maps and was assured that stacks were available in the back of the shop. He left after having a quick browse around, telling the shopkeeper he would return soon. To find out if anyone was following him, he entered a few more establishments of a similar kind before walking up the winding streets toward the crescent of the hill.

He arrived at a beautifully overgrown and disused graveyard—a sure indication that all traditional burial practices had ceased long ago. The view over the town and into the valley was enjoyable, so he walked around pretending to look for a specific burial ground, bending down in a false display of curiosity to read the inscriptions on the moss-covered gravestones.

The girl called for him out of the shadows of a large tomb, asking him to step inside quickly. Erick, never without his instincts on high alert, looked around cautiously, making sure he had not walked into a trap of sorts.

Judging by her looks, she was not more than seventeen, slender, pretty, and of a slightly darker complexion. Without introducing herself, she began to tell Erick straight away, in her French-accented broken English, that he and his beautiful girlfriend were in great danger! Madame ran a high-class prostitution business and was keen on acquiring healthy, young, attractive women. Her enterprise could be summed up as classy slavery of young women. The emphasis was on healthy because venereal diseases had become rampant in and around Paris, with effective treatments now in short supply. Furthermore, the wealthy paid very high prices for healthy breeding stock and classy mistresses.

Madame's methods were implemented without scruples! As long as she could lure Elena with luxuries, entertainment, and presents, she would keep up her pretence of joviality, acting like the wolf before Red Riding Hood entered the house. If coercions of the softly-softly method did not achieve the desired results, Madame would use drugs and violence to ensure the 'product' performed to her specification.

For Erick, there might be a special offer of money or a position in her entourage as a bodyguard. Madame had a particular liking for athletic men, but he would be killed immediately if he could not be convinced with money and special favours.

'Well, why did she not do that straight away?' Erick wondered out loud.

The answer was simple: damaged goods are less valuable, and good fighting men are hard to come by. Diseases were now widespread, spreading, and uncurbed. Consequently, self-interest and survival were left as the last moral barometer. For Madam, it was the only characteristic that counted around here, so she expected everyone else to live by a similar moral code to hers.

A chill went down Erick's spine on hearing a young person already having such a dark perception of reality. He had to admit her bland statements and directness about Madame's character did not surprise him.

'So, what do you expect us to do then?' he enquired, somewhat stupefied.

'Run, and take me with you,' was her simple, bland answer.

Erick could not help but laugh. But there had been not a trace of humour in her voice. Wasting no time, she laid out the details of her plan:

'The only way to get out of here is to take one of the helicopters and blow up the other one, or take Madame as a hostage and drive the Rolls Royce out of here. Since your arrival Madame has given orders not to let you go and all guards at the gates are on high alert. If you try to leave, they are ordered to kill you! You have no time to waste; your only chance of success is to act as soon as possible. Because you have just arrived, Madam does not yet think you already suspect her sinister intention. Furthermore, they are not expecting a bold attempt to escape right now.'

Still somewhat suspicious about whether it was not just another of Madame's ruses, Erick enquired how she was so well informed.

'Why should I not think you are trying to trap me on instruction from Madame?' he asked.

To disperse his suspicions, the girl rolled up her sleeves to show him metal bands, one welded firmly to her left wrist and one on her right leg.

'These are sensors and they are activated if a slave tries to leave the town. Does that not tell you enough? I have been a prostitute since I was twelve and locked up in that mansion since. Unfortunately for them, I have caught the disease and now I am only useful as a maid. But I know of others who met the same fate as me before. They were disposed of without hesitation! If my condition gets worse, I too will disappear without a trace. I am only still alive because I used to be Madame's favoured girl! Please take me to Paris where I can hopefully find a cure.'

Now that he had listened to the girl, Erick understood that the situation appeared far worse than he had anticipated. However, there was a seventeen-year-old girl that had given him a simple, straightforward plan of action. It was apparent the girl had thought of and planned this course of action for quite some time. She had been waiting for someone like Erick to help her put it into action.

Could he have asked for more under the circumstances?

There was one apparent weakness in her plan; she would need to obtain the car keys with the help of one of the male servants she trusted to be on her side. After she had got hold of the keys, Erick would have to handle the abduction and the rest.

He decided, for now, to listen further. Since his army days, he knew plans never worked out how they were expected to. But time was in short supply; their chances of escape were diminishing as they spoke. He had to make his moves as soon as possible! If Madame discovered he was unwilling to agree to her terms, her henchmen would try to kill him, leaving Elena at her mercy without any chance of escape.

As on most nights, Madame attended to her brothel, but over the weekend, expecting very influential clients, which would most likely arrive by helicopter. After playing the gracious host, she would leave her clientele to their pleasures and retire around midnight to her quarters, handing over the supervision to a dedicated mistress. The girl followed up with more detailed descriptions of how to proceed:

The time it took Madam to walk from the mansion to the villa would be the best moment for the abduction. She had to be subdued and quickly dragged into her limousine, which the girl would have opened beforehand. Once Madame was securely tied up, they would use her as a hostage and order the guards to open the gates. The rest should be an easy drive to Paris.

Of course, they could get in trouble once they reached Paris because Madame was well connected and the word would be out, but everyone had enemies, and possibly did Madame, so they might get some help on their arrival. However, as soon as they let her walk, she would pull every possible string to have them killed. Under these circumstances, it would be advisable to kill her first before they reached the city, considering that she would not hesitate to do the same to them. The girl's eyes began to glow suddenly with hatred. 'Or, it might be a good idea to sell her on the slave market in the outer suburbs to let her experience what she has inflicted on so many others,' she added gleefully.

Erick had to realise Paris was now a city of 27 million people, a human anthill ruled by many warring factions.

'But for now,' she concluded, 'let's make sure we get out of here safely.'

Erick shook his head in disbelief. How much must such a young girl have been through to reach this clear-headed ruthlessness? He could not help but admire her for her courage. Under the circumstances and being pressed for time, he had no doubt that this was a desperate plan riddled with numerous unknowns. But what choice did he have? Erick agreed to follow her strategy, and without further words, they parted. Both chose a different path to return to the manor house.

There was just one big obstacle for the plan to work without delay: Elena's obstinacy in not wanting to see the evil intentions of Madame's actions. Erick would have a lot of convincing to do during the following evening!

On his way back to the shop, Erick sensed many eyes again spied on him. Should he not be worried about the young girl? Indeed she must have understood the risk to her life by approaching him. Doubtlessly, all of the citizens in this town were under Madame's control and would inform her about every one of his moves.

Erick began to rush down the hill back to the second-hand shop, now more urgent than before. He entered the former shop again and nodded to the man who recognised him as he made his way into the back room, focusing on finding some maps of Paris, no matter how outdated they might be. Erick had no intention of revealing his search's genuine interest, casually mentioning his love for old books about Paris's architecture and historical plans. Everything in the man's behaviour indicated that he was under instruction to observe Erick closely but could not make any sense of Erick's historical interests.

The air was filled with dust and the smell of rotting paper. Numerous unpacked boxes were piled up all over the floor. The walls were covered with a shelf holding books in a highly disorderly manner. At first, it appeared hopeless to Erick to even start his search. It could take hours to find what he was looking for. Time was in short supply!

Nonetheless, he rummaged through the shelves and soon was lucky. He found several old city directories and maps featuring Paris and its surroundings, most of which were dated back fifty years. However, he knew from experience names of streets and suburbs usually did not change much over hundreds of years. He bought a few other books about the city's history and architecture to camouflage his genuine interest. Erick was sure Madame would receive the message about his acquisitions as soon as he had left the shop.

If she had been suspicious previously about his intentions around town, Erick's passion for books would prove to be a convincing diversion. She knew they had been on their way to Paris, and his obviously shown interests would only confirm that they intended to continue their journey without expecting any danger.

The shopkeeper simply nodded when Erick paid with a silver coin. The coin displayed Madame's face and had been minted by herself and handed out generously by Madame to all her guests. For a moment, he appreciated her generosity because he did not have to use his own gold coins, which might have aroused unwanted attention. The man, obviously no antiquarian, charged Erick the same price for every book without even looking at the titles.

20

The best-laid plans do not always succeed

On her return, Elena was ecstatic and would not stop praising Madame's exceptional charm and generosity. It was the first time ever she had hunted on horseback. Elena had felt very unsure at first but had been fitted with a special saddle for beginners and, after an hour, felt confident enough to join in the chase after a wild beast across open grassland. Once they rounded the animal, she brought down the massive beast with her bow and arrow. Her skilful handling of the weapon had earned her the admiration of the entire hunting party. A nearby waterhole, fed by a clean spring, offered the pleasure of cooling off afterwards.

The hunt was concluded with a lavish picnic in the afternoon, at a forest hideout, with a feast of roasted hare and pheasants, and washed down with delicious wines.

'Oh, can we not stay here with Madame and live a life without worries and trouble?' Elena exclaimed excitedly.

Erick was not at all amused, nor had he time for the excuse of her youthful foolishness. On the contrary, Elena's report made him even more determined to leave as soon as possible. He gesticulated with his hand for her to be quiet and follow him into the bathroom, at which point he turned on all the taps before he addressed her in a muffled tone, having expected all along that their suite might be bugged! Finally, after the arguments had been thrown backwards and forwards, he became fed up with her stubbornness, which indicated at the depth of Madame's manipulation.

Surrounded by the sound of the gushing taps, Erick, in a low voice, began to tell her about his encounter with one of Madame's young maids the previous afternoon. At first, Elena looked at him in disbelief, still unrepentant and unwilling to see reason. Instead, she expressed her disappointment by accusing Erick of making up wild stories because she had enjoyed herself, claiming he was just jealous and selfish. How could he suggest leaving the coming night when she had just started having such a good time and made so many new friends, and for what reason? A wild story told him by a girl he had just met that afternoon!

For a moment, Erick had doubts about the sanity of the girl he had nurtured and educated to be critical and see the truth. His blood was brought to a boiling point.

Despite his quiet voice, he managed to put enough emphasis into his words, asking her rather harshly, 'Have you lost your trust in me?' whilst shaking visibly with impatience and anger. This was the moment of truth for Elena. Knowing Erick, she instantly accepted the validity of his words and the danger they were in. She blushed, shook her head and began to cry quietly, realising her foolishness for having doubted Erick's words. They were both quiet for a few minutes. He took her into his arms whilst letting their nerves cool down.

As soon as she dried her tears, he explained his plan.

'But why does it have to be so sudden, can't we...?' she interceded several times, but looking into his eyes, she understood this was the only workable solution.

He continued unperturbed, telling her first that the girl would organise the car keys, and then he would drive the car towards the mansion. Elena would already have gone ahead, having abducted Madame at midnight on her way to the villa, forcing her at gunpoint into the vehicle.

They prepared without delay, ensuring that all their belongings were packed. It was a straightforward plan for Erick, but it felt different for Elena. Taking aside all the negativities she had heard about Madam, Elena could not help but feel she was betraying her new friend, who, after all, had shown so much interest in her wellbeing. Erick had no time for her sentimentalities, expressing his impatience and reminding her plainly their lives were at stake.

Just an hour before dinner, Erick could hear the distinctive sound of two helicopters arriving. The helipad at the front of the house was now brightly lit. Six men in designer suits and small briefcases disembarked; obviously, one-night stayers were walking towards their villa. Erick kept watching, hidden behind the curtains. His focus was now on the pilots. He needed to know where they would go and stay for the night. These enquiries were part of his plan B. As Erick had learned from experience, the only fair chance of an operation to succeed under any unforeseen circumstances was when you had made preparation for a contingency plan you could fall back on.

Seeing the pilots entering the building, Erick rushed down the stairs. He needed to catch the pilots before they disappeared to find out where they were staying for the night. Asking later about their whereabouts would only raise suspicions. There were too many doors to choose from, so he entered the kitchen, pretending to be disorientated and trying to sound as innocent as possible. Erick mentioned he was looking for the pilots because some minor problem had occurred with one of the helicopter's landing gears. He was directed to a side corridor with three doors. Having opened one of the doors, he saw one of the pilots had just reclined on the bed having a drink. Erick, all smiles, excused himself for opening the wrong door.

Dinnertime was at eight. Erick, his strategy in place, played it cool, pretending that it was business as usual and engaging the newly arrived dignitaries in a lively conversation about the current conditions of life in Paris. In contrast, Elena left the table before dinner, excusing herself for having drunk too much this afternoon and suffering from a headache. Her face did not appear wholly convincing for Erick's taste.

By ten o'clock, the newcomers, now slightly drunk and showing unrestrained sexual arousal, retired one after another to the mansion. Madame, smiling wickedly as usual, also generously extended her invitation to Erick.

For a moment, Erick felt himself to be in some kind of a pickle. On the one hand, he had to avoid Madame's suspicions that he might be up to something, but at the same time, he had to give her a valid reason for not wanting to join the others at the brothel. Returning her smile with all the innocence he could muster, he openly declared to be homosexual unless she had something special on offer. Instead, he preferred to stay behind a bit longer and nurture one of her excellent whiskies.

The following two hours appeared to pass excruciatingly slowly. Shortly before twelve, dressed and ready for action, they both let themselves out of the window in anticipation of Madame having posted a guard outside their door, using a rope Erick had organised from one of the downstairs storerooms. The ornate facade made the climb down easy. While Elena posted herself in the shadows of a bush beside the mansion's entrance waiting for madam, Erick made his way towards the garage to meet the young servant girl.

Erick, approaching cautiously, using every shadowy corner to stay as undetected as possible, saw a human shape lying near the car, and his senses sharpened instantly.

Something must have gone wrong! He could not call out for the girl in case a trap was laid out for him. Coming closer, he saw it was unmistakably the body of the girl. She was lying in a pool of blood, her throat cut.

At that moment, Erick could hear feet quietly stepping on gravel; someone was approaching from the direction of the barn opposite the house. He wheeled around instinctively and countered the heavy metal pipe just in time with his prosthetic forearm, continuing the move by ramming the flick knife into the man's throat. Checking the man's and the girl's pockets, he could not find any car keys. The option of escape by car was now out of the question.

Without delay, Erick proceeded with his plan B, simple as that. There was no time for second thoughts or to contemplate how the girl's plan had failed; instant action was required, and analysing could be left for later. Only one man had seen him speaking with the girl—the bookseller! He blamed himself now for his carelessness, which had undoubtedly caused the girl's death, reminding himself he would make Madame pay for it.

He hurried towards the mansion, fearing for Elena. Madame had just left the building, her face showing sudden surprise and terror when she saw Erick. She had been sure that her man would have taken care of Erick, so she saw no need for extra protection.

Elena knocked her unconscious from behind before she could scream for help. Erick instructed Elena to carry the limp body of Madame into the first helicopter, bind her, store their stuff and be ready for take-off. He turned towards the villa and entered the sleeping quarters of the pilots. Waking one of them up, putting his revolver to the man's head and not allowing him to dress, forcing him to walk in his pyjamas towards the helipad.

The pilot, all confused, tried to argue when Erick, without warning Erick jammed his flick knife into his upper thigh while instantaneously shutting the man's mouth with the other hand, telling him if he wanted to live, he had better follow his orders without delay.

Everything was going smoothly until two men suddenly appeared from the villa's rear entrance, one shooting into the air and asking them to stop. Erick turned slowly without letting go of the pilot and pointed at the helicopter, where Madame was already sitting with Elena, a gun to her head. Now two more men appeared brandishing weapons and moving closer before realising their matron was sitting in the firing line. They had no choice but to lower their guns and look on passively for the situation to unfold.

Once Erick had taken his position in the cockpit beside the pilot, he fired a blast of shots into the cockpit of the second chopper beside them, disabling the instrument board and thereby taking away any chance for Madame's men to follow them.

Madame awoke from her head trauma while the blades were already rotating, slowly coming to terms with the situation of her captivity. Her face displayed sheer terror. Vile threats could be heard from the hapless stooges, soon to be drowned out by the rotating blades of the rising helicopter.

Half an hour into their flight, the night sky ahead began to lighten up, reflecting the endless sea of flickering lights on the ground, stretching into the distance. It might not be what the city's nightly illumination once was, but the vastness made up for the lost intensity in its centre.

Finally, and only on Elena's insistence, Erick tied a tourniquet around the pilot's upper thigh. Even so, the man's wound was bleeding steadily, but Erick had no intention of stopping it. His cruelty had a method. He wanted the pilot to understand that any funny business would delay his arrival at one of the city's hospitals. Any secretive diversion would increase the pilot's chance of bleeding to death. Under these circumstances, Erick counted on the pilot's fear to follow their plan.

So far, the darkness below was still absolute, apart from some occasional vehicle headlights. It unsettled Erick to have only a rough idea of where they were heading, despite having studied the outdated maps of Paris for most of the afternoon.

During their relatively short flight of one hour, they had to endure a barrage of vile-sounding words from Madame's mouth, unrepentantly ordering the pilot to turn around. At first, she offered him mountains of gold. The pilot, unable to respond to her ridiculous demands, was threatened with his immediate execution on their arrival. At one point, Erick lost his patience and told Elena to gag Madame. The pilot knew his choice was made for him. If he did not follow Erick's orders, he would undoubtedly bleed to death; also, whom could Madame tell about the incident once she was dead?

Unfortunately for the pilot, the situation did not develop as straightforwardly as he had hoped. Erick insisted on getting rid of Madame before the pilot could find his hospital. Erick had no intention of killing Madame or of bringing her along into the city centre, where she was, without doubt, a well-known character and had connections. Erick's mind was already working on a more devious plan of how to dispose of Madame and all this for one reason: to avenge the young girl and the many others who had died before her.

During the previous night's dinner, Erick had gleaned some fascinating information from one of the guests but, disappointingly, nothing new about the mysterious technology hub in the city centre.

He soon realised those were not the right people to draw into a conversation about that subject. However, there was other, equally exciting information to be gained. Seven rings of suburban settlements apparently surrounded the city of Paris, each with its own administration.

It gave Erick a rough idea of what to expect ahead of them. Each of these rings was approximately 5 to 8 km wide and surrounded by a defence system against the next outer ring, maintained accordingly to the strength of the administrative power. The city centre, comparatively small, comprised the twenty original nineteenth-century arrondissements and was highly fortified with walls that were apparently impossible to overcome.

Three tunnels led into the old part of the city; one for bringing in the supply trains, and the two others provided the in- and outlet of the Seine. Those walls were constructed from reinforced concrete, five-meter-thick and fifty-meter-high, and topped off with electrical wiring, permanent guards, and cameras. Although most of the Seine's water had been diverted around the walls to form a hundred-meter-wide moat.

The river's entrance into the city could be closed by massive sluice gates during heavy flooding, leaving the outer rings to the mercy of the elements.

In Erick's opinion, they had left nothing to chance.

The ruling elite and their service entourage occupied the entirety of the centre. Visitors were permitted to enter the centre only by invitation, and a few lift towers or helicopters usually conducted their movements. The two innermost rings were still controlled and administered by the centre, functioning as buffer zones and housing the better-paid workers for the service and supply stations. The barracks and training centres of the mercenary troops were also located here. Consequently, these two areas required strict controls, and permits were needed for everyone who wanted to get in or out.

The five outer rings were administered to different degrees by lessened governmental oversight. They were more or less notorious hotbeds of crime and lawlessness, kept in check by poverty, disease, and constant rioting among its inhabitants and ruled over by tribal clans, crime syndicates, and political factions of all kinds; constantly making and breaking alliances, fighting each other, and all were willing, for the right price, to do the bidding of the inner city's ruling classes. With its power and resources, the government manipulated these outer rings at will and to their full advantage, regularly playing them off against each other and undermining any possible long-term alliances.

However, out of this melange of humanities dregs, they also recruited the mercenaries they needed to quell any possible uprising, or they would be contracted for the occasional overland raids to quell rebellions in far-off regions.

The descriptions Erick received about the last or seventh outer circle stood out in unimaginable contrast to the inner part. This suburb was apparently populated with ten times as many people as all the other rings combined, stretching seemingly limitlessly as far as the eye could see. In this area, which was without any kind of administration monitoring or policing, the rule of law was entirely in the hands of the powerful gang bosses, who could be only marginally manipulated by the city's administration. Because of its vast, population mass, this area posed a long-term threat to the inner city. Lacking the manpower for physical interference, gold spoke a clear message. The seventh ring was described as equal in appearance to the landscape in the times of the industrial revolution, its population mainly consisting of North Africans and southern European immigrants.

Any combined uprising or unity among these clans needed to be undermined at any cost, assuring that the discontented population, while having nothing to lose, was always ready to engage in violent skirmishes against each other for no other reason than out of utter hopelessness, and starvation played the central role in that game. Simply put, killing undesirable people was not against any law, and precious metals and slavery were the only real currency. Unfortunately, to Erick's irritation, Madame de Bois' had interfered at that point in the conversation and abruptly ended the possibility for Erick to gain more detailed information.

One specific aspect of the outer suburbs had caught Erick's attention and had stuck in his mind. The seventh ring housed one of the city's largest slave markets, especially notorious for its uncompromising and humiliating treatment of its slaves as non-persons. It was run under the motto 'Anything goes'.

Erick instructed the pilot to set them down at that particular slave market. It was now that Madame understood this detour was solely for her benefit she started to shake all over in desperation, and her eyeballs appeared to pop out.

At that moment, the pilot tried to make one last attempt at resistance. He pretended not to know in which direction the market was to be found. But he changed his mind instantly, screaming and causing the helicopter to swerve dangerously when Erick jammed his gun into his wounded leg. After that last feeble stunt, the chopper began to lose altitude and changed direction.

They landed, somewhat shakily, on the roof of a large, disused factory building. The pilot informed Erick that the slave markets were located on the ground floor of the building, where trading was conducted twenty-four hours a day, every day of the week.

Erick tied the pilot to the helicopter's underside—Just in case, he thought. He also took the key for the chopper whilst instructing Elena to stand guard.

Having dragged the struggling Madame out, he told her to strip, showing his most sinister smile. When she stubbornly refused, he used his knife, roughly slicing open her expensive dress, stripping her down to her underwear and collecting a few pieces of jewellery. Erick, ignoring Elena's protest, was undeterred. He continued his procedure by giving Madame a crude haircut using his knife and finished off by kicking her down and dragging her along the ground, covering her with oily dirt until he was satisfied. Madam finally began to sob and begged for mercy, while Elena winced and held her breath watching the drama unfold; she knew it was pointless to interfere when Erick was enraged like that.

Madame began to repeat the same sermon as she had done before, her voice now shriller than ever, simultaneously realising there was no way of escaping her fate. Begging, crawling, pleading for him to let her go, she could pay any money, make them rich beyond belief, and open all the city doors for them.

Erick did not listen nor laugh, telling her that if she kept annoying him, he would gag her again. He tied a rope around her neck and pushed her in front of him towards the nearest iron staircase. Three levels down, Erick heard the commotion of a large gathering of people—shouting in different languages mingled with screams of desperation. He dragged Madame along until they arrived at a vast hall. In the middle stood a large platform. Here, bound, naked and semi-naked people of all ages were lined up. Numbers were shouted from the audience, and fingers were pointed. Once bought, the slaves were pulled down, and others took their place.

Erick approached one of the dealers standing beside a line of cages behind the podium. By now looking rather unattractive, Madame did not even get a glance from the dealer. As soon as Erick approached the man, Madame began to address a barrage of words to the slave handler in French. Erick could easily guess that she was trying to persuade the dealer to buy her and let her go afterwards, possibly promising him handfuls of gold and jewellery.

Unfortunately for her, the man, an experienced slaver, had heard these kinds of stories all before. Increasingly agitated, he slapped her hard across the face, sending Madame to the floor, bleeding from her nose, with nothing more to say. Without giving Madame one more look, the slaver held up five fingers, to which Erick agreed without further haggling and not even knowing what kind of currency this payment was based on.

The dealer handed him five silver pieces cut from a rod, and Erick did not look back when he heard the door slam shut after Madame had been pushed into one of the cages.

While returning to the helicopter, he thought keeping Madame alive had been a mistake, as his feeling for vengeance had got the better of him. He regretted not having slit her throat and thrown her out of the helicopter. Now there was the likely possibility they would see Madame again, and then it might be on her terms.

Back on the roof, he told the pilot to take his chosen direction and get to the nearest hospital, if possible, near the city centre. The man now looked very pale, his blood loss beginning to affect his ability to fly the helicopter, but he also knew his life depended on the quickest way to get help.

However, they would not be allowed to land at any hospital without radioing in first. Erick hoped it would not be the second mistake of the day, and the 'bad news' had not yet come through when he allowed the pilot to inform the hospital. It was a gamble.

Shortly before landing, the pilot informed Erick the hospital's location was in the second circle; if he crossed over into the centre, they would be instantly arrested for violating the restrictions, as no special permit had been issued for their landing. He could still be charged with treason for smuggling in illegals if found out. He begged them to not mention to anyone how they had arrived if caught.

Erick gave him his word while the pilot, suffering from extreme blood loss, tried to land the helicopter without crashing. The machine came down, tilting to one side and then slithered across the roof, only just being prevented from falling over the edge by the solid barriers. Erick dragged the now delirious pilot from the cockpit, threw him over his shoulders, and walked towards a waiting nurse at the door to the fire escape, who directed him down three flights of stairs as the elevator was out of order. Here a pulley system was installed in the central stairwell's eye, where a platform was lifted and lowered by hand, with a stretcher on standby.

Elena was behind him, carrying their rucksacks and all their other paraphernalia. Erick told her not to get too precious about their stuff. They had to get out of there as quickly as possible before someone wanted to see some papers.

They had nearly made it to the foyer before the nurse recalled them and asked for the pilot's credentials and corporation stamps. Without proof of identity, no treatment was possible, and the pilot would be discharged immediately. Erick had no choice but to return to the chopper and retrieve the man's personal bag. Knowing nothing about the procedures required, he decided to hand over the lot and let the nurse deal with it.

Unfortunately, Erick's nerves began to suffer; he did not like being in enclosed spaces for too long and didn't know how to get out quickly, as a situation like this large hospital building presented to him.

Elena tried to divert Erick's mind as well as possible from his claustrophobic attack, reminding him that they had just avoided being killed in a helicopter crash. Erick's tension was still increasing, expecting the sirens to go off any moment. As he had observed, everything appeared out of order, apart from the strategically placed state-of-the-art surveillance cameras. The report of a crashed helicopter on the roof might have triggered alarm bells already. Where would the authorities look first? A hospital might not be rated as their first priority, possibly the entrances to the city, but how could they tell who was watching them?

All they could do was hurry down the fire stairs, diving deeper into that monolith of a hospital before finally finding an unguarded side door into a deserted service area. The scene changed dramatically when turning the corner into the hospital's forecourt. Here they were suddenly confronted with a long queue of people, most of them looking wretched, all lining up in front of a gate, a red neon sign above, saying '*Du Sang*'. Erick did not need a translation to understand its meaning.

The line extended backwards to a heavily guarded entrance gate, separating the forecourt from the street, where another long queue was awaiting permission to enter. Elena spoke to one of the women in the line and asked how much they were paid for their donation. Three silver pieces for a litre of blood and one hundred for an organ was the woman's sullen response without looking up.

Seconds later, the alarm went off, easing the tensions between them. It was time to act. They saw a large military truck pulling up outside the gate, spilling out a troop of twenty heavily armed men rushing through the now wide open gate and advancing towards the hospital building. Spurred on by adrenaline, their survival skills instantly took charge.

Fortunately, no one was examining the queue yet, and Elena and Erick pretended for the time being to be part of the waiting clientele, shuffling along and holding down their heads. Their weather-worn leather suits made them blend in perfectly with the rest of the people. But there was no telling how long their camouflage would hold. They knew they had to escape from the hospital forecourt as quickly as possible. The pilot's interrogation would start soon, and the descriptions of their appearance issued at once.

Elena whispered to Erick that a stampede might be the best solution to get out unnoticed. If all the people suddenly surged towards the gate, driven by panic, there would be no way of stopping them. Erick spotted a small door at the side of the building, which led into the blood bank. Elena instantly came up with a plan: she would use that door to find a way towards the reception area, and from there, she would suddenly storm out in panic, shouting repeatedly 'yellow fever' in French. They would have to split up. Each would rely for the time being on their ability to make a dash for the gate. This would ensure that if one of them were caught, the other could free the other afterwards.

Having been out of use for quite a while, the door opened only after several failed attempts. Elena then found herself in a cleaner's storeroom, where she could enter the blood bank's reception area. To her relief, here, no security guards were to be seen.

An orderly was taking names and credit credentials from the prospective donors when Elena, pretending to have come from one of the donation rooms, rushed past the line of waiting people and suddenly started to shout in a desperate high-pitched voice, *'Jaune fièvre!'* again and again, and running out of the entrance onto the forecourt.

Erick had to admit every time, it was an exciting experience observing how panic played out. All orders in the queue collapsed instantaneously. People turned around and desperately surged towards the most secure place, the gate. Under these circumstances, not even a machine gun could have stopped these terrified people.

21
Swallowed up by the maelstrom

The scene on the streets outside the hospital stood in stark contrast to the situation in the courtyard. Even now, in the early morning hours, people were everywhere, and the majority were enjoying themselves and appeared completely unfazed by the panic-driven people spilling onto the street. There was music, bright lights, cafes and restaurants full of people. What they saw seemed like a human anthill, a dense river of people flowing along, which instantly swallowed them up and carried them out of sight.

They might be out of trouble for now, but the tension of the last few hours had begun to take its toll. They needed a resting place as soon as possible. Hotels were out of the question, considering how well the spy system seemed to work around here.

Despite being highly paranoid by now, their optimism appeared not to be dented. They told themselves they had survived a very critical situation, and it deserved a bit of self-congratulation. And to Erick and Elena's delight, they both fitted in surprisingly well. Both felt extremely hungry, and the seductive smells around them contributed to their desires. All they could do for the moment was to let themselves be pushed along and try to conserve their energy as best as they could, increasingly weighted down by their heavy backpacks and concealed weapons.

Masses of people and a few vehicles moved slowly, sharing the streets with makeshift bicycles and the occasional motorbike. Here and there, a few horse-drawn carts were possibly the newest addition to progress. Clearly, walking was now the predominant form of transport. Most buildings were occupied on the ground floor by small shops, food stalls or cheap restaurants overflowing with goods for sale. But their shiny, busy appearances could not disguise the ruinous conditions above. Without a doubt, this was a favourable hideout for the homeless. By now, the stream of people had flooded them into the open of a large square surrounded by tall buildings. Just like everywhere else, only a few levels above ground appeared to be occupied. On the opposite side of the plaza stood a well-maintained structure featuring a vast and busy eatery. The place caught their attention because they could easily mingle among the many customers without drawing attention to themselves. Everyone was doing just one thing—indulging in the plates filled with foodstuffs in front. Elena, feeling wholly famished, was magnetically drawn into that place.

As soon as they entered the premises, they realised you had to be extremely hungry and poor. The place was filthy and smelly, but the hungry customers were not bothered by the lack of style and cuisine. The affordability was the obvious drawcard that attracted so many customers. Without any hesitation, they joined in the cue of the waiting. To their dismay, they soon discovered no one paid with money. Everyone handed over a coloured card that was stamped at the counter. Elena, pretending to be a newcomer to the system and saying she had lost hers, enquired as naively as possible how she could obtain a meal without a card. In response, she received a rude grunt of disbelief and the order to piss off. However, as much as the situation felt uncomfortable, no one in this place appeared inclined to call for the authorities.

Under the influence of her ravenous hunger, Elena was unwilling to give up so quickly and decided to find a candidate who might be willing to sell the food voucher for some of their gold. She could not imagine that any of these people would refuse such a lucrative deal.

An elderly, grey-haired man dressed in a coat that had seen better days but who still managed to hold himself with some dignity caught Elena's eye. He had just swiped his red card and retired with his bowl of rice and some watery soup to a remote corner of the greasy interior of the restaurant. Elena followed him, waited until he had seated himself, and then pushed next to him on the bench. Some of the other customers at the table started to voice their irritation but retreated quickly when Erick's intimidating bulk took his place on the other side of the old gentleman.

The man was immersed in his meal and had not yet noticed them. Elena decided, for now, she needed to respect the man's privacy and let him eat his meal undisturbed. When he had finished and was about to leave, Elena held him by his arm, asking him kindly if she could speak with him in private.

Obviously intimidated by her request, he told her he could not pay for her meal if that was what she was after. When he tried to move away to the other side, Erick gave him a stern look not to make a scene, assuring him they did intend no harm; they simply wanted to ask him a few questions.

Resigning himself to his fate, the old man sank back onto his seat. Looking at these two strangers, he understood this was not just a simple matter of begging for food. Elena did not waste time on the preamble and asked him directly if he would sell his food allowance card.

At that suggestion, the man looked confused, and then suddenly understanding, he nodded, 'You must be unregistered immigrants, I assume,' he replied, showing no surprise about the question. Obviously, such requests were not uncommon around here.

Elena continued unperturbed in her appeal, telling the old man they would pay him generously for his troubles. He just had to name a price. In response, the man nodded and quietly asked them to follow him outside around the corner to a quiet place. Here he explained to them that any violations of the general order, no matter how trivial, were punished with extradition to the outer rings. Most people would have preferred prison, but there were no prisons. The only charge for any offence against the general order was immediately enforced exile.

Now he looked closer at the two strangers in front of him, finding their appearance neither thuggish nor ignorant. They had behaved well-mannered and non-threatening, and the girl spoke with dignity. It appeared they had finally attracted the old man's curiosity, and it was as if their challenging request somehow energised his spirit. A moment of soul-searching passed before inviting them to follow him to his small watchmaker's shop nearby, suggesting negotiating in the privacy of his home. It might be more suitable to conclude a satisfying agreement for both parties.

As soon they arrived, Elena was unwilling to hold back her graving for food any longer and asked the man if he had some edible items to offer. When he handed her a piece of stale bread and a small block of cheese accompanied by a glass of red wine, Elena nodded her thanks and wolfed it down without delay.

The watchmaker began explaining the logistics of the cards. These came in different values, in yellow, orange and red, and they were only handed out to the citizens of this particular ring. They were also issued with the person's fingerprints to make theft and transfer impossible. So, even if he sold them his card, they could not use it. Yellow, the card for the poorest, provided the bare essentials; tinned food containing only five per cent of protein, the basic survival ration. Orange provided twenty-five per cent protein and twenty per cent fresh food; red, fifty per cent protein, and thirty per cent fresh food items. The rest would account for the beverages. All cards were issued for three months only. However, sudden food rations, seasonal changes, and the effects of interruptions by the raiding parties also influenced the issuing dates. It was as simple as that, no food supplies, no cards.

For now, he strongly recommended they buy only a fake yellow card as they were the least controlled. If they had exceptional needs for something else, there was always the black market. Life in sector two was not cheap, and unforeseen circumstances should be expected at any time.

For the first time since they had escaped from Madame's compound, Elena voiced her frustration with some derogatory Spanish swear words. She simply could not believe that, after they had managed to dodge just about every danger possible, they were brought to a halt by the tedium of bureaucracy.

The outburst caused the elderly man to smile, who lifted his hands in a calming gesture and said, 'Everyone can be bribed, so please relax dear mademoiselle.'

The watchmaker explained finding suitable lodgings was challenging at all times, the two inner rings were under constant pressure to accommodate new arrivals, and that accounted only for those with legal documents. For the time being, they could stay for a small fee in the storage room behind his workshop until a solution had been found. If they had any precious metals to trade with, he could immediately get them food from the black market, lasting them for the next few days. Hearing this, Elena's eyes began to glow. She instantly wrote a list of her desired food items. Their host could not help but smile after he had read it and replied that the real deal would cost her a fortune, but he hoped to find a few less expensive substitutes.

Erick handed him the five pieces of silver he had received in exchange for Madame while thinking to himself, how fitting! The old man looked in surprise at the small fortune and assured them that the sum would pay for two weeks of food supply.

After their host's return, all three sat down to a surprisingly satisfying meal, further enhanced with a bottle of red wine, doubtfully brewed from grapes but rather from some fermented vegetables. Even here in the city, alcoholic beverages appeared to be the only available products in plentiful supply. Small breweries all over the suburbs were busy using whatever was available to produce the desired wares.

Even though Erick and Elena had been dead tired, the meal had revived them somewhat, and desperate for information, they began to ask questions. Under uncertain and possibly dangerous circumstances, getting a clear understanding of their current position was vital.

The old man was only too willing to talk and did so with obvious enjoyment. This was a sudden but welcome interruption to his drab watchmaker's existence.

Elena's most burning questions were, how was the status quo maintained and managed? What kind of institution ran the city? What was the political leaning of the people there? Why was no one instigating a revolution against such dire living conditions?

Listening to the girl's idealistic stream of questions, their host shook his head and began to describe the city's current state of affairs.

As had become evident during their extended stay in the wilderness, Erick and Elena had been left behind by the significant developments of the disintegrating civilised world of middle Europa. Both experienced a bout of doubts again as to whether it had been a sensible idea to leave the wild reaches of the north. Despite its harsh climate, what could compare with the unrestrained freedom offered by a life in the tundra?

Apparently, Paris and, to a lesser degree, Rome and Madrid had become buffer zones, giant holding pans, stemming off and absorbing many migrants intending to move into the north. All had streamed into Europa wanting a better existence, but for most of them, it turned out that they were trapped under the current circumstances. Leaving that chaos of the mega metropolis was nearly impossible once people began joining a particular ring's societies. They soon became obsessed with wanting to move further inwards and, if possible, become citizens of Paris.

The still-functioning administrations were under extreme pressure holding the dam against the continuous waves of immigrants from the south. Their preventive measures' failure would unleash a human wave towards the north, bringing chaos and increasing competition. Consequently, the supply chain and food distribution from the north were vital to keeping those people in place. If the dam broke, the flood would swamp the north, and it could be expected that all the support for southern Europa would be under threat and might completely cease.

London had lost its position for quite some time, gone under owing to constant flooding by the rising oceans. The city was now fragmented into many separate small towns. Only Paris, because of its medieval layout and structure and due to its administration's foresight, had managed early on to become a successful bulwark. Fortunately, all this had only been possible because of the immense gold reserves still held by its ruling elite.

Madrid was now struggling, mainly because of the desertification of Spain and the subsequent dwindling water resources. But more threatening were the marauding bands that were increasingly interrupting the vital supply chains from the north.

Erick was puzzled by the extraordinary possibility of the city's existence despite the current dismal situation.

'Where does the city draw its energy supply from to run the place so effectively?' he asked.

'Ah, a man who sees beyond external appearances,' the old man replied.

'The first and second outer rings not only supply manpower and protection for the city, it also harbours four small, nuclear power stations, which are highly protected and the main source of income for the inhabitants of the two rings. Of course, you might have already noticed, windmills and watermills are in use everywhere, energy is now a currency. There are also a few small manufacturing plants in the outer rings; using whatever material they can scavenge to produce solar panels. Of course, the bottom level of the poor has reverted back to making candles from animal fat, or worse, human remains.'

He added that Paris had managed very well so far because of its enterprising leadership, which continuously invested in the maintenance and defence of the delivery trains. Also, special conditions apply to the two inner circles. By degree, they received preferential food provisions and limited medical attention in exchange for military support, carrying the heavy burden of defence against the outer rings, which displayed a gradual increase of desperation towards the fringes and received only the bare minimum for their survival.

The inhabitants of those habitats relied on raids into the surrounding countryside and, if transport was available, even further afield. However, their primary source of food supply was the breeding of caged animals, especially the raising of pigs, easily fed by the endless supply of people who starved to death or the victims of violence.

Hearing all of these gut-wrenching details, Elena could not help but feel sick.

The old man continued with his descriptions of gory details with undeterred enthusiasm. Rats, for example, were the only affordable protein items for the people at the bottom. Even sewer rats had now a very slim chance of survival, being hunted mainly by the children of the poor. Everything that could be turned into foodstuff was processed, especially in the outer rings. Dead slaves were apparently minced into food for the vicious guard dogs trained on human blood, but generally, they were fed to pigs.

Elena, feeling increasingly depressed, asked where all the slaves came from. Without changing his demeanour or the narrative, the man continued to give an account of one of the most usual daily events:

'We abolished the death penalty ten years ago. Any kind of rule-breaker who acts against standard regulations but who does not qualify for extradition into a lower ring is now condemned to slavery. Because of the endless supply of slaves, most of them are usually worked to death, owing to the scarcity of food. Under these circumstances, sentences like that are more feared than death. Death sentences create only unnecessary costs, and so as a deterrent, the prospects of enslavement work well enough.'

He concluded dryly, 'Hard times demand hard solutions; so far, these measures have found approval by all levels of society,'

Elena's revulsion about such inhumane practices began to turn into anger. She was boiling up inside. Hearing about the treatment of slaves had planted a seed for a new mission in her mind, but she was not yet consciously aware of it.

Erick, in contrast, usually the pragmatic realist, saw it as unavoidable timely progress towards chaos and had passed the age when one still had a taste for revolution long ago. Erick agreed with the watchmaker, already in his mid-sixties, who had seen and experienced enough horror. Uprisings had come and gone, leaving him without illusions about the positive outcomes of such events. The powerful always won in the end. For him to survive meant to take society as it had developed and deal with its daily challenges to the best of his abilities.

However, he sensed that the flames of a revolution were just starting to heat up in Elena. Being of a younger generation, she seemed to lack tolerance for consolidation with the so-called status quo.

Suddenly and to the surprise of both men, Elena burst out into unrestrained passionate screams, addressing the old man, 'Is there no one willing to fight and change that system of such degraded humanity?'

For a moment, the old man looked at her, his face expressionless, before he quietly continued:

'Of course, there are always people who intend to change the system. As it stands, they are hopelessly outnumbered, poorly organised, cannot agree on a modusoperandi and most of all, have no alternative concept to offer that could replace the current state of affairs. Their uncoordinated violent attempts, to bring on change is giving the system an excellent excuse to continue with their harsh methods of suppression. The realm of these so-called insurgents is the sewer systems of the city; a subterranean world, impossible to penetrate or control by any adversary, but also easily blocked and regularly gassed out by the authorities from above. On top of everything else, these outlaws have all the criminal gangs lining up against them. These gangs also profit from the status quo, especially from the constant supply of the condemned, feeding their highly lucrative slave markets. To be honest, mademoiselle,' he continued, 'I have lived through good and bad times in this city, but I have to admit, these are the best times so far of the bad times. Of course, I cannot speak for the people in the outer rings, which may right now be sliding towards the Dark Ages. But we also know, nothing lasts forever. When one day these dissatisfied hordes breach the walls, God help us!' he concluded.

Erick had listened with fascination to the old man's narrative, but was now too tired. He decided to leave the inquiries about his most precious subject, the mysterious technology hub the city was supposed to house, to another day.

Erick retired to the small back room, and while drifting off into sleep, he mused quietly to himself; the journey might, after all, not have been about his search for a bionic arm. Maybe it was Elena's mission to bring that long-awaited solution how to challenge the status quo for good or bad? The young woman was still boiling with rage, all fired up and not feeling remotely tired, appearing like an avenging angel ready to strike fire into her enemies' hearts.

PART 4
THE RISE OF THE HEROINE

22

Uncertainty

Erick and Elena spent the next few weeks of their time familiarising themselves with the layout and social structure of the second ring. Also, that uncomfortable feeling of being watched did not leave their mind, expecting Madam's assassins to be already on their trail. It was time to change their appearance. Replacing their leather garbs, they wore bunched-up, dishevelled dresses and boots without laces. Erick regrew his beard, making him look older, and Elena cut and changed her hair colour into blonde, giving herself a doll-like look.

Accommodation had been found in one of the many cheap and illegal hotels, proliferating in the upper levels of those disintegrating, disused office blocks. The manageress, Madame Lupin, a stout middle-aged woman, was a distant relative of the old man. He had assured them of her trustworthiness and reliability, as she had once been a fugitive herself. She clearly understood that, in a world overcrowded by fugitives, fugitives had no choice but to look out for each other. After she had heard about Erick and Elena's story and their plan to enter the inner city, she immediately offered to help.

She took particular delight in the ironic story of a high-class slave trader ending up as a slave herself. The news of this specific abduction drama had already been circulating for a few weeks among the disenfranchised of the inner rings, where Madame had enjoyed a 'special' popularity after having abducted many young girls from unsuspecting families.

As the proprietor of an illegal establishment, Madame Lupin was used to the occasional raid by the authorities, despite the bribes she paid. However, to ensure her customers were not caught, she had installed a hidden tunnel system at the rear of the building, which opened up into a maze of overgrown ruins, thus offering plenty of ways to escape.

To ease their concerns, she assured them all illegal businesses bribed informants in the governing administration, so they would be warned beforehand of any possible raid on their premises.

Lately, Erick and Elena had started to go their separate ways and spent less time together. They had reached their destination, and so it felt as if there was no need to seek out each other's constant protection. Both, for different reasons, were increasingly enjoying some loosening up of their tightly-knit companionship.

However, Erick wondered about Elena's recent habit of returning late, looking exhausted and tired, and showing physical strain. His questions were answered evasively, so Erick kept his curiosity to himself, not wanting to sound controlling. Their trust in each other was complete; he expected she would tell him when she felt the time was right.

Erick himself had not much to report. His own enquiries, which centred mainly on the day-to-day activities in the second ring, did not supply him with the information he was seeking. Some people might have heard about the giant skyscraper in the fifteenth arrondissement of the city centre, but no one had any specific knowledge about its reputation or purpose. That information had no real value anyway as long as they could not enter the city. For the moment, his curiosity concerning the fate of Madame took up most of his investigations. Erick expected that only a woman like her would have the cunning talents to escape the shackles of enslavement. He imagined the most likely scenario was that the pilot, after being interrogated, would have revealed Madame's whereabouts. If Madame was free by now, Erick had no doubt she would move mountains to get her hands on both of them. But so far, all seemed to be quiet, and he had not seen any images of himself plastered on walls as a wanted man.

Something else was lingering in the back of Erick's mind. How could he contact Monseigneur Moulray? For more than one reason, he liked the man! Of course, he had no knowledge of his new acquaintances' whereabouts, but with Moulray being a public figure, it could not be so difficult to find him. The only person of reference he could have used, Erick, had sold into slavery. Just mentioning her name alone would surely endanger his life. For the time being, making contact with Moulray would have to wait until Erick had found a way to get into the city centre.

These days of inactivity made Erick feel like a fish out of water. There were moments he was not quite sure what he was waiting for. An opportunity to get into the inner city, of course, but so far, they had found no one to help them overcome the obstacles.

Erick also struggled increasingly with this unique, alien environment, and his age-related inflexibility was not helping. This enclave of abandoned eccentricity might offer richness in new experiences for a young, adventurous spirit and a pathway into a more sophisticated existence or the leadership of a powerful clan. Still, for Erick's taste, this place was not far removed from a prison camp. Even in his wildest imagination, he could not have created an alien territory like this. Only his dreams comforted him occasionally with the solace of the wild tundra. Erick avoided discussions about his nagging thoughts, not wanting to appear indecisive or show the weakness of regrets towards Elena, who seemed to be wholly absorbed in some mysterious project she had refused to discuss.

But Erick could not help the increasing irritation towards Elena. After failing to deal with his emotional discomfort, Erick finally decided he needed to address the subject of Elena's secretive behaviour.

To Erick's surprise, it was the exact moment when she revealed what had lately so intensely occupied her. Was it because she had recently sensed his uneasiness? He couldn't tell. So Erick decided to keep a lid on the sensitive issues that had risen between them for the time being.

Elena, incredibly excited, presented him with a selection of delicious cured meats and a bottle of genuine red wine.

'What is there to celebrate?' he asked in a curious tone.

Elena, enjoying the moment of suspense, smiled and began preparing their dinner. As soon as she had filled their glasses and raised hers in celebration of new opportunities before she excitedly reported on the latest development in their life.

'Erick, I can get us into the city very soon!' Elena declared, displaying a broad smile as she waited for his response.

Erick, somewhat unconvinced, could only mumble, 'How?'

Of course, it was not a reaction the overexcited Elena had expected, but although he had asked rather grumpily that he wanted to know what was going on, his response was not unexpected.

'Erick, you must understand, I have been working on this project for over four weeks by now for both of us! During that time, I have risked my life on several occasions. Considering how protective you feel about me, I kept all this hidden from you, fearing that, if I told you what I had planned, you would have without doubt stopped me from going through with it!'

While Erick was still trying to find his voice, Elena continued:

'Erick, the time has come for me to forge my own path! I intend to do it with or without your consent and help. I needed to prove to myself that I am not anymore just an extension of Erick! It does not mean that anything between us has changed. But dealing with the challenges of life and its dangers from now on is going to be based on my own decisions.'

Finally, after having taken a large gulp from his wine glass, Erick managed to speak. Putting aside his own issues, he asked her calmly to tell him everything.

After a few explanatory background details, Elena laid out her plan and the implications involved.

'Erick, remember those people who live in the underground; sewer rats the old man called them? I have managed to make contact with them. They know the underground better than anyone and they are willing to help us get into the city centre! And after weeks of negotiations and test trials, they have finally accepted me into their ranks.'

Now surprised but alarmed about the nature of this new development, Erick forced himself to stay calm and inquired what she meant by 'joined them'.

'Are you saying you are taking part in their action, that you are now one of them? Do you intend to fight together to challenge the status quo? Do you intend to risk your life for a ridiculous and hopeless cause?'

'Yes, that sums it up, more or less!' Elena replied nonplussed and defied him with laughter. 'By the way, Erick, when did we not risk our lives for all kind of courses since the day we left the lodge?'

Her words made sense and brought reality back into their discussion. Erick knew she had him there! Theirs had never been a life of tranquillity, not even in the remote forest mansion. It never made much difference when either fighting for a principle or fighting for their survival.

At that moment, it was up to him to take her into his arms and apologise for doubting her integrity.

'Elena, I am very proud of your decision to fight for something that you believe in and you can count on me to support you all the way.'

Having found each other again, Elena laid out the details of her plan. But the more he heard, the less Erick was convinced that Elena's passionate stance would lead to the outcome she envisaged. So he suggested several alternative ways to deal with the new situation, which would still achieve a similar result. Erick wanted her to apply a dose of pragmatism, see reason, and understand that revolutions never delivered the expected outcomes and the powers to be always won out in the end. She might want to consider those historical facts before she rushes off and try to save the world. He reminded her again what the old watchmaker had told them: Paris provides a buffer, a holding pen for the people streaming up from the south to escape the increasing desertification of the continent.

'Furthermore,' Erick continued, 'this place still holds enough attraction for people who have fled from even worse living conditions. If they all begin to migrate north, the precarious balance, which has established itself in the last thirty years, will collapse. Many will die on their way, and the North's organised food supply may cease, creating starvation for all the people left behind.

'I know this setup of increasing savagery is not ideal, and the people in charge are no better than the most brutal slave traders outside the city. But, do you really believe that once you have overrun their walls, smashed their institutions and administrations, the victors will not behave in a similar fashion? Has any revolution in history really brought the hoped-for liberation? Don't get me wrong; I don't advocate doing nothing, Elena, but I have difficulty seeing a workable alternative for the current situation. See for yourself, the power of the city barely extends further than the third ring. Beyond that, numerous violent gangs are fighting for supremacy. Any new vacuum will be filled instantly. This system is only controllable through holding up the current status quo, and it comes for a certain price. Any new administration will have to make arrangements again with the gangs. New supply chains will need to be established and, what is worse, who will stop the flood of immigrants in the meantime, possibly destroying even what is left worth of preserving? So, what will be achieved between now and your new utopian administration?'

Erick, by now, nearly at the end of his wits, played his last desperate card.

'Elena, remember up north, when living among the untamed elements of nature, nothing happened overnight. Everything happened in its own time. The beavers took years to build their water world. The permafrost disappeared not just in one year, but slowly as well, over many years. So it was the same with the reintroduction of the pine and birch trees. Without question, the time will come when the cities ruling classes will run out of gold reserves, unable to increase the height of their walls, or pay their mercenaries. But they will not depart overnight, they will plan everything long before and by the time the walls fall there will be nothing left behind that is worth conquering. After that the place will begin to reinvent itself out of the ruins until a new equilibrium is established.'

Erick had hardly taken a breath before Elena launched her passionate response. Erick, watching her expression, came to terms with the fact that his opinion was a lost cause. Her passion for fighting for the underdogs, for creating a new reality, had taken a solid hold in her mind over the last few weeks. In the end, the discussion had only one outcome for Erick; he abandoned all lingering thoughts about returning to Finnmark! He would never leave her side, no matter the circumstances. This was now Elena's world; her time was just beginning, and he would help her build this world according to her imagination.

'You are so right, Erick, and you are so wrong,' she began.

She explained in detail the reasons for her absence over the last few weeks. The contact with the sewer rats had come accidentally rather than by choice. She had encountered an altercation where one of their female members had been cornered by a few thugs from a local street gang. Of course, being Elena, she had not been able just to stand by. After having messed up the attackers very severely, the woman invited her to meet her friends, and everything went from there.

Over the following weeks, she gained their trust bit by bit. She was let into their intricate tunnel systems, which extend in all directions under the suburbs of the rings and also under the city proper. She had witnessed these people's misery, deprivation, and strength. These adverse situations were more or less a result of the institutionalised manipulations of the inner-city bourgeoisie.

'Erick, you need to understand there is no equilibrium! This is disinformation to placate the populace about their true intentions. Poisoning their food and water supply systematically decimates these outlaws. Childbirth is rare; if it happens, most newborns die in their first few months of life from diverse causes. The mercenary army of the city is being recruited from the constant stream of desperate newcomers. Those chosen are selected only for their physical strength, brutality and willingness to obey orders. Everyone else will join the masses of the outcast undesirables, condemned to a slow death. I have witnessed people being ripped apart in daylight by giant dogs for entertainment, not unlike the games during Roman times.

What's more, out there, it is all centred on survival of the fittest! Human rights are non-existent; women are the primary victims, either enslaved for sexual purposes or worked to death under horrendous conditions. Erick, if you had seen what I have seen, knowing you, you would have started a slaughter instantly among these savages.

'So now you tell me, shall I leave these people to their fate of that so-called equilibrium or return with you to the North? Shall I not instead make a last stand for humanity, by holding up what is left of consciousness and integrity?'

Having listened to Elena's impassioned speech, Erick did not dare reply and nodded quietly in agreement. He knew that Elena being Elena, had no choice but to follow her conviction. Erick also admitted that he might have been too excepting of the status quo and out of touch with what could be counted as the real world.

Elena continued less emphatically now, conciliatory, admitting she also understood his position but could not accept it.

'Erick, believe me, I am not making this up. I have witnessed too many atrocities during the last few weeks. There is no alternative for me. I just needed to remind myself that there are these characters, like Madame, who are behind all this, profiteering from the suffering of others and getting away with it. I know that I am doing the right thing.'

Finally, Elena sighed; having spent all her energy convincing him of her position, she fell back and closed her eyes. Erick admitted quietly to himself he was impressed by her passion and conviction. Leaving him without any doubt, she had found her calling among these underdogs in their fight for human rights.

23
Contestants

His name was Guillaume, the current leader of the sewer rats, a slim, wiry man of sly character. Until the day Elena joined their ranks, none of the women had the physical strength or determination to fight Guillaume. However, since Elena's arrival on the scene, with her debut as an experienced street fighter, the female faction, nearly two-thirds of the underground army, felt emboldened to challenge Guillaume's position.

During her time in the underground, Elena had impressed her new friends not only with her athletic build and fighting skills but primarily with her charismatic charm, honesty, idealism and the way she treated all members without judgement. She was approached by some of the elderly women in the council if she was willing to stand as their champion in a leadership contest. Dissatisfaction had been brewing for quite some time over Guillaume's dictatorial style and increasing brutal willfulness.

After a few days of negotiation, Elena agreed, and the women's faction made their bid to dispose of Guillaume. However, despite Elena's popularity, most men stuck to their traditional ways of wanting to be led by a man. To ensure those traditions were maintained, the fight over the leadership had to be a life-or-death contest.

After Elena had filled him in on the customary details of the fight, Erick went into a total meltdown! His support for her revolutionary ambitions was one thing, but a life-or-death combat, so she could gain leadership for a lost cause was out of the question. Yesterday they were fugitives; today, she stood to become the leader of an underground army of desperados! This was crazy. Where was the sense in that?

Erick tried to change her mind all day. Could she not be satisfied being second-in-command? At that suggestion, Elena pointed out his ignorance and accused him of not wanting to understand the situation. His male attitude prevented him from seeing clearly. This was not a leadership issue. This was about women's rightful place in society, the right of the majority to rule! She had given her word of honour to fight for them. To change her intentions or to refuse would not only dispute her integrity but everything she had worked for in the last few weeks.

By winning the contest and becoming the first woman to lead the underground army, she would give them a chance to raise their self-esteem and stand as equals to the men. Most of these women had previously escaped from slavery, battered women, subjugated and tortured. This might be the first time in their lives to have the chance to gain some sort of dignity through the representation of their own kind.

Erick's last desperate attempt to change her mind was his offer to take her place, become the leader, and make her his deputy.

Elena shook her head in disbelief, stating, 'Erick, hampered by your patriarchal way of thinking, you still refuse to understand the situation, this is my fight; I am proud to be chosen and look forward to it. If we want to start a new era, this is one of the first necessary steps.'

All that Erick could do was grunt disapprovingly. Elena laughed, assuring him she felt absolutely confident about defeating her opponent. After all, did he not remember she had been trained by an expert in hand-to-hand combat? Was he now doubting his own expertise?

All the crucial gatherings were held in the most massive catacomb of the underground city. The place had been built during the great plague to house thousands of its victims. During the reign of the sewer rats, the site had been continuously enlarged, and galleries had been added to accommodate about fifteen hundred men and women. The remaining members of the society, nearly five thousand, were crammed together in the adjacent tunnels.

The duels for leadership were regarded as most vital, guaranteeing that only the best and most formidable of their fighters would gain the leadership. Being the lowest of the lowest, their principles were entirely based on the natural law, survival of the fittest, and an eye for an eye. These people had no time for whimsicalities. Savagery was their second nature. Their diet consisted of rats and leftovers that could be scavenged from above. Their knife skills were feared and regarded as the tools to guarantee their survival. Even the youngest and weakest were trained from an early age to handle their knives expertly and in total defiance of death. This was just one of the many reasons why they were feared and despised by the populace above ground.

Elena had made light of the contest to deter Erick's fears, but she had no doubt that her life would hang on a fragile thread once she entered the arena.

Just before the fight, she wondered how she could have let herself be talked into this situation.

Both combatants had to strip down to the barest of clothing to prove no trickery or protective armour was involved. Anyone who observed the two contestants would have, without a doubt, put their money on Elena. There she stood: tall, athletic, and charismatic, in total contrast to her opponent Guillaume, wiry and emaciated.

She had been warned over and over again that this man was the most vicious of knife fighters. Despite being injured many times, Guillaume had come out on top in every contest he had entered due to his relentlessness and cunning. There was more at stake than just her survival. Her victory would be a victory for all women. Elena had been urged to kill him as quickly as possible. Otherwise, Guillaume would wear her down and, without a doubt, kill her!

Ten meters in radius, a circle had been drawn on the ground in white chalk. If either of the contestants stepped out, she or he would lose. No matter how the fight proceeded, there would be neither interception nor wiping away the blood. The fight would only end with the death of one of the contestants.

Twenty minutes into the duel, both combatants showed the first signs of fatigue, the blood from numerous cuts turning their bodies and the ground slippery.

Elena had taken her time and studied her opponent's moves until she knew his weaknesses. She was ready for the final stroke. However, Elena had no doubt Guillaume must have done the same.

Trusting in her skills, she had used one of the methods Erick taught her, which she acted out in a particular manner repeatedly, hoping to give Guillaume the assurance he knew all her moves by now. Then, in a split second, Elena switched her knife hand, followed by signs of insecurity in Guillaume's facial expression. She was expecting Guillaume to come for her in that instant before she could unbalance him!

It was the move she had been waiting for; that predictable fighting technique used in the slums of the city, lacking in finesse but performed with all-out death-defying savagery.

Guillaume suddenly ducked low, falling down on his left hand and using his legs to swipe her off her feet. Alas, before he had shifted his weight onto his left hand, giving him a chance to put the action into his right leg, Elena was already in the air, catapulting herself above him while slamming her knife into the top of his skull. Guillaume was dead before she had landed back on her feet. There was a long silence, followed by a roaring applause from all the women in the audience.

24

The Underground

Paris has been known globally as the city with the most extensive underground system of defunct tunnels, sewers and catacombs. Tales had been told that one could easily get lost and never find a way back into daylight again.

Erick was utterly unprepared for his first encounter with the fastness of that system. In his imagination, he had expected a labyrinth of narrow tunnels, reeking with dampness and populated by myriads of rats.

He found a city under the city, equipped with a functioning water supply, cosy niches covered with drapes, kept dry, when necessary, with an electric heater, run by power usually siphoned off from the city's supplies above.

Of course, there was a lot of dampness in some places, and of course, there was the occasional rat that had gotten away from the children, who were constantly on the hunt for a meal. Those rodents were often the only meal of the day, a valuable protein source! If Elena had not informed him rats were part of these people's staple diet, Erick would have questioned why he only saw so few.

Most impressive were the vast caverns, which had been dug out and continuously extended downwards, reinforced with steel and anything that could be salvaged from above. While expanding the system, the underground inhabitants ensured that invading troops would be met with their worst nightmare.

Dead-end tunnels were fitted out with spiked traps or would close suddenly behind anyone who had entered, burying them alive. Warning signs were placed in such ways to be understood only by the locals.

Despite all the tunnel dwellers' advancements, Erick found the darkness oppressive and claustrophobic. This was the antithesis of where he came from. He had to remind himself repeatedly how much these people must have endured being willing and able to live under such conditions and perceiving this kind of environment as their home.

Many years ago, before these people had begun to organise themselves, the central administration raided these tunnels regularly, using gas and explosives. But in time, more often than not, fewer and fewer members of the raiding forces had made it back to the surface. Furthermore, the intensive gassing had also begun to affect the people above ground. Mounting costs, protests from the citizens, and increasing unwillingness for the mercenaries to enter the underground finally ended the eradication program.

Having chosen an alternative approach, the authorities began to seal off the surfacing tunnels, not realising how futile such an exercise would be. So, whenever a tunnel had been filled with concrete, new ones were dug parallel to it. The flooding of the system had proved to be equally disastrous. The sewers had overflowed and spilt excrement into the street, creating an unbearable stench and inflicting epidemics on the citizens above. After years of low-level warfare without any gain, a truth packed was agreed on for the time being.

Food and material supplies would be delivered to the underground in exchange for those living there not attempting any attacks on the citizens of the inner city. Of course, this deal excluded the suburban rings; the underground people were allowed to act out as they wished. Despite constant renewals of diverse agreements, both sides knew this was only a temporary solution. With their constantly increasing population, the sewer people would one day see no other option for their survival but to rise up with devastating consequences.

Erick's excursion into the city centre was still on hold. Only two or three new exit tunnels opened monthly for a limited time and for a limited number of people. Once those exits had been used up and their location was known, they were sealed off immediately. Two new tunnels were currently under construction. But the queue of people waiting for entry permits was long. Erick had been given temporary living quarters. Because of Elena's leadership position, these could be described as a royal suite by the sewer rats' standards!

It went without question that Erick soon had to accept this lodging came with strings attached. To his initial irritation, Elena had informed her new friends of his unique fighting qualifications, expecting him, for the time being, to teach the young every possible combat technique he knew! He had also been told that if he treated them too softly, they would despise him for not being the real deal. So it was all knives out with blood flowing generously. During those sessions, his respect for those people grew day by day. He never heard anyone complain about injuries or having been treated too harshly. On the contrary, they asked relentlessly for more.

Erick soon appreciated training people with this kind of mental disposition. However, his underground stay slowly got to him—it became difficult for him to deal with the constant darkness and the confined spaces, trying as hard as possible to keep his lingering claustrophobia at bay. To his surprise, after a few weeks, he unwittingly had adapted to the conditions.

For the necessary sunlight exposure of every underground citizen, secret enclosed spaces had been established, allowing Erick to experience the positive effect these short moments had on his psyche. However, because of the risk of discovery and the steadily increasing numbers of their members, everyone was permitted only a short sunlight time per day.

Erick also wondered how Elena could stand it. So far, he had never heard her complain about the darkness and questioned to what extent could human beings live under such conditions before their psyche displayed detrimental effects? Then again, he assumed the places where most of these people had come from offered even worse conditions.

Apart from everything else, the illumination of that underground world posed a constant challenge. Initially, electrification was installed and illegally siphoned off from the city's power stations, but recently the power supply became a challenge. All for one reason: technological advances above were demanding more and more of the limited supply of the city's energy, resulting in improved surveillance by the city's authorities about the power theft behind the scene. Apart from the illumination of the large assembly halls, all the lighting for the personal cave dwellings and tunnels was now the individual's responsibility.

Consequently, the lightening of private spaces had reverted to the simple handheld lamps, mostly burning alcohol as fuel. In areas of possible methane ignitions, those were strictly forbidden. Instead, ropes were installed along the walls leading through the darkness.

Erick could not help but be impressed by the versatility and innovativeness of these people. How quickly they could adapt and find new ways to cope! Undeniably, many had paid with their lives in previous years by contributing to the collective knowledge until a reasonable equilibrium had been established to deal with their inhospitable environment. While the underground had grown consistently in strength, the city's ruling classes had also become aware it was now impossible to overpower them with those brutal methods previously tried and failed. The residents below had no doubt; the challenge would arise as soon as the city's administration had acquired the technological know-how for a full-on assault that would solve the problem of the rats once and for all; until then, a precarious peace prevailed.

The awareness of the unpredictability was feeding the enthusiasm for a preventative assault on the city and its establishment. But, no one had come up with a workable strategy for how they could defeat their enemies, and furthermore, how would they run the city's administration after their victory? Erick clarified that the destruction of one system does make no sense as long the replacement only offered an equally dysfunctional system without suggesting improvements for the ensuing period.

As far as Erick could judge, their warmongering was simply fuelled by hatred for the city's upper classes and an unrestrained bloodlust. The young he was training accepted predominantly without much questioning that their futuristic vision might be just a variant of their chaotic presence. What else did they know?

Considering the circumstances, Erick quietly pursued his own agenda, collecting necessary information about the types of people and their lives in the city centre. He wanted to be as ready as possible and blend in with the populace when the day of his entry came.

All those preparations took time. First and foremost, the need to acquire the right outfit, particularly a designer suit and a fashionable hairstyle! Soft leather gloves were also on the list so his metal hand would not be noticed.

Under the current circumstances, Erick avoided inquiries about the well-known personality of Monseigneur Moulray. It might be better to wait until he was in the city. Any connections with one of the bourgeoisie might jeopardise his relationship with the people from the underground. Even though patience was one of his greatest strengths, Erick felt tensions rising during the weeks of waiting. His mind was again overcome with doubt, the increasing discomfort of not belonging, and most of all, an instinctive feeling Elena was slipping away from him. As time lingered, inactivity led to negative thoughts and, in turn to depression. Something needed to shift! Also, Elena had not yet confirmed if she could accompany him on his first excursion into the city.

Of course, there were many reasons for the holdup. The biggest obstacle so far had been the impossibility of obtaining false identity papers for Erick. No one could move around in that highly technologically controlled city without documents. The difficulties did not stop there. Their own spies occupied the two safe houses permanently. Crammed, as they were, their job to collect vital information ranked as the highest priority. In addition, Erick had been informed as soon as he came out of one of their secret tunnels he had to navigate the situation by himself. If one of their own people were caught on the streets, they would most likely be executed.

Erick had never had trouble losing his nerves when confronted with a violent full-frontal assault. Still, when he stepped out into the light of this alien civilisation, it was precisely what happened.

He had been briefed about this eccentric, technologically advanced environment, but nothing in his imagination could have prepared him for what he was now seeing. A pseudo-liberal society under the absolute control of a high-tech security apparatus! Gleaming shiny surfaces everywhere, superlatives in every form and colour, ostentatious displays of wealth, and no sign of poverty.

PART 5
THE CITY OF PARIS

25

Culture shock

Erick was unable to move and stood there motionless, letting the scene play out in front of him. An otherworldly city, Erick thought; one might as well have been visiting a space station! Regarding architecture, this was a city of the past and the future. Without exception, everyone was dressed outrageously stylishly. This environment, which displayed unrestrained consumption and leisure-seeking activities, instantly disturbed Erick.

On the positive side, no one took notice of him, and no one moved with any kind of urgency or even purposefully. If his memories did not deceive him, the whole place seemed like a leisure park on a Sunday afternoon.

A few electric cars could be seen, but most people used tramlines. Skin colour or race appeared to be no issue. Black, brown, or white skin, everyone walked with confidence and wore equally luxurious outfits. One aspect left a somewhat favourable impression on Erick: no religious distinctions could be made. As Erick found out later, any overtly displayed signs of religious expression had been outlawed by mutual consent from all parties. That included any sacred symbols in churches, mosques, or temples.

Furthermore, anyone proselytising spiritual beliefs would be instantly expelled from the community. On the other hand, religious freedom was paramount but regarded as a strictly personal issue. In that way, all religious tensions among the many congregations were eliminated from the onset.

No police or security guards showed their presence anywhere, which made Erick highly suspicious. It could mean only one thing; control through the city's cyber security net must be absolute and capable of spying into every nook and cranny!

As soon as Erick had left the shelter and started to walk the streets, he was instantly overcome with paranoia, adding to his already high mental stress. Any behaviour trait that could single him out as an alien intruder had to be avoided, expecting face recognition technology to set off alarms at any moment, leaving him hopelessly exposed; Erick saw no alternative but to get moving and act like everyone else.

As if that was not enough to put him on edge, Erick spoke hardly any French, and he had no idea how to find a place to settle down for the next few days. Without secure accommodation, his stay in the city might be short-lived. None of these small details had been mentioned previously. For people like the undergrounders, who were constantly on the move and could hide and sleep anywhere, these were unimportant details to be considered a minor inconvenience; consequently, those aspects had not arisen in their discussions.

Slowly getting his bearings, Erick concentrated on how to fit in. This meant learning how to walk at a leisurely pace, avoiding falling into a hurried trot, trying to let go of his paranoia, and at the same time, asking for directions without inhibition.

For security reasons, Erick made sure he moved with the crowd, joining the endless stream of people moving about in the direction of the Eiffel Tower. He needed this point of reference so he could orientate himself better. Trying to introduce some irony, he imagined how an African desert dweller would feel when suddenly transplanted into a space station.

Turning a corner and walking into what was supposed to be the open expanse of the Parc du Champ de Mars, he suddenly stopped in his tracks.

Before him, a vast monolithic building of incredible massiveness rose into the sky. Erick estimated it must be over three hundred meters high and possibly a thousand meters long. Erick had only one answer for such an aberration, 'Absolute power!' Once a park surrounded by elegant structures, the whole area had lost its identity.

Erick, entirely absorbed by the monstrosity's presence, suddenly felt that someone was standing close next to him. His instinctive response initially was to take a defensive position.

When he turned, he saw a very tall woman, a somewhat outer-worldly creature, in appearance not at all unusual for this exceptional environment. An abundance of lime green hair was piled up in a turban, and highly stylised make-up was accentuated with a pair of outrageous sunglasses. In addition, this creature wore a jacket in black combined with a pink miniskirt, lime green leggings, and blue boots featuring immensely high heels.

Gracing him with her generous smile, Elena asked how he was coping. Did he really assume she would let him go alone into this zoo? Was he not scandalised by that ostentatiously abundance that stood in such a contrast to the outer rings of the city? Erick could only nod, still gob-smacked about Elena's transformation. But Erick's mind was distracted. The question that shot out of Erick's mouth was, 'Elena, what is this monolith doing in the middle of this beautiful city?'

'Oh?' she replied in surprise because it was the last thing she expected Erick to ask. 'I thought they had told you? This is the illusive technological research centre we had come for. What is actually going on in there, no one could tell me. It apparently contains the 'holy grail' of their defence project, but let's leave that to another time,' she concluded. While their conversation continued, they had been moving along with the stream of the *flâneurs*. A small green square ahead of them promised more privacy and rest so they could engage in a proper debrief. Elena gave him a detailed description of her position as the new leader.

She explained that it had taken some convincing for her tribe to let her go, as her leadership was still in a fragile, untested state. Most men had not yet come to terms with the new situation of being led by a woman. The women feared the male faction could stage a counter-takeover as soon as Elena was out of sight, leading to a renewed contest. Her presence among her closest allies was vital for now. She was required to give speeches, convince the wary, act decisively, and suggest new directions; the demands were endless.

But she also had good news for the still somewhat stunned Erick about the where about of his new 'friend' Monseigneur Moulray, a political figure who stood at the head of a new experimental political movement. The Monseigneur would give a lecture at the Théâtre des Bouffes Parisiens that night, its focus being 'Do religions still need leadership?' Unfortunately, because he was a top-rated speaker, all tickets had been sold out weeks before the event. No great surprise here, being gay, a Catholic, an atheist and a Darwinist to boot! A man of his intellect must know the dissatisfied hordes at the gates could not be held off forever. Fortunately, Monseigneur Moulray always held a discussion forum afterwards, which would hopefully be less crowded. How to contact Monseigneur Moulray had been on Erick's mind all day. Elena had solved his problem with a few inquiries of her own. The unexpected chance to meet his new acquaintance infused him with optimism.

Erick marvelled at Elena's organisational talents and abilities to deal with the new environment and its challenges as if she had been residing in this place for years, causing Erick somewhat to relax.

She was undeniably in her element here—in contrast to Erick himself! Doubtlessly, she was a woman of her time, being able to make immediate sense of unexpected challenges while keeping her eyes open, driven by a curious spirit that might be only reserved for the young, reading every billboard, finding interest in the grotesque and the banal equally.

Elena had arranged a pre-booked hotel for both of them, putting Erick's mind at ease. These arrangements were not straightforward, but she forgot to mention that minor detail. Visitors to the city had to be registered, not only with photos and fingerprints but also with their DNA. Their gold reserves had again saved the day!

The women's factions, now only too willing to help out in every possible way, had managed to abduct a couple, a few days before, who had been on their way to the city with a visiting permit. The IDs had been altered to match Erick and Elena's personalities. Erick felt discomforted by the thought of what might have happened to these people. But Elena assured him that no harm had been inflicted on these people and that they had been well compensated for the inconvenience.

Before going to the theatre, they decided on a nearby restaurant for a sumptuous meal while watching and waiting from across the road for the crowds to leave the venue.

26
Monseigneur Moulray

Erick would have liked to hear Monseigneur Moulray's lecture. Despite his long absence from mainstream culture, he had not lost his taste for sophisticated entertainment. He hoped for a private audience with the Monseigneur, followed by plenty of interesting conversations.

One hour before midnight, the doors to the performance hall were opened, spilling people into the square. It was time to make their way to the small anteroom. As expected, the room was already tightly packed on their arrival, predominantly filled with people from the press, excitedly flashing their cameras. Everyone was talking at the same time, keenly fishing for more information. It was impossible to get close to the stage where Monseigneur Moulray stood like a maestro playing the audience and unmistakably in his element.

On listening to people around him, Erick became convinced that this had not been a lecture about a particular philosophical subject, instead of a political campaign. Monseigneur Moulray was clearly running for a post in the city's assembly. Knowing nothing about the city's governing body, Erick could not make much sense of the affair. So instead of following the discussion, he began to study the people around him more closely. Also, with so many cameras in operation, it appeared wise to wait out their time to not draw unnecessary attention to themselves.

Elena, on the other hand, was becoming increasingly impatient. After all, it was nearly midnight; she felt tired and decided to take matters into her own hands. Towering just above everyone else, Elena struck an imposing, outrageous figure and had no difficulty pushing towards the stage. She addressed him with a few unrelated questions, earning her a few derogate responses from the audience, such as why he was making these regular leisure trips into the countryside until the Monseigneur finally paid attention.

A slight change in facial expression told Elena he had recognised her, but he did not interrupt his eloquent oration for a moment. That was all Elena wanted; recognition and his attention! She gave him her most winning smile and slowly, followed by many staring eyes, retreated to the back of the auditorium. However, her appearance had unsettled him as he brought the interview session abruptly to an end after less than ten minutes, charmingly giving his apologies for being fatigued and departing amidst flatteries and loud cheers for more.

Before leaving the stage, he wrote a note and handed it to his secretary with instructions to give to the beautiful lady with lime green hair standing at the back of the room. Waving jovially once more to his admirers, he disappeared through the back door. The message was: Rue Etienne Marcel no. 123.

As soon as Elena had read the note, they walked separately and swiftly around the block in opposite directions before any reporters could ask her uncomfortable questions or take her picture. Erick perusing his city map, recognised that their destination was not far off.

They arrived at a small exquisite restaurant. The concierge, already informed, showed them without delay to a table towards the back, situated in a cosy niche, unobservable from the street. Monseigneur Moulray greeted them with his winning smile, bowing to Elena courteously and warmly hugging Erick, showing his unrestrained delight.

'Please call me Jean-Philippe,' he began his introduction. 'I had expected you two to arrive much sooner in the city! Then again, I thought you might be too busy dodging Madame's hunting dogs. Of course you did not know, but she has unleashed an entire army of spies and assassins all over the city since her return from that all-embarrassing encounter with reality. She is out for total annihilation of you two as you can probably imagine after the ordeal you put her through. Unfortunately, it didn't help her see the falsity of her own ways. Instead, it made her even more evil!'

Their late-night snacks arrived accompanied by a good bottle of red wine. After a toast, Jean-Philippe continued with his story about Madame.

'It cost Madame a fortune to get released from the bondage. After that she had every one killed who had intimate knowledge of her ordeal. Having to send a troop of cutthroat mercenaries into that hellhole of the slave market could not have come cheap either. Apparently, it was a massacre. Only a few of her stooges got out. As the rumours go, she was treated lavishly with her own medicine during her 'holiday' in that slave trader's paradise. The first thing they did to her was branding her forehead with a capital *S*. Immediately after her return Madame consulted the most expensive cosmetic surgeon in town to get it removed. She would probably have liked to kill him too. They must have done some awful things to her because, as a consequence of that experience, she has given up sex for good! Not that I have much sympathy for characters like her,' he concluded.

Despite having eaten earlier, their food was so exquisite that Elena could not resist and did ask for a second serving.

Jean-Philippe continued to mention that one essential aspect played now in their favour. Since the scandal broke free, Madame has lost the sympathies of her favoured acquaintances in the higher echelons of the city; it has become unfashionable to be part of her circle, and her invitations are increasingly ignored means diminished protection. On the other hand, Elena and Erick had violated every city regulation and would, without a doubt, be sold into slavery if caught. However, they were publicly admired for their daring and skills in defying the system and avoiding detection.

'After all,' he continued, 'the populace of this city is not only made up of yes-men or spineless bureaucrats. This is a melting pot of eccentrics, extremely intelligent individuals and, above all, survivors who, through their wit and know-how, have managed to hold out against the odds for more than twenty years. Make no mistake you might be deceived by their looks, but most men and women are in constant training for combat and self-defence. If under siege, we are able to mobilise an army of one hundred thousand well-trained women and men in a matter of hours; not to mention the technological advantage in weaponry we still have.'

What you might perceive as decadence is simply a way of releasing widespread anxiety about being overrun by the disaffected masses outside the gates.

Elena and Erick said nothing; everything they had heard challenged their minds while their host ordered another bottle of red wine, which undoubtedly was of the best quality.

Noticing their contemplative, questioning faces, Jean-Philippe continued:

'I could use people like you around me if you are interested in staying. I will organise your citizenship application, which will make it impossible for Madame to touch you, as long as you reside in the vicinity of the city of Paris. Of course, I cannot guarantee that she will not try. You can be sure that, as long she can breathe and can hold a kitchen knife, she will not stop until her revenge is complete.'

Erick took a deep gulp of the wine and moved it around in his mouth, letting it permeate his senses before he swallowed. This was not unexpected, but still disturbing news. He was now berating himself for his leniency in not killing Madame right away and for failing to avenge the dead girl. He promised himself that if he was ever given a chance again, he would not hesitate to cut her throat.

Elena had turned quiet for reasons of her own. The impression she had received about the city from her new friends, the sewer rats, had not been entirely truthful and objective. How was she going to agree to the destruction of a community apparently run by people who were thinking as bluntly, directly and rationally as herself? People, who were highly tolerant towards every race, religion and belief, and who practised a system of society that deserved admiration and not condemnation? Elena felt unsettled, at the very least! Was all the information she had been given simply the consequence of that kind of thinking; underclasses versus ruling classes, refusing possible compromise solutions out of pure hatred for those they blamed for their suffering?

Elena took her time before she was able to ask for more clarifying details, but just as she was about to speak, Jean-Philippe came up with another unsettling remark:

'By the way, my congratulations for winning the sewer rats' army leadership title, Elena!'

Elena's face turned white and then red. This was followed by an angry outburst of flaring arms, which nearly knocked the bottle and glasses off the table:

'How on earth did you get this information? Who told you? Who is the traitor?'

Jean-Philippe, completely surprised by her sudden outburst, lifted his hands in a pacifying gesture and smiled generously to indicate no harm was intended before he began to explain:

'I am sorry to tell you, but the city's administration is kept informed just about everything that is going on above ground, underground and around the city! Our surveillance apparatus is extremely effective. We employ spies in every level of society, making sure the balance of power stays in equilibrium. Of course, all is done in the end to preserve the interests of the ruling class.'

This was as blunt as it could get. Elena sat there, still fuming and not at all pacified.

'Please hear me out, before your youthful idealism does you more harm than good,' Jean-Philippe replied.

'We originally created that underground movement, and we had excellent reasons! In the days when the old administrations were being swept away, religious fanatics militarised their followers, intending to establish their new kingdoms of god. Outside of the city, tribal warfare, marauding bands and many other challenges were rocking the countryside.

'Millions were on the move. We had to find ways to secure the city and its citizens. The first step we saw as necessary was securing the underground network of tunnels, catacombs, and sewers. No one knows the true extent of that system; not unlike a honeycomb, it reached far beyond the city proper. Bands of marauders constantly broke through our defences using secret tunnels. So, we began recruiting and paying people willing and able to patrol these tunnels. At first, we had to overcome great difficulties to find enough individuals ready to take on those duties. But, with the increasing influx of desperate people, their ranks began to swell in random numbers. In exchange for certain privileges and payments, they guaranteed, no one could enter the city through those tunnels again.

'As the underground army grew, taking on more and more of the unwanted and disaffected, fighting and overcoming rival factions, their confidence and power increased. Since the beginning, we have supported and, at times, even helped to enhance these underground dwellers' myths of invincibility and viciousness. What we did not anticipate during the early years was that they would someday become a power in their own right. At the same, their demands have increased, and so has their hatred for our lifestyle as city dwellers. Forgotten are the original contracts and now ruling their realm as if it had been theirs from the beginning. However, make no mistake, we still have the means to wipe them out in a matter of hours!

Unfortunately, it would be a Pyrrhic victory. Immediately afterwards, we would have to establish a new force because our Achilles heel would again be exposed! So, the solution for the time being is holding out with conspiracy, bribery, and the occasional threat that we might give material support to the gangs in the outer suburbs. But everyone knows the line has been drawn. We are currently in a stalemate, and so the demands are rising. I can assure you that we have no intention to weaken their forces, as we rely on them to hold the underground against anyone who dares to invade the city.

At the same time, we are showing them that, if they go too far in infiltrating the old Paris, retaliation will be swift and devastating.'

Seeing Elena's glum facial expression, Jean-Philippe chose a more conciliatory tone:

'Please, Elena, do consider the situation. If the city gets overrun and destroyed, what will be left? Do you think any of these fanatical religious leaders will make peace with whoever is administrating the city currently? Or do you expect one of these tribal warlords will impose a fair go for everyone, after all its rivals have been eliminated? Not to mention that array of small potentates, who want to bring back the kind of fascism represented by the Third Reich in Germany? Or consider the worst: there might be nothing left after everyone has had a go at each other.'

Silence descended on their table after being presented with such a gloomy outlook. Unperturbed by Elena and Erick's grim expressions, Jean-Philippe continued:

'Make no mistake, we have been pondering about these questions for the last twenty years. Of course, over time the conditions in the outer rings have been worsening dramatically. We also know very well that we will not be able to hold off the rampaging hordes at the gates forever. Once our technological superiority fails us, or we run out of gold reserves, we are doomed. We will have no choice but to fight a rear battle to get out of here alive. In the meantime, we still have a life to live and admittedly, not everyone in this city lives under the highest moral code. If one of you can come up with a workable solution, better suited to the present state of affairs, I will be the first one to promote it. Until then, we need to survive as well as we have so far.'

Now Jean-Philippe had stopped smiling and was also looking rather solemn and exhausted.

Suddenly he stood up, 'This is not the night for thoughts of doom and gloom,' he pronounced. 'I assume you must be starved of good entertainment. The night is still young and I think a good jazz performance will cheer us all up. Let's continue with these serious matters another time. By the way, have no fear that you will come across Madame and her henchmen tonight. She has never had any citizen's rights in the city. With an unfailing surveillance system in place, any assassination attempts from her side would immediately spell the end of her!'

Jean-Philippe had not promised too much. For the next few hours, they felt as if all the world's weight had been taken off their shoulders. After having downed a few of his favoured single malt whiskies, Erick let his amorous side come out of hiding while Elena watched him, delightfully amused.

After three hours in that ostentatious jazz club, listening to the most superb performances ever in her life, Elena was slowly getting drunk. For a while, engaged with bantering, laughs, and amorous gestures, she decided to leave the two men alone. On her way back to the hotel, Elena unexpectedly felt jealous. Despite his sexual preference, she would have been content to share the rest of her life with Erick more than with any other man. Tonight, however, after having experienced Erick's amorous side in full swing, her still lingering illusions met their tragic end. She was far too young to settle for a platonic relationship! Elena understood it was time to re-evaluate her friendship with Erick, let go, and seek her own satisfaction as a woman.

27

The fortress within the fortress

During the next few days, Erick and his partner in his first love affair in over twenty years shared every possible moment together. Wanting to be reassured that Erick had not lost his mind completely, Elena showed up occasionally, politely asking if she could do anything, knowing only too well that the best she could do was to leave the two of them alone for the time being.

Nonetheless, she was still troubled by her jealousy. Erick had never looked so gentle and serene. This contrasted with that tough, uncompromising survival exterior she was so used to. She knew, and so did he, that his honeymoon period was somewhat limited, so she wanted him to enjoy every minute of it, despite her slight irritation at seeing him in this condition.

After the initial sensual overload had been satisfied and channelled into a more level-headed time-sharing arrangement, all three came together to discuss their further steps towards acquiring a bionic arm. However, they found themselves hugely disappointed if they had hoped Jean-Philippe was in a position to facilitate the necessary connections.

He explained that despite being a member of the council of elders and receiving certain privileges, the true power was in the hands of five oligarchs. The committee merely had the function of discussing and advising. When it came to the dealings of the powerful among themselves, holed up behind their fortress walls, he had only vague ideas about what was going on in the inner circle.

The monolith was the centre of their power, housing their administration and research facility. Whatever those black glass walls were hiding, Jean-Philippe could not tell. There was talk about a robot project underway—the ultimate weapon, as rumours had it. The scientists at the facility were specially selected, screened and housed in a secret location, and of course, well paid. None of them would divulge any insider knowledge; if they did, they knew their lives and families would be forsaken.

Jean-Philippe did not deny the facts and the possible truth of this information. What the public did know had possibly been leaked by a few disgruntled scientists, who had sold their knowledge before they had managed to escape from the city. Only to what extent their research had progressed and what direction they were taking was anyone's guess. All in all, he told them fragments of conversations he had overheard.

Their intention to enter the facility without permission appeared somewhat reckless to him. The monolith was completely sealed under and above ground as far as he knew. The main entrance at ground level, protected by heavily armed mercenaries and the helipad on the roof were the only visible entry points.

Erick and Elena went quiet for some time. They could not hide their disappointment at having come so close and seeing all their expectations evaporate in the face of reality.

Elena, as usual, unperturbed by any difficulties, was already one step ahead in her response. Thinking creatively, excluding impossibilities for the time being, she began to enquire about structural details, staff members' housing, how many secret entries points the building might have and so on. All of it unrealistic sounding ideas, to which Jean-Philippe could only shake his head. Only when asked about the supply chains, he finally revealed, also somewhat reluctant, as if he feared having already said too much, the existence of an underground train system.

Even so, feeling surprised, Elena left it at that for the time being. She was sure her people from the underground would know more about what was going on down there and come up with a few solutions to excess these tunnels.

Seeing no point in discussing the issues concerning the secret entrances of the monolith any further, the conversation turned towards the possible cost of a sophisticated mechanism like the bionic arm they had in mind. Jean-Philippe shook his head disappointingly when he heard they had only two kilograms of gold left. It would be just enough to bribe one of the officials—if they could find one willing to put them in contact with the scientists working on the specific project.

'Whatever you plan, two kilograms of gold will not be enough to get what you probably have in mind. Not to mention, how much you will have to pay to obtain such an item. You would need to bribe many already well-off people. You run out of gold before getting to the decisive person in charge.'

'I am sorry to tell you,' he continued, 'but you will not be able to buy your way into this building, not to mention the extra cost for the arm. Your only chance will be if you steal it yourself!'

Now Jean-Philippe addressed Elena directly for the first time since they had begun their discussion:

'Mademoiselle, you'd better make sure you stay in power as the leader of the underground league as long as possible. Your position there might provide the solution to acquire what you two are after,' he concluded, smiling rather wearily at her.

Despite the setback and rather disappointing result of the discussion, for Elena, when it came to Erick's wellbeing, there existed only one motto: whatever needed to be done to help her friend, she would do it! Consequently, she might fight more duels and overcome intrigues and compromises with uncertain outcomes. Elena understood what she was getting into.

Jean-Philippe had just opened another delicious bottle of wine when Elena swiftly bade good night, leaving the two men somewhat disappointed. Her mind was now set in a new direction, and there was no time to lose!

She returned a few days later, Erick reading her face, understood the expression was not promising! Elena fussed around a bit at first, having apparent difficulty in approaching the subject, side tracking with the mention of a few personal issues she had with some of the underground people, her own wellbeing and the general tensions in the catacombs.

Erick waited patiently and did not probe until she had collected herself to give him the bad news.

'As you can imagine, I've been busy getting as much information as possible, and my investigations are on going. We already know the scientists are not citizens of the city. They are flown in from a special compound outside the perimeter for the week and then return for the weekend to their families. The security set-up for those specialists apparently depends on their performance and willingness to stick to their contract of absolute secrecy. If they do not perform as expected, the protection of their families will be withdrawn, and they will be thrown to the dogs, so to speak. If they were citizens of the city with rights for individual freedom, they could not have been manipulated in such a manner.'

'So, they are being kept outside and forever vulnerable. Anyway, the building can only be entered from the top—by helicopter, as we already knew from Jean-Philippe and the heavily fortified main entrance. Apart from those two options, the building is an impenetrable fortress. The first hundred meters of its height are covered with steel plates, thick enough to withstand a rocket attack! The basement structure extends apparently forty meters into the ground and has two train stations below. One line is connected to the interstate delivery train for raw materials. The other, and here it becomes sinister, is a small tube connected exclusively to the largest slave market on the outer ring! Both tunnels are hermetically sealed with two double-sliding steel doors after the trains have entered the underground stations. Also, in an emergency, the tunnels can be flooded between the gates.'

'My informant also hinted at sensors and all sorts of technical whizz bits. No explicit details have been obtained yet. Considering the technical facts alone, I don't see any possibility of getting in there. I would describe it as a dead end. And we don't even know yet if what you need is even provided there. In addition, where do we start in finding a person we can bribe, not to mention someone who will go through with the procedure?'

Here Elena paused, appearing disillusioned, waiting for Erick to respond. In a curious undertone, Erick asked her what was being delivered through the entrance of the small tube? He could sense at that point he was touching on an uncomfortable subject for Elena to talk about.

'People,' she replied reluctantly. 'Slaves, to be specific—the best the slave market can supply, the young and strong! Furthermore, what happened to the poor souls once they arrived at the science labs is a mystery?' To my great disappointment, the whole enterprise is organised by the underground people, a kind of tacit agreement with the city administration and an opportunity for extra income. This new information has put the whole revolutionary movement of the sewer rats into question for me and was particularly hard to swallow.

'No one was able to answer that question. I am just beginning to grasp their dog-eat-dog perception of humanity and the influence it had on their general psyche. Of course, I made no secret about my contempt for their hypocrisy! Then again, I have not lived long enough in this place to judge them.'

To Elena's surprise, Erick seemed not at all despondent about the state of affairs. He sat without uttering a word, mulling over what had been said in his mind, and finally replying optimistically, 'We will use the small tube and pose as slaves. That's how we will get in, Elena!'

Surprised by his simple but undeniably pragmatic response, Elena wondered why she had not come up with that idea herself. It showed that Erick, after having appeared somewhat distracted over the last few days, was once again on top of things.

'By the way,' he continued, 'don't mention anything about our further planning to Jean-Philippe; he might be a liberal in mind, but when it comes to questions about the status quo or a revolution, he will choose the former. After all he is a pragmatic bourgeois and not an idealist! He might tolerate your idealism and listen to your reasoning with sympathy, but nonetheless, reject any alternative to the current status quo. Change would mean chaos for him and the end of his comfortable lifestyle.'

28
A reversal of fortunes

Elena's hope that the leadership issue would stay out of the way for the time being was dashed as soon as she returned to the catacombs. From the beginning, the male faction had made no secret of their discontent about the new female dominance in their ranks. But they could not stage a coup d'état until they had built up their numbers again. And so they had been scheming quietly behind the scene, waiting for the right moment to launch their bid for a new male champion to take over the leadership again.

It was announced to Elena a new male champion was challenging her!

When initially hearing the news, Elena regarded the issue as not too serious. Also, she lately had been pondering about her role as leader after the conversation with Jean-Philippe, now doubting if she could still wholeheartedly agree with these people's methods and political direction.

Despite the warnings of her female friends, it appeared that not everything was being conducted in the usual manner this time. A sinister undertone could be sensed when it came to the discussions about the new contest with the male faction. So far, all information about who the new challenger would be was kept secret from her. Still, Elena was unperturbed; in her mind, it would be just another man who would bite the dust. However, no one had seen or heard of the new challenger, so the rumours about the sinister circumstances persisted, continuously stirring up lingering fears of gloom and doom among the women. All the underworld citizens were on edge as if expecting the immediate onslaught of a deadly virus to be pumped into the tunnels by the city authorities at any moment.

As the days went by and the time for the challenge was finalised, Elena felt increasingly uncomfortable. Not everything appeared how it was supposed to be. The whole affair might have be instigated by Madame to get back at Erick and her.

Madame would have paid well for any information that could have led to their discovery. And the 'Wanted' messages had probably been out for quite a while now. As his spies about Elena's leadership had informed Jean-Philippe, so could Madame's informants have gained the same message. Here the woman might have seen a chance for revenge. If she could not get to Elena and Erick personally, at least someone else could have been contracted to make the killing. But so far, those were all speculations stirred up by paranoia; she had to avoid letting those rumours undermine her confidence.

The situation changed dramatically for Elena when she walked through the tunnel towards the arena. She was overcome by a sudden bout of anxiety on observing the faces surrounding her. She knew then that something was not quite right; the women, in particular, did not show their usual enthusiasm when in Elena's company. They now looked downcast and avoided her gaze.

This behaviour stood in direct contrast to the hard-core male faction, most of whom were now occupying the upper balconies, voicing vulgarities and insults towards Elena.

She understood what had set her on edge as soon as she reached the arena surrounding the fighting pit. What hovered there on the other side of the ring was not a man; it was a human aberration, a monster! His torso, in the shape of a barrel, featured arms of extreme length that nearly touched the ground. Despite standing on very short legs the size of tree trunks, this monstrosity still reached a height of more than two meters. Besides the small strip covering his groin, he was completely naked.

A male chorus began to shout in unison, 'Strip, strip, strip', to the beat of a drum, obviously designed to intimidate and demoralise Elena. She had no doubt this had been orchestrated to the last detail. They were out to humiliate the female faction and destroy her specifically.

If Elena had ever felt desperate, this was the worst moment.

Suddenly, there was a lull in the intensity of the screams. Elena, turning around, saw the reason why. Erick was walking out of the crowd towards the fighting pit. Here, he raised his prosthetic arm, calling out in his powerful voice, demanding silence. Having gained authority in the previous few weeks through his masterful training of the troops, the audience obeyed respectfully. He did not speak until the hall had fallen silent. Now everyone was waiting curiously for what Erick had to say.

'As the rule states for all leadership contests, the reigning leader can nominate a champion to do his or her bidding. I am Elena's champion in this contest.'

All of a sudden, uproar exploded throughout the hall. Cheers could be heard from the ranks of the women's league and protests from the men's quarters, which were soon snuffed out by the women's majority.

Without waiting for any further responses, Erick began to strip. The display of his well-built Herculean physique, with its rippling rows of muscles, now earned him cheers of admiration from all sides. However, having observed the hulk he intended to take on, Erick was instantly overcome with doubt about whether he would survive the challenge. No matter how one interpreted the odds, Erick was in no way a match for that aberration of a human standing on the other side of the ring.

The creature had been surprisingly motionless throughout the preliminaries. It appeared to Erick as if something was entirely mechanical and unnatural about his opponent. He seemed not wholly human, somewhat robotic in his stoicism. Because all odds were stacked against him, Erick needed to come up with a quick assessment of this monster's weaknesses.

He had no doubt that the only chance for survival was to knock out his opponent as soon as possible. He would have to invest all his strength in one decisive blow! The challenger's bulk would make him slow to react, and the extreme reach of its arms might take him quickly off balance.

The gong sounded, and the monster came slowly towards Erick, head and shoulders forward. In his right hand, a long blade was held in a stabbing position, the most unprofessional way to use a knife in a fight. Quickly countering the first attack, Erick smashed his fist with all his might into the face of the oncoming giant. The grinding sound of broken bones could be heard, followed by outcries of disapproval from the male audience. Any other man would have gone down on their knees after that powerful blow, but the beast only grunted as if having been objected to some kind of minor inconvenience. Without stopping, the monster kept going at Erick, who now knew it was no use trying to knock his opponent out.

While parading the monster's attacks, a thought flashed through Erick's mind that this contest must have been orchestrated by Madame to bring them down. Only she could have been financially capable of initiating such a devious plan!

For now, all Erick could do was play for time. He had to save his strength because anything he had so far thrown at his beastly opponent proved futile. To defeat his adversary, Erick had to find weaknesses in his opponent's abilities as soon as possible, or he would be done for. Still swift, Erick danced around the hulk while parading the clumsy but powerful attacks with his metal arm. The prosthetics were his only real advantage in the contest he would have lost otherwise.

Erick noticed that the skin began to shred where he had hit his opponent's arms, exposing a metal structure underneath, confirming Erick's previous assumption. However, he had no doubt that his opponent's prosthesis was of a higher quality than his own, which was beginning to show dangerous signs of wear and tear.

To make things worse, he felt the constant battering was affecting his right shoulder, whereas the monster showed no signs of strain. The pain began to affect Erick's ability to concentrate, an increasingly dangerous situation in which he could quickly lose focus during the attacks. Erick knew then he had to come up with a quick solution, or he would be slowly battered to death. He decided in an instant the only decisive strategy to bring the monster down would be cutting off its head! He moved back as far as possible, positioning himself for a mini spurt.

So far, Erick's only advantage was the cyborg's slow mobility and lack of creativity, as his movements were predictable, and his knife movements were always the same. It appeared as if the whole body was being controlled remotely. This 'aberration' had only one purpose: to destroy Erick while completely disregarding his own life.

For a moment, Erick congratulated himself for maintaining his fitness over time, for enduring tedious repetitions stoically and not giving in to aching muscles due to the unavoidable ageing process.

Once he had manoeuvred the beast as far as possible from him, he sprinted the short distance. He somersaulted before the cyborg's blade could graze his chest, turning in mid-air and slamming his own flick knife deep into his opponent's neck, instantly bringing him to the ground. Erick twisted his blade several times and moved it around until the head was completely severed from the still-thrashing body! Whilst holding up the head in a victor's pose, he kept his foot firmly planted on the creature's torso; its four limbs still moving violently, trying to get up.

Not in the least surprised, Erick noticed that, besides the blood, a thick green liquid had begun to drip from the wound. This confirmed his theory that not everything about the monster was entirely human.

Despite his fatigue, Erick could not help but smile, immensely relieved that he had survived the contest against all the odds, proving once again his opinion that, in most instances, intelligence triumphs over brute force.

All Erick could hear now was the absolute silence all around, suddenly interrupted by a high-pitched piercing sound! It came from one of the balconies—possibly from a malfunctioning radio transmitter? Everyone looked in that direction, seeing a few men hurrying up the aisle, trying quickly to retreat from the scene before their complicity was discovered.

As if given a signal, a small group of men nearby also got up and followed without delay.

Having expected foul play all along, Elena did not waste any time. She called out to a large contingency of women and men to go in pursuit.

Erick, who was still standing in the arena, too stunned to make any moves, took the situation in slowly. As soon as the novelty of the interruption had evaporated, the spectators began to cheer, including most members of the male faction. After all, this was an undeniably heroic performance.

But for Elena, it was more important for the moment to catch the conspirators than to congratulate and attend to Erick. Soon it became clear to everyone the entire contest had been a setup—a conspiracy instigated from the outside to bring down their leader for reasons unrelated to their own cause.

In the meantime, Elena and her followers saw it as the highest priority to catch the traitors! This had been a violation of their tradition. Betraying that tradition was perceived as an attempt to undermine and destroy the underground society. For every sewer rat, respect for the results in the fighting pit was paramount, no matter with whom they felt aligned.

Now on the run, the conspirators knew they would meet certain death when caught. Under those circumstances, their reactions would make them even more dangerous and unpredictable. Their best chance of escape was to use the tunnels leading into the countryside. Elena immediately gave instructions to block these first. But even if they could make it out from the underground alive, their escape from punishment was improbable even whilst in the sanctuary of their paymasters.

Gunshots could now be heard coming from all directions. Some of the escapees had already been trapped and were now fighting to their death, while others might have preferred suicide after being cornered. A handful escaped deeper into the tunnel system, intending to hide and wait out their time, hoping for an opportunity to slip through the darkness.

The only one the pursuers managed to capture alive was the man with the radio transmitter—possibly one of the leaders in charge of the conspiracy. Unfortunately, he poisoned himself before they could get any information about the instigators of the plot.

29
The slave market

Erick could not have imagined ever returning to that hellhole in the outer ring where he had sold Madame into slavery. However, to exclude any possible danger from her, they had come well prepared, heavily armed, and with enough men to repel any aggression.

Elena was still unsure how their plan to get into the tech building would work. The men in their company, who were in charge of scouting for suitable slaves, had informed them that the train would usually be loaded up with their purchases over the following three to four days. The timeline merely depended on how quickly they could collect the right amount of quality subjects—because their buyers were only interested in young, healthy, athletic specimens. Consequently, the acquisition process, being very thorough, was unpredictably slow.

Once the allotment was complete, the slaves were drugged and loaded into specially prepared containers. Erick and Elena were troubled as they witnessed the inhumane practice of sending these young people to an unknown, possibly fatal situation. For the sewer rats, this was just one of many ways of making a profit out of others' suffering, living by the rule of them or us. However, having come so far and not wanting to dishonour their follower's efforts to get them there, Elena and Erick went along quietly.

The train was remotely operated and consequently driverless, but other issues must be considered. To enter the train unnoticed, they would have to avoid the permanently running cameras, possibly instigating a short circuit in one of the compartments.

Of course, they could not be drugged like the slave's consignment to be ready for any necessary action on arrival. However, to look convincing, they would be placed in the usual trunk without being locked up.

They felt extremely uncomfortable when they heard that the compartment doors automatically closed once the loading had been completed and would only open after their arrival. Finding two conscious people among the shipment of drugged slaves would surely not go unnoticed. But because no one could tell them what to expect at the other end, everything from here on was pure speculation.

Erick's suggestion of hiding under the train was instantly dismissed because, owing to security reasons, the train would run for a long distance whilst submerged underwater. Unless they could provide their own diving equipment, the chance of survival by travelling that way was zero. So far, this was all they had to go on, but they still had three days to improve on the current situation.

The three days passed excruciatingly slowly. To distract their minds, they both decided it might be helpful and informative to participate for one day in the slaves' selection process.

Accompanied by their entourage of sewer rats, they went to the market. Their troop, distinguishable by their black leather outfits, was noticeably given a wide berth on their walk through the slums. Erick and Elena observed the fear in the eyes of the passers-by. It was well acknowledged throughout the outer rings that the sewer rats were short-tempered and skilful in using their knives. But despite being feared, they were treated with contempt. Insults could be heard wherever they went, and people spat on the ground because the rats were known for their opportunistic allegiances and disregard for any life.

By the time they entered the slave market, Elena was already highly distressed. Old memories were welling up in her mind, and her hands repeatedly clenched and called for the knife more than once in a reactive manner. When she suddenly heard the crack of a whip, she froze instantly, clasping Erick's reassuring hand. It was again one of those moments when Elena promised herself that she would end all that suffering one day. She also knew that to get there, she had to play along by becoming more brutal and less affected by other people's suffering. All the while, she was in no position to change the current status quo. This was unquestionably the wrong time for an emotional outburst. She had to focus on the plan ahead.

The gates to the market were heavily guarded. Despite being a neutral territory, there were ongoing threats from gangs roaming the countryside beyond the city limits. Occasionally, these gangs would launch a bold attack to free their captured members. In most of these incidents, they were killed or captured and turned into slaves.

A deafening soundscape greeted them when they entered the enormous former factory hall. Here the slaves were displayed in heavy steel cages all around the walls. Some were stacked up to five storeys high, only to be accessed by ladders or fire stairs. Breaking into these cages was a challenge in itself. The slaves were arranged in order of quality. The less healthy, the old, and the children were usually kept in the lower levels, where the air was foul and thick. As it appeared, the rat infestation there provided their primary diet. The young, attractive, and healthy were stacked according to appearance. The upper level housed the most precious wares, the young beautiful women and men, who were regularly auctioned off and bought by wealthy visitors from the city and used as human toys or for prostitution in classy brothels.

These clients would usually arrive by helicopter on the rooftop landing pad. As they were being told about these wealthy buyers, Erick and Elena instantly had the same idea: to go to the upper platform and capture one of the helicopters, which they could then use to land on top of the monolith in the city.

Unfortunately, those visitors were usually surrounded by a heavily armed entourage of highly paid mercenaries equipped with the most advanced weaponry. Any attempt to challenge their firepower would be fatal! After concluding that overcoming those troops of mercenaries was a dead end, not to mention the undoubtedly violent welcoming reception on their arrival, they quickly let go of the apparently outrageous idea.

The dealers had been waiting with their merchandise of quality slaves ready on display, knowing they would only be paid for the high grade of subjects. Three men and a woman in their team made the selection and the follow-up bidding.

As Elena and Erick recognised, all the slaves were in exceptional health, young, athletically built and good-looking. Elena had no doubt these young adults must have just recently been captured from one of the caravans moving north, people in search of a better future, now enslaved and to be traded as wares, not dissimilar to her own tragic experience in the past.

Money was obviously no issue here. The corporation's pockets were deep. All in all, the order for this shipment was twenty people of both sexes.

Despite the readily available cash flow, the sewer rats had their own agenda, always seeing a chance to make some extra profit on top of their already generous payments. They would usually bargain and bring the price down as much as possible. But it was not the only reason the deal took hours to complete. Dealers and customers enjoyed the part of bargaining and haggling, accompanied by drinking and swearing, all to the detriment of the slaves, who had to stand upright, heavily shackled and obviously drugged. When the deals had been finalised, the naked slaves, shivering and barely able to walk, were whipped to get them moving again and loaded onto a truck to be delivered to the underground station.

Throughout the procedure, Elena had more than once been close to throwing up. She wanted to leave that horrible place, as she increasingly felt her senses were pushed to their limits of endurance, but Erick repeatedly reminded her that she was now the leader of the sewer rats. Any sign of squeamishness on her behalf would again be interpreted as a reason for another leadership challenge.

The general rule among the rats was never to split up their troop when in foreign territory, which could expose them to attacks by rival gangs. Only their strength in numbers guaranteed their safety in this alien territory. Elena and Erick had been warned not to leave beforehand, not only because of their unfamiliarity with the surroundings but also because they would be recognised as newcomers. Such people were usually the preferred easy pickings of the local street gangs.

They should also not forget Madame had by now increased the bounty for their heads to ten kilograms of gold.

During the third hour, Elena could not take it any longer despite noticing that not even half of the consignment of slaves had been bought. The only excuse she could come up with was to claim that she had suffered heavy blood loss from her recent menstruating cycle. She felt demoralised using such a pathetic excuse, receiving unashamed looks of contempt from her troops.

They agreed that four of their best fighters would accompany them to their hotel, ensuring their travel through alleys of the least populated areas and avoiding any challenging provocation.

Of course, how could they have known that Madame's spies had already picked up their trail before they even had arrived at the slave markets? As soon as they had stepped out of the gates, Madame's bloodhounds were on their path. Not far into the maze of the sprawling slums, they found themselves suddenly trapped in a small alley. At both ends of the passage stood a group of thugs wielding knives, clubs, and shotguns. Guns were not the problem here, as their use inadvertently would also kill their enemies on the opposing side.

However, these goons were aware that they were confronting some of the city's best fighters, and reinforcement could be called upon very quickly. Slowly moving closer, the attackers stopped only a few meters away on both sides. Their leader demanded boldly that the man with the prosthetic arm and the girl be handed over, declaring they had no interest in fighting the sewer rats and were willing to share some of the ransom. Before they had finished their sermon, however, the rats had thrown their knives, and at both ends of the alley, six of the want-to-be attackers fell dead on the ground. It was a clear answer, so their adversaries immediately stormed at them.

The alleyway did not allow for more than three men abreast to fight, a perfect setup for Erick and Elena's little troop. Fortunately, those reckless thugs were not particularly good street fighters either. Elena, already feeling she was losing control over her nerves after her experiences at the slave market, welcomed the sudden physical distraction. This was the perfect chance to relieve her anger, giving her fury free rein.

Two surviving attackers were on the run only a few minutes later. Erick could not help but smirk at how Elena had proved again when it came to a battle about life and death; she was without scruples.

Despite being victorious, there was no time to celebrate. A more considerable troop could arrive at any moment, most likely a better-equipped and trained company. As soon as the news spread about a local gang's defeat, the call to arms would be shouted all over the precinct. Their entourage hurried them along, only too aware of the build-up of danger.

Passing along a few blocks, they arrived at a dead-end alley. Here the rats pushed a car wreck aside, exposing an unassuming sewer grill. They lifted the heavy lid with a particular key then everyone hurried down the iron ladder into the subterranean world below.

Their guide suggested it might be the safest decision to make their way to the underground station and assist with loading the slaves. As much as they detested being involved with the drugging and boxing up of the slaves, now was no time to claim the moral high ground. It was also a chance for Elena and Erick to get acquainted with the situation in the carriages.

Walking swiftly along the tracks, Erick and Elena soon arrived at the station ahead of their entourage and were greeted by an eerie silence. There was no loading of slaves in progress. Instead, several corpses could be seen lying on the platform. Some appeared to be recently acquired slaves due to their nakedness, and others clad in black belonged to their troops. For a moment, Erick and Elena halted, dumbfounded, when beams of blazing lights suddenly fell on them. A unit of at least twenty men stepped out of the shadows, their guns unmistakably trained on them. Madame among them was all smiles and showing unrestrained hatred, but she did not say anything.

It was out of the question for Erick and Elena to reach for their weapons, but they were also hugely surprised not to have been gunned down instantly. They were relieved of their weaponry and were ordered to enter the waiting train carriages.

As their four companions came up slowly from the dark recesses of the tunnel, having stayed behind to secure the rear in case their escape hatch had been discovered, remained in the shadows and watched the drama unfold. Outnumbered and outgunned, they opted to retreat, slipping silently under the train and trying to disappear unnoticed into the opposite side of the tunnel.

They had nearly made it into the darkness when one slipped, causing his gun to clatter on the rails. The noise alerted the man standing guard at the end of the carriages. The bullets sent after them failed to reach their target, and luckily, they got away.

The incident raised Madame's anger, bombarding her mercenaries with an avalanche of swearwords of the vilest nature. Letting the four rats slip away had been, with utmost certainty, the signing of her own death warrant. She would have to leave the city immediately, and even her outpost in the countryside might no longer provide her with safety. It was generally known that no one could escape from the under-grounders once someone had become their enemy. Especially under those circumstances when it involved the capture of their leader!

While still stunned by the turn of events, Erick and Elena did not doubt that someone on the inside must have tipped Madame off.

Despite the irritating interruption, the pleasure was all Madams. The last thing they saw was Madame's face displaying a delighted, vicious grin. After ensuring Erick and Elena were securely locked up in a compartment, she waved them goodbye when the train started to move.

30
The slave delivery

Both could not help but wonder why Madame had not left a scratch on them, nor had she taken time to savour her victory. It could only mean one thing; she knew a fate far worse than she would have ever been able to inflict on them lay ahead.

Elena expected the incident would set off a major battle between the sewer rats and the gangs from the outer fringes involved in their capture. Many more lives would be lost, and both were only too aware; they were partly to blame because of their ignorance.

The lights went out as soon as the train had picked up speed, leaving them in absolute darkness. Luckily their captors did not know. Having been relieved of their larger flashlights, their captors had not bothered to search their pockets for the smaller emergency lights. Life in the underground required every member to carry torches of various shapes and sizes.

In contrast to Elena, Erick had not yet come to terms with the new situation they had suddenly found themselves in. On top of it, Erick was smarting about losing his most valued weapon, his 357 Magnum. Then again, Erick was glad he had left his two sawn-off shotguns and the second handgun behind in his underground lodging. Nonetheless, Erick now blamed himself that because of their carelessness and impatience, they had given Madam the opportunity for the ambush.

Being irritated about himself made it difficult for Erick to concentrate.

Elena shook her head and sarcastically reminded him there was no time for such antics. This situation demanded quick and decisive action before they arrived at the other end of the line. After all, it was a mess of their own making, and it was left to them to find a way out. Clear thinking was now required, as their life was at stake! Knowing the ride would take an hour, they had approximately forty-five minutes to devise a plan and react to whatever awaited them at the time of their arrival.

After a short heavy silence between them, Elena suddenly snapped her fingers. 'We need to create chaos,' she exclaimed excitedly. 'We'll throw the entire contents of the train into a big mess, empty the boxes and smash them. Let's make it look like Madam's men purposefully created it. It will throw the blame back onto her, and might give us a chance to slip away during the confusion about it.'

Erick's response was a dull nod, having no doubt that any plan was better than no plan, considering they had neither weapons nor any idea about what was to be expected. Although still slightly irritated with himself, he managed to respond with that broad grin Elena loved so much about him, lifting her spirits as it had done so many times before.

'At least we're free now from the pressure working out a solution how to get into the monolith,' Erick remarked sarcastically.

To blend in convincingly with the rest of the slaves, they decided to strip and planned to play along as if they were slightly dazed. They piled up all the smashed boxes in front of the two sliding doors, intending to push the rubble over as soon as they opened. Elena and Erick would then create a stampede amongst the disorientated and drugged slaves, trying to take advantage of the ensuing chaos to quietly slip away. Hopefully, the confusion among the welcoming party would last long enough, allowing Elena and Erick sufficient time for their plan to work.

Time was draining away fast. Elena took over the organisation of the slaves, cutting their bondages and bringing them back into a semi-wakeful state. At the same time, Erick put his metal arm to good use, smashing before piling the debris up. Their work was nearly finished before the lights came on, leaving only a few boxes behind that had not been cut to pieces. The train slowed down, entering a brightly lit station.

Most of the slaves could stand up but were disorientated, some even voicing their relief at having been freed of their shackles.

Erick kicked the pile of boxes as soon as the doors had been fully opened, and Elena started to scream hysterically behind the semi-conscious group of slaves. Instantly overcome by panic, they rushed through the open carriage doors.

The men and women waiting on the platform with their trolleys, dressed in white lab coats, were pushed aside, fell to the ground, and trampled over. Unfortunately, the stampede was over in just a few minutes. The slaves, who had nowhere to go, soon stopped and stood around in their sullen stupor.

At first, it all appeared to work to plan. Erick had joined in the first wave of general confusion and intended to make his way towards any visible opening or staircase. He had just knocked out one of the assistants and taken the man's lab coat when, out of nowhere, a group of heavily armed security guards appeared.

Still holed up in one of the carriages and trying to make her way through the rubble, Elena realised the sudden danger and so dived instinctively back into the train and hid under the pile of smashed boxes. Through a small opening, she observed, powerlessly and overcome with horror, how the struggling slaves, including Erick, were rounded up. The mercenaries were using their rifle butts to subdue any resistance, and in no time, the newly handcuffed slaves were rushed towards the elevator doors.

Elena heard the doors closing automatically, and the train began to move again, returning to the station at the slave market.

PART 6
THE MONOLITH

31
Misery

Distraught, Elena hid away in her underground dormitory. She ultimately blamed herself for a badly improvised operation that had put Erick now in mortal danger. She still could not fathom how it could have gone so wrong.

It took her a few days in self-isolation before she realised that time was not on her side. She had considered all possibilities to break into the building, apart from dropping out of the sky—a point of entry that was to be disregarded due to the lack of opportunity and the heavy guns on top. She now regretted having wasted time pathetically pitying herself. And as a consequence, she could not help but drive herself mad thinking about Erick's uncertain situation. A new plan was needed, and she needed it immediately! Once calmed, having found her rational footing, all hope was now pinned on Jean-Philippe, who had previously suggested he might be able to develop a new strategy.

In the meantime, Elena was looking for a distraction from her torment. Sabotaging the train station used for slave transportation appealed to her as a rightful kind of revenge. While she organised a team of explosive experts, she also demanded the discontinuation of the slave trade with the corporation. The loss of revenue would be considerable and not easily compensated by other income schemes. She was told this was a very controversial decision and not received with great enthusiasm by most leadership team members.

It took her some convincing, arguing that it might be wiser to recruit the slaves for their own army to swell their ranks. In addition, she reminded everyone that, as things stood, they could soon be embroiled in a conflict with the city's mercenary troops. To take on the corporation in a long-drawn-out battle, they would need a far larger army than they could currently muster. Her arguments had not quieted all the voices of discontent, but she had given them something to mull over for now.

Until she could consult with her friend Jean-Philippe, Elena kept her mind busy with all kinds of organisational matters. However, nothing seemed to calm her down for long. At one point, her frustration had boiled up to such a level that she suggested storming the slave market, opening all the cages and leading away all freed slaves. An overly romantic idea, raising doubts about her current state of mind among her lieutenants, pointing out to her that such intervention in the status quo would unite all gangs of the outer rings against them, which would lead to an all-out war among the tribes and play further into the hands of the corporation.

Accepting her limited understanding of local customs, Elena devised the plan of ransacking Madame's fortress town and wrecking it completely. Not only would such an attack have been foolish, given her emotional instability, but also because of the current shortage of manpower and the lack of appropriate hardware. Nonetheless, she soon became aware her desperation led her to make reckless and unreasonable demands. She needed to pull herself together before her people lost faith in her. In discussions with all team leaders,

Elena came to terms with the fact this attack would require more long-term planning, and not only because of the need to acquire adequate weaponry. She was advised that, for now, all her energies must be focused on freeing Erick.

As expected, Jean-Philippe was equally devastated about the failed attempt to penetrate the plant and to learn of Erick's capture, having dismissed it as folly from the onset. But he did not let the dire situation dampen his optimism and willingness to help. For his light-hearted suggestion that Elena might have to prostitute herself to gain exit into the plant, Jean-Philippe received a heartfelt barrage of insults and an outright rejection of the idea.

After she had calmed down and without taking much notice of her ravings, he explained to her in more detail the plan that he had in mind, reminding her at one point with dry humour, that he had heard her once proudly announcing to him that she lived by the motto 'whatever it takes.'

Paris's high society usually came together on a Friday night for dance, cabaret and music at the inclusive Club de la Roche. Of course, being one of the members, he would introduce her as his consort to all who had access to the venue. Elena's attractiveness and charming abilities were the necessary assets to get what she wanted, to open the forbidden doors she was so desperate to enter.

A request like this immediately brought to mind dark memories from her life as a slave girl. Listening to such outrageous suggestions, it took Elena all her self-control not to storm out of the room. But she managed to keep quiet. After all, she had no one else to ask for help except Jean-Philippe. So she endured giving her friend the benefit of the doubt and listened with increasing curiosity while he unfolded his previously well-thought-out plan. She would need a certain kind of preparation, sophisticated conversational manners and the cultivation of specific sexual techniques. Such suggestions, such words, and spoken by a man of the cloth! He was, without question, a character of many facets.

Finally, when she had heard enough, Elena told him that under no circumstances was she willing to play the role of a concubine; instead, she would storm the building and turn it into rubble.

Jean-Philippe waited until Elena had finished letting off steam. He reminded her again that they had been at the same point in their discussion previously. Such ideas were pointless. Had she forgotten the physical impenetrability of the building? He shook his head, showing an expression of increasing frustration. Was she serious about needing his help, or would she prefer to summon her troops and go to war? If she found his propositions impossible to digest, she should leave now. He wanted no more of her theatrics.

Elena's resistance evaporated when she came to terms with the hopelessness of her position. She resigned herself to the utterance of a few Spanish swearwords and agreed to listen without any further protest.

The plan was to seduce the general manager of the factory, the Comte de Deauville, the wealthiest man in Paris and the most wanted bachelor, known for his exquisite taste in women but also for his aloofness. It would be no easy feat to seduce him, and to succeed, Elena would need the kind of education he had previously suggested.

She must understand she would have to compete against all kinds of sophisticated women well-versed in the seductive arts. Here was more required than Elena's youthful charm.

He suggested she should have an interview with his friend Madame de Bovoire, who was the proprietor of one of Paris's most exclusive brothels. They would have an none committal conversation about the preparation she would need to become a convincing seductress. It was the course of action which promised the highest success.

Later on, Jean-Philippe admitted reluctantly that he had already consulted with Madame de Bovoire about the need for her training. Madame, one of his closest friends and political allies, had wholeheartedly agreed to take Elena under her wings. Madame was ready to begin immediately with training her in the fine art of seduction and sophisticated sexual mannerisms. It was another one of those moments where Elena had to take a deep breath so she would not lose her temper again.

Finally, with some effort succumbing to the demands of reality once more, her hostilities abated, she accepted her friend's plan.

Elena could not help but respond with growing curiosity in her voice. She wanted to know how long it would take to acquire the specific skills Jean-Philippe had in mind.

Seeing that she had finally come to her senses, he was satisfied and said, 'Dear Elena, it is absolutely up to you how quickly you are able to acquire what is necessary and how much you want to learn. Of course, it is also up to Madame de Bovoire to show you how to be a convincing courtesan. Let her be the judge of the moment when you are ready to play the sophisticated seductress.'

Even so Elena had agreed to this unexpected new avenue on how to proceed, in her heart, she was unsure about the new direction her rescue mission was taking. However, she felt relieved that something had shifted and satisfied that a new plan had begun taking a realistic, pragmatic form. Hope entered her heart for the first time since the disaster of Erick's capture. Elena wanted to get on with it now that she had agreed to Jean-Philippe's strategy. They arranged a meeting with Madame de Bovoire early the following day at her establishment.

Utterly exhausted after such a battle of minds, Elena gladly took up Jean-Philippe's offer of sleeping at his place.

Elena could not say what she had expected, but on no account had it been a six-storey mansion designed in the most exemplary art nouveau architecture of the late nineteenth century.

The concierge greeted them with all the refinement expected from an aristocratic setting rather than a brothel. A second woman guided them into the matron's office, a lavishly furnished salon about the size of a cottage.

The matron received Elena with a warm, welcoming smile, greeting them with embraces and kisses. Somehow, she reminded Elena of Madame de Bois without having Madam de Boise's fierce eyes and deceptive, manipulative dishonesty in her attire and manner.

As soon they had taken their seats in very comfortable armchairs, coffee was served, and Madame complimented Elena on her ravishing beauty. With a humorous undertone, she immediately offered Elena a highly-paid position in her establishment. All laughed at that remark, eliminating any kind of inhibition Elena might have felt up to that moment.

Jean-Philippe had already filled Madame de Bovoire in on most of the details of their plan from the previous day, and due payment was arranged without mentioning it to Elena. Under these circumstances, there was no need for further explanations, so the discussion went straight to how to acquire the necessary skills.

As time was precious, Elena agreed to start with the first lessons the same day as soon as Madame de Bovoire made the necessary arrangements. She would sit in an adjacent room and observe the rituals of some courtesans through a peephole.

On the second day, she would have an extensive conversation with the most experienced courtesans of the establishment, thereby acquiring a few insides about the trade secrets of the profession. On the third day, she would be taken under Madame's wings to refine what she had learned, and she would initiate Elena in the Karma Sutra of lovemaking. Those teachings were intended to free Elena's mind from moralistic inhibitions before she entered the practical part of her training. From then on to the end of the period, Elena would have a few sexual encounters with one or two courtesans at a time. In the final few days, she would have to show that she was ready to perform the art of sexual seduction with a male client—a prospect Elena quietly dreaded already.

In light of the urgency of the matter, Elena had made it clear from the beginning that she could not afford more than two weeks. In Madame's opinion, the time should suffice after observing Elena with her professional eye.

Without further comment, her friend left Elena in the wise hands of the expert, promising to pick her up in the evening. He planned to take her out for dinner afterwards, all in anticipation of what Elena would have to tell him. He expected expressions of disgust and horror about the intimately performed acts she had observed. And true to his expectations, the young woman, who usually drank good champagne pleasurably slowly, had hardly sat down before she had drained her glass.

Jean-Philippe was left without a doubt; the day had turned out to be full of exceptional experiences for Elena. In addition, he hoped those experiences had some kind of distracting effect on the painful thoughts about Erick's fate, which constantly overshadowed Elena's mind.

There was no need for him to probe, and to his great delight, the words tumbling out of her mouth were all very positive. Observing the performances of the courtesans had blown her mind and rectified some of her misconceptions about all matters of seduction. She had not imagined that lovemaking could be such a skilful art form and so much fun.

Jean-Philippe knew from Erick's account about Elena's time as a slave and the deep scars it had left in her psyche. He admired the girl for burying those memories for the time being so they would not become a hindrance to her mission. Besides, he hoped these exceptional experiences might offer her an opportunity to heal somewhat psychologically and enjoy all kinds of sexual pleasures for her own sake again.

While she described her observations, he could sense a certain kind of curiosity in her voice, more than just the satisfaction of accomplishing the first step leading up to the task ahead.

After day five, the matron was full of praise for Elena's progress. Smiling modestly, Elena received the compliments with relish. In the matron's opinion, the young woman was a natural. Once again, she offered Elena employment with the promises of great wealth and influence over the male citizens of the city.

However, for Elena, those compliments were just building blocks towards fulfilling her mission.

On the evening of the eight's day, Madame de Bovoire called Elena into her office just when she was leaving and bade her sit down. This was the moment she had secretly dreaded during her training all along. Elena knew what was coming owing to a lengthy discussion earlier in the day about her progress when Madame de Bovoire had hinted at the final touch of her training. The dread had not dissipated.

'Well, my dear,' Madame de Bovoire began somewhat reluctantly, 'it is time for you to participate in the practice of the real thing. I have arranged for two lovely young men to join you in the art of lovemaking tomorrow afternoon and the day after.' She put a particular juicy slant on the word *lovemaking*.

Elena's breathing stopped for a moment. She thought she had made it clear beforehand that she had no intention of being actively involved in any sexual act with a man.

'No, I will not. I cannot have intercourse with someone I do not love,' Elena burst out defiantly.

Madame de Bovoire gave her a smile full of sympathy and then, using a more decisive tone, asked her if she was sure she could seduce the targeted person she did not even know yet and have sexual intercourse afterwards? How did she want to address that lingering reluctance regarding the real thing? How confident was she about her ability to participate convincingly in a sexual encounter with someone she did not love? She could hardly expect to fall in love with that specific individual on the spot! Also, there was no telling how long it would take to reach her goal of winding that man around her finger until he would willingly do her bidding. In the meantime, she would be required to act convincingly every day as long as it might take. To enjoy sex for pleasure was one thing, but pretending she was in love and having sex with passion was a far more significant challenge to her psyche. So now was the moment to prove she was up to the task, or had she forgotten why she had sought help with the matter?

Elena nodded quietly, admitting her foolishness and thanking Madame de Bovoire for clarifying the situation for her once again. She assured the matron she would be there at the required time and left without further comment.

Jean-Philippe got his ears full at this night's dinner, reminding Elena repeatedly of the presents of the other guests and controlling her voice while in emotional overdrive.

'I still don't know if I can do it,' she began. 'After all, I have promised myself to stand up for the rights of women. Acting like this would expose me as a hypocrite, not to degrade the ideals I hold in such high regard, and to act with integrity when it comes to the emotional truthfulness between the sexes.'

'Elena,' Jean-Pierre replied with a smile, as always the epitome of a diplomat, 'there is no such thing as emotional truthfulness between the sexes. It is a nice romantic notion one indulges in after having fallen in love, but without any chance of it enduring.'

His cynicism infuriated Elena even more, once again a reason to raise her voice. Both were breathing out with relief when their food arrived, giving Elena a chance to rein in her passion. She knew Jean-Philippe was a connoisseur who liked to concentrate on his main course and preferred to leave the densely emotional matter for dessert.

After his share of indulgence, smacking his lips in appreciation, he wiped his mouth and began to probe tenderly into Elena's emotional turmoil.

'How old are you now, Elena, twenty-three, twenty-four? You have experienced and achieved a lot in your short life, more than most have during their entire existence. I admire you for having not yet sacrificed your idealism, despite what you have been through or maybe because of it. You are still holding onto to your principles and believe in the good of people. Unfortunately, if you want to succeed, especially in freeing Erick and whatever comes after, it is time to infuse your idealism with a dose of pragmatism. As irritating as it might sound to you, this is not a world where idealism has a place and possibly never had—even before it all turned into chaos. You might distrust my diplomatic talents and ways of scheming, however, in times like these, the alternative would be brute force, as you have witnessed being practised in the outer circles.'

He took a long sip from his glass, looking at her nonchalantly, expecting no further response.

32

Unexpected pleasures

Early the following day, Elena received some satisfying news. The train tunnel used to deliver slaves had been wholly destroyed over several kilometres, burying the train carriages under the rubble.

The matron was surprised to see Elena in a somewhat better mood than when she had left her the day before. She concluded that the young woman had come to terms with the necessary arrangements and maybe even looked forward to an exciting sexual experience.

Elena did not mention the reason for her positive mindset but readily agreed to go ahead with the matron's plan. After a few more hours of instruction in the art of intimate pleasure giving, the matron presented Elena with corsets, suspender belts, dresses and more illustrious items to support the seduction ritual. With great satisfaction, the matron observed Elena choosing and trying on several garments, the young woman expressing her admiration for the beautiful lacework and the many ways they could transform her bodily appearance.

Both of them enjoyed the fashion show, not realising how quickly the time had passed. In the end, Elena had no choice but to wear the outfit she was already dressed in.

The moment of truth had arrived, and she was again overcome with anxiety. In her state of panic, she quickly downed two glasses of champagne before entering the boudoir.

Before Madame de Bovoire left Elena alone, she gave her some last instructions about draping herself on the bed and not letting her panic stiffen her posture. At that point, she reminded Elena again that she was being watched over and safe. Unfortunately, this extra piece of information did not improve Elena's sense of comfort at all.

To Elena's delight, the matron kept her promise. The client was a middle-aged man of good looks who displayed divine manners and behaved courteously throughout their encounter, helping Elena put aside her insecurities.

She surprised herself at how well she managed to ease herself into the situation. Her client appeared in no rush; money was obviously no concern to him, he was an exquisite conversationalist, entertaining her with sophisticated anecdotes and witty remarks. Elena did suspect the client might be in with the plot; then again, had the matron not insisted the test had to be absolutely real?

More than an hour later, the second bottle of champagne was half emptied. Elena felt it was time to take the initiative as instructed, and she started to perform a very slow striptease, watching her client's arousal with satisfaction.

Of all evening dinners over the last two weeks, this was the one Jean-Philippe had been looking forward to with great excitement. After all, he was the only one who knew about the 'experiment' outside the establishment.

Had Elena triumphed over her inhibitions? Was she ready for the task ahead? He had purposefully not consulted with the matron, preferring a first-hand account from the young woman herself. Now it was all about the question: was she comfortable in her role as a seductress?

Elena's smile and relaxed demeanour spoke volumes, and she eagerly expressed her excitement about the experience. Still, he had to probe a bit to encourage her to reveal some of the more juicy details of the encounter. To loosen her tongue, he ensured her champagne glass was filled regularly.

'We went at it all afternoon,' she told him, blushing without inhibition. 'He couldn't get enough and nor could I. I surprised myself in the act,' she added, smiling contentedly.

Jean-Philippe complimented her repeatedly with a hearty laugh. His efforts had paid off! He was satisfied and convinced that Elena was now ready for the next step in their plan to free Erick.

Later in the evening, after they had exhaustively discussed all aspects of her surprising success story, Elena, despite her slight inebriation, turned to a more serious subject. She desperately needed advice on approaching the issue of her tenacious position as leader of the sewer rats. And who was better suited to guide her in manipulating the masses than her friend Jean-Philippe?

33

The Comte de Deauville

There was no doubt; the sexual experience had been a welcome distraction from Elena's inner torment. However, she could not shake off her dark mood for too long. Nearly four weeks had passed since Erick disappeared inside the dark monolith. Without any information of his whereabouts and no progress in getting closer to the prospect of rescuing him, her desperation was beginning to consume her from the inside.

Adding to her tragedy, new trouble was brewing among the opposing factions in the underground army. Disagreements about her decision to discontinue the slave trade with the corporation and the subsequent loss of revenue had not helped to improve her position as their leader.

There were moments when Elena felt most vulnerable without Erick at her side. Also, at this point in time, she could spare very little energy and patience for dealing with any kind of instability among the factions.

A quick solution was needed about how to divert another leadership challenge among her tribe, or everything would blow up in her face, which would result in the loss of the support she now needed more than ever while pursuing her plan to free Erick.

As she stood in front of the assembled faction leaders, it took all her resolve to appear in control of her emotions.

Despite the difficult challenges Elena had endured and overcome in the last few weeks, she felt they had somehow boosted her confidence. She had gained diplomatic insight and a better understanding of human nature. Through Jean-Philippe's teachings, she acquired new skills on how to influence the minds of her audience without the need to revert to threats or seek out factional favours.

In her mind, she also thanked the matron for showing her how to use her voice seductively and providing her with the necessary vocabulary to go with.

Elena took her time before she began to speak as she had been advised and observed the audience's mood whilst quietly contemplating how to approach the issue, studying the faces of outcasts, thieves, cutthroats and lost souls, counting those who showed hostility and those on whose loyalty she could still count.

Elena remembered what Jean-Philippe had said recently when she touched on the issue of need and greed defining the characters of the sewer rats. His answer had been straightforward: 'Just mention the word *gold*, and they will all move over to your side!' A plan formed in her mind during the previous days of rising tensions on how to address the issue.

A society made up of the lowest of outcasts usually aspired to simple riches in the form of gold and jewellery—all those items they could feel, see and possess physically and could easily trade with. He also pointed out that offering a solution to the most uncomfortable issue would allow them to reduce their discontent and create the necessary contrast before she landed her convincing blow.

Elena waited patiently until the crowd had calmed down; ignoring the provocative shouts that could be heard occasionally, she began to speak.

'I know some of you disagree with my decision to discontinue our slave trade with the corporation,' addressing the most pressing subject immediately, ensuring her voice sounded calm and in control of the situation. 'What I can suggest instead is…' here she held her breath… a far more lucrative deal and a constant flow of revenue, without having to debase ourselves any longer by selling our own kind to the enemy.'

The immediate response was laughter and a barrage of insults. Elena paused, letting the crowd puff out their steam before continuing to stimulate their curiosity. Demands for clarification could now be heard repeatedly, so Elena lifted her hand for a call of silence, introducing a moment of suspense before unfolding her plan, and announced they would raid the fortified town in which Madame de Bois was holding out. She had been there and had observed its riches and prosperity. Despite Madame's personal wealth, there was a highly lucrative supply chain the townspeople had to offer on a long-term basis. Now that Madame de Bois had lost the support of the city's elite, the town would be vulnerable because they relied entirely on a few mercenaries and the townspeople to defend her.

The audience still appeared unconvinced by her statement. Provocative shouts could still be heard, mixed with accusations of madness and incompetence. But Elena held her nerve, following Jean-Philippe's advice to provoke the 'beast' to react erratically, massaging the audience's minds and preparing them for the final assault before eliminating their resistance.

When it appeared Elena was losing control over the assembly, she paused before she announced: 'There is also a large store of gold in that fortress.'

Her words created the anticipated effect; a sudden silence had overcome the crowd, followed by a roar of frantic voices, drowning out all sensible responses. But the cries had been transformed from dismissiveness to enthusiasm; they were the voices of greed and the hope for riches.

Smiling with satisfaction, Elena listened to the differing opinions thrown back and forth between the opposing factions. By the time the fracas had calmed down, only one question remained:

'How big would the loot be?'

Elena used the same tactics as before, asking confidently for calm and waiting until all voices had eased. She had led them where she wanted them to be. They were hooked; it was the moment the bait would be swallowed unconditionally. Elena had no idea how much gold would be available or if there was any, but for now, it was irrelevant. Any inflated figure would incite their passion for going into battle.

'It will be more than one thousand pounds,' she proclaimed confidently, unsure if that made any sense. The roaring enthusiasm that followed confirmed her leadership position once more. But her strategy was not yet complete. As Jean-Philippe had advised, implementing emotional attachments to a cause was as crucial as monetary gratifications. She would also need to inflame their passion for revenge.

Finally, Elena set out to win over even the most reluctant souls, reiterating that it had been Madame who had attacked them in the underground station, killing many of their own and consequently sabotaging the slave trade in the first place.

Did they want to let that effrontery go unpunished, and did they want to become known to their enemies as a people who did not avenge their own? This strike at their hearts and pride eliminated the last resistance to her plan. The crowd roared, filling the hall with shouts of praise and approval.

The contest was won. Elena had overcome a long-brewing discontent and, in addition, had fired up their spirits, which gave them a new focus to channel their frustration. She could return to the surface and concentrate on her mission to free Erick.

Her lieutenants, satisfied at having a new exciting proposition to look forward to, gathered around Elena for a more detailed discussion. She gave them a preliminary account of her plan and what kind of hardware was needed for a successful assault on the town. The list included assault rifles, explosives, protective gear, and a few armoured cars, if possible. The distance of the village from the outskirts of Paris was about 90 km, which meant undetected arrival before the gates were most unlikely. Introducing a slow build-up of their forces around the town, with small groups, would be the most sensible approach.

'Under no circumstances can we be seen marching along the highway like an army,' she said with sarcasm when some of the younger members of her officers were presenting too much confidence.

'However, you must be aware, the information about the attack will seep out at some stage for a handsome reward. The only advantage we have is to keep the date of the attack on the compound secret amongst the leadership. In the meantime, I advise you to disperse mixed messages to confuse the enemy about our intentions. Also, I expect you to limit all details of our preparation to the top ranks alone.'

On her return to the surface, Jean-Philippe was already impatiently waiting for her. He hugely disapproved of her meetings in the underground. For the time being, Elena needed all available energy to prepare for her mission. For example, the most pressing need, for now, was to acquire the necessary outfit to make the right impression.

In Elena's eyes, the dress designer's parlour would have been a very pleasurable experience at any other period in her life were it not for her current inner torment. But she managed not to let her feelings show and went along without objection to any of the suggestions her friend and the dressmaker had for her.

During the week before the event, Elena was only too aware of Jean-Philippe's scrutinising eye. His face showed great concern for her, constantly looking for signs that might indicate Elena was losing her nerve or sinking into depression. Undoubtedly her face must have shown the strain she was under despite trying to cover it up. He remarked several times it would be better to postpone than to risk failing in their mission at the beginning. Elena blankly refused even to consider such an option.

Later in the evening, Jean-Philippe pointed out again Elena's lack of resolve to focus on Erick's rescue alone. She listened quietly to his reprimand that if she continued to divert her powers, she would not be able to pull off her stunt on the coming Friday and in the ensuing period. And because, until the day she could free Erick, she needed to look extremely desirable, radiating energy and seductiveness. How did she think she could attract her target and appear worthy of being pursued under the current circumstances of her divided interests?

Time was running out to find Erick alive, and this might be her last chance to make it inside before it was too late. How would she cope afterwards if the rescue failed because she had exhausted herself and consequently was unable to seduce the targeted individual? However, there was plenty of time later for her to take revenge if Erick had been killed. Now she had to stay focused and radiate her most attractive talents.

After this sermon of reprimand, Elena nodded quietly and agreed to everything he said without further objections. She assured her friend she would not return to the underground until she had completed her mission. Her initial stroppiness had all but evaporated.

For the next three days, Elena spent several hours every day at the dress designer's parlour, making every possible effort to push dark thoughts aside, looking radiant and appreciative, visibly enjoying the fussing about her in this stylish establishment. She sensed the staff had been instructed to be extra attentive to all her whims and needs. Coffee and sweets were presented at all hours, and she was greeted with a glass of champagne on her morning arrival.

Despite all the pressure her friend put on her, Elena was most grateful for his efforts. He was, without doubt, trying not only to transform her outer but also her inner condition.

Her appearance at Friday's venue drew the eyes of everyone present. Elena stood on high heels, towering nearly a head above Jean-Philippe and radiating supremely. Her dress, fashioned to the last detail to accentuate her seductive figure to the finest degree, stirred up the envy of all female guests. Even in a place like this, where beautiful women were aplenty, heads repeatedly turned, questions were asked about who this unearthly creature was who accompanied Monseigneur Moulray?

The art deco palace was oozing with style: soft lights, seductive forms, soothing jazz music, slowly seeping under the skin. Elena was instantly taken in. Limiting club membership prevented overcrowding, creating an atmosphere that assured patrons of their standing in society, as Jean-Philippe had pointed out.

Elena managed to rein in a comment of criticism just in time. For a moment or so, she felt sadness gripping her heart. How would the experience have been with Erick by her side? Jean-Philippe, noticing the dark shadows rising, seized her hard by the arm, whispering, 'Snap out of it, Elena. Focus!' From that moment on, he made sure not to let her out of his sight throughout the evening, repeatedly reminding her this was not the time to let herself go.

They moved towards the bar, followed by charming greetings, heads nodding, and little kisses here and there. They looked around, drinks in hand, expecting the carousel of introductions and heightened curiosity further to intensify.

While enjoying the exciting allure, their target subject had still to arrive. Elena, feeling anxious, tried not to empty her glass too quickly. But her tension was soon alleviated when several attractive middle-aged men surrounded them, acquaintances of Jean-Philippe, playing their usual game of charm and seduction, intending to get a bite off and maybe even a night with this mysteriously beautiful woman at his side.

Elena, now on her second glass of champagne, was beginning to feel her smiles come easier when Jean-Philippe suddenly alerted her by turning his head in a specific direction, indicating at a flock of attractive young women who were trying to win the attention of a middle-aged man of average height and not of a particularly outstanding appearance.

'He has just arrived, but he has not yet spotted you,' Jean-Philippe muttered quietly. 'Be assured his nose is already up in the air. It will not take long before he will be on your tail.'

From a comfortable niche, they were observing the audience and listening to delightful tunes. Elena continued to smile generously in response to teasing complimentary remarks coming her way.

As if by accident, Monsieur de Deauville casually sauntered past their table, shaking Jean-Philippe's hand and kissing Elena's before focusing his gaze unashamedly on her. At that instant, she understood this man's smile and voice could have melted a glacier in an instant. His act was played out with an irresistible boyish charm. Suddenly and just for a moment, Elena wished she had met this man under different circumstances.

He was a smooth operator. The conversation evolved as if they had known each other before, making it easy for Elena to elaborate on the storyline she had previously rehearsed with her friend, describing herself as the last surviving member from a distant Spanish lineage who was now residing with Jean-Philippe in Paris for the time being. While at university in Madrid, she witnessed the country's slow slide into chaos, followed by a tenuous existence on their country estate near Burgos until her recent arrival in Paris. She had not yet decided on further arrangements to stay for good or travel north.

Louis de Deauville's unabashed interest in her signified that the snare began to tighten, offering to call him by his first name, all to Elena's delight. He appeared not to concern himself with detailed descriptions of her tragedies, making it easy for Elena to avoid embarrassing questions. His mind was obviously focused on amusement and not misery.

The rest of the evening flew by in a flirtatious tête-à-tête. Like a true gentleman, Louis de Deauville did not try to overplay his cards, which indicated his serious intention towards Elena. By the end of the evening, they had agreed to meet for lunch the next day. Surprising herself, Elena had to admit Louis de Deauville was not the only one who had been hooked after this evening encounter.

Something had shifted in her heart, a conflict of interests without a doubt, and highly irritating when considering her intention.

What she had expected was a snotty, arrogant, degenerate aristocrat. Instead, she had come across someone who had changed her outlook on the opposite sex, a someone who was hard to resist not falling in love with!

34

On the inside

It took a few days before Louis ate out of her hands and treated her like a princess. During those raunchy nights following their first encounter, Elena ensured that her new lover would not want to see any other woman. She had also told him from the beginning that she was unwilling to accept any competition, taking on one of the matron's valuable advice: 'You are laying down the rules from the beginning and do not accept any compromises.'

Elena had very little doubt; being Louis' latest conquest, the dominant factor here was his obsession with her. Alongside her appreciation for his devoted attention and the sexual pleasure he gave her, Louis had the exceptional talent of making her feel special under all circumstances. Elena could have convinced herself that Louis truly loved her, but again the matron's wise words rang in her ears: 'The hotter the flames burn, the quicker the heat will turn into ash.'

During those few days, time passed in a flurry filled with passionate intensity.

In the mornings, after leaving Louis' residence, Elena usually went straight to the underground in defiance of her promises to Jean-Philippe. She needed to keep up her fitness and fighting skills to be able to deal with any kind of possible violent confrontations along the path of her mission.

Regarding the constant simmering discontent brewing among the sewer rats, Elena kept the tension manageable by showing up regularly. Her presence was necessary to ensure everything was running to schedule for the planned assault on Madame's compound.

On most afternoons, she visited Jean-Philippe to discuss her progress and receive continuous instruction in diplomacy, intrigue and sophisticated behaviour and how to prevent any rising suspicion on Louis' behalf.

Despite becoming irritably impatient, she had to be careful not to move too quickly and unintentionally give her true motives away. Every new step forward had to be backed up by her previous actions.

While listening to Jean-Philippe's sermon on how to manipulate minds and the art of filtering out information from the innocent without provoking distrust, Elena began to have an uncomfortable feelings about her friend. Was he really the man of integrity she had believed him to be?

She had no doubt he was a great puppet master and expert in manipulation. Elena suspected that his generous helping hand might be guided by ulterior motives. No doubt, it could be dangerous to have him as an enemy. However, those insights should be kept for future reference, now was not the time to engage in such troubling thoughts.

Ten days into the affair with Louis, Elena began to feel ill at ease. Nearly seven weeks had passed since the disappearance of Erick, and she had come no closer to knowing anything about his fate. It was time to get access to the 'forbidden fortress'.

'We promised to be honest with each other,' Elena began innocently, 'but I don't really know what you do. You said you are the first chairman and major shareholder of a technology empire, but what are you actually producing?'

In response, Elena sensed a certain discomfort in Louis's demeanour for the first time in their short affair. The subject of the internal structure of his company appeared to be a rather touchy issue. His reply sounded unconvincing and reflected an apparent lack of enthusiasm. He limited his responses to a discussion about his workload and the constant organisational challenges, which burdened him with immense responsibilities.

But Elena wanted none of it and verbalised her disappointment, accusing him of not taking her seriously. Or was he trying to hide something from her? Cunningly playing on her emotional side, she feigned that she suspected him of having an affair with one of his secretaries.

Visibly put on the back foot by Elena's brash accusations, Louis did not know how to react at first and appeared insecure and irritated while avoiding defending himself, knowing only too well it would have been a dead giveaway under the circumstances.

Elena kept up the pressure. Was his intention for her not to see the cohort of attractive secretaries that surrounded him, she implied with a slightly jealous undertone, pushing him further into the corner he had made for himself?

'You do love me, don't you,' she stated with emphasis as her final assault.

With glee, she watched him crumble. Utterly defenceless, he replied rather meekly, 'Of course. I will organise your visit to the plant as soon as I can find a slot in my schedule.'

'Tomorrow afternoon after lunch would suit me perfectly,' Elena replied with determination, having no intention of letting him off. She pushed her advantage even further, making clear she was not in the mood for negotiating and leaving Louis no way out but to give in to her demands.

Cold sweat began to run down her back. That 'psycho' assault had just about burned up all her reserves despite her mental preparation for that standoff. Sudden doubt infused with insecurity came over her. Had she gone too far? Was she giving away too much about her true motives by insisting on seeing inside the plant?

To ease her moment of doubt, Elena followed another one of the matron's valuable pieces of advice: in case she feared she had raised suspicions after believing she'd gone too far with her demands, the seductress' best weapon is to throw herself into the arms of the man, asking him to fuck her with all his passion.

At their next meeting, Jean-Philippe, diplomatic as always, recommended not to rush and instead proceed with caution. This time his words fell on deaf ears. Elena's patience had been spent; she was willing to walk in with all guns blazing. Of course, Elena knew he was right. She had gained permission to enter the plant; she had a chance to research the locality, but simultaneously, the challenge of maintaining Louis' trust remained. Elena had to be convincing in the show that her interest in the plant was related entirely to her love for him, of wanting to know him intimately. She would start with the administration levels and proceed toward the elusive basement. A new performance was asked for.

Arriving at his office the following day, it was only too apparent, Louis had prepared the place for her. First, he introduced her to the present board members and to the teams at the administration level.

Flowers were everywhere, with soft music and overly attentive staff. In addition, the secretaries all appeared somewhat of mature age. Louis instructed them to be as helpful as possible if his girlfriend had questions or needed assistance. Elena dispensed many warm smiles all around and voiced her appreciation.

Louis took great care to make the right impression, and Elena took the chance to be shown as much of the complex as possible, encouraging him with compliments about the stylish interior and the impressive view over the city from his offices.

The top level's most outstanding features were the staff facilities, which included a small shopping mall and a stylish restaurant adjacent to a greenhouse for workers to wander around and spend time in quiet contemplation. The recreational complex, including a sauna, a swimming pool and a gym, was most impressive. Much to Elena's excitement, the service level was as exuberant as her imagination could have allowed, offering the complete experience of a small village. All that was missing was an accommodation level. Undoubtedly, considerable efforts have been made to care for the workers' needs during their breaks.

Louis received her compliments with visible pride. His aim had been to create a multifunctioning facility, providing a complete integrated experience of work and pleasure to the highest satisfaction of his employees. The building comprised twenty-two levels above, most of them workshops and six below, reaching nearly 50 m deep into the ground. And yet, in Elena's eyes, the apparent socially attractive amenities appeared somewhat like a blindfold to camouflage the most sinister of secrets hidden away in the lower grounds of the building.

Elena, to get as much out of Louis's current cooperativeness, made a great show of her enthusiasm, praised, admired and voiced her curiosity with all the passion she could muster, telling Louis after the first tour that she would like to see the entire building if he ever had the time. She was convinced she had him there, so now she needed to drive her demands home as fast as possible.

However, Elena realised only too soon she had miscalculated the depth of her seductive achievement. Time was slipping away. Even so, after she had employed the full range of her feminine talents so that he would accede to her desires for more, Louis showed no signs of willingness for another guided tour. He vaguely described the lower levels as a research and production facility for advanced defence systems, including remote-controlled flying gunships, fighting robots, rockets, helicopters and a vast arsenal of guns. For that reason, there were limits on public viewing. Most of the merchandise was shipped to the cities still holding out against the human tide from the south. The export revenues provided the necessary financial support for further research projects to safely retain the city's status quo.

After those last disclosed details, Louis became very serious and evasive whenever she raised the subject of her interest in seeing the actual manufacturing levels. His main argument against further downward excursion was that the contractors controlled the production and the know-how. Those individuals were very cagey about their patents and feared industrial espionage. The company used a large part of its resources to attract many cyber technology specialists from all over Europa, who were willing to sell their expertise, but unwilling to part with their patents.

Seeing that her probing for more information fell increasingly on deaf ears, Elena, although disappointed, finally let go of the subject. She had to use the knowledge she had obtained as best as possible; further probing might raise unwanted suspicions.

At least, all information confirmed Jean-Philippe's previous speculations so far.

Elena had hit a roadblock, despite having pulled every possible register of her seduction repertoire. All she was left with was her fuming inside.

It was time to be bold and go against her friend's 'better' judgments, take the initiative into her own hands and employ her personal style of action. Even so, in that moment of disillusionment, she was not quite sure how to proceed.

35
Bribery

'I am getting nowhere with my current approach. Louis does not budge, no matter how many magic tricks I pull out from my seduction cabinet! And to be honest, I am beginning to get tired of it,' a highly emotional Elena expressing herself compellingly the next time she met her friend.

'He claims the lower levels are off limits for all public viewing according to the regulations of industrial espionage. And I fear, if I push harder, he might suspect an ulterior motive behind my love interest in him,' she concluded agitated.

Jean-Philippe's response to her ravings somewhat baffled her as he asked her how many gold reserves she still had. Elena gave him a curious look, not knowing how to answer.

'Possibly around two kilograms,' she replied with a questioning undertone.

'There is your solution, Elena! In this city, gold opens all doors! You will have to bribe your way down below. Getting in the door was the biggest obstacle. Now you will need your wits to penetrate deeper into the lair of the beast. Find a technician who, for the right price, is willing to take you on as his off-sider and show you around. Many of the corporation's employees are not satisfied with their work conditions or their salaries. Furthermore, no one dares to leave before having accumulated enough for sustainable a future existence outside the city. However, here comes the tricky part: you have to make sure you find the right personality who is greedy and desperate enough not to sell you out. So, you must offer a reasonable sum to keep the person hooked.'

Jean-Philippe continued, 'I am not well informed about the numbers, but to my knowledge, there must be more than three thousand people employed in that building. In an operation as large as this, many of those single, middle-aged characters are lonely and dissatisfied with their lives achievements. How do you make them out? They are usually sitting alone! With slumped shoulders, looking like wet dogs coming in from the rain. If a young, beautiful creature like you approach one of them, it will be as if they are seeing the first ray of sunshine after an arctic winter. Such an individual might even help you for free, just to impress you or out of spite to make up for his dissatisfied existence. I guess I do not have to tell you how to attract a man's attention. The canteen for the technical staff is possibly a good place to start,' Jean-Philippe concluded.

Elena took a deep breath, nodded appreciatively and left without further comment.

Louis had planned a lunch meeting with his executives the following day, conveniently suiting Elena's plan. Louis did not mind that she took off by herself.

As expected, the canteen was crowded at lunchtime; no free tables for single people, so Elena had to wait for the less social characters to take their turn.

Finally, she spotted a man who fitted the profile perfectly: he was bald on top, displaying a sullen face, shoulders hunched, and sitting motionless. Elena walked past him, dropping one of her earrings right under his table, then suddenly clutching her ear and crying out, 'Oh dear, where has it gone?' whilst searching the ground around his table. Meeting his eyes in the process and looking at him pleadingly, she cried out, sounding desperate, 'They, they, were my mother's; oh god, I cannot lose them. Can you help me find them as my eyesight is not very good?'

The man was on his knees in an instant rummaging around under the table and, seconds later, holding the earring up, a triumphant expression on his face.

Elena made a show of her gratitude, thanking him profusely. Then she took his hand and introduced herself. The man melted visibly in front of her.

'François,' he humbly replied.

Elena did not let up. 'Can I invite you to have a coffee with me?' she asked, using the softest of voices while looking deep into his eyes and smiling.

'Ahhh, aah, yes please,' he stuttered.

'Milk? Sugar? Black?' she enquired sweetly.

'Black, please,' the words squeezed out from the man's dry throat.

She went to the counter, making sure she walked as seductively as possible when returning with the cups. Not taking her eyes off her victim, she casually mentioned she had been employed by her boyfriend, the general manager, to redesign the interior of the cafeteria, sounding casual as if it was of no importance. François was slightly taken aback by her influential connection.

Elena began to probe into his professional status immediately, soon becoming disappointed to realise that François' position allowed him only to enter the top four factory floors. Apparently, he worked as an engineer on electronic guiding systems for the various weapons assembled further below. François had no specific knowledge of the military hardware developed and tested on the lowest levels, an area highly classified and restricted to most employees working on the upper levels. Of course, there were rumours about experiments in artificial intelligence involving human cyborgs, but he had no know-how about the specific technologies involved. At this point, he looked around before he lowered his voice and whispered that just talking about it could get him into trouble.

Elena noticed how proud he was having dared to reveal this information, despite his claim of the risk involved when talking about such a delicate matter. Unfortunately, this information only increased Elena's anxiety level. Nonetheless, she kept pushing on with her inquiries to extract more specific details, aware of the need to improvise to accomplish her goal.

Seeing François brimming with enthusiasm to divulge as much as he knew, Elena kept up the pretence of her fascination with the man's expertise. No matter how trivial any of the facts, any specifics could make a difference regarding the success of her mission. Of course, she had to be careful and make out as if all her curious inquiries were related to the design issues she was responsible for. Cunningly, she directed the conversation towards the subject of the floor layouts and access points, spinning the web of deceit tighter and tighter around François' mind.

When she was sure she had him snared tightly enough, she asked flippantly, smiling seductively, if he could show her the inside of some laboratories. She would be most delighted to have such an excursion, with him as the expert at her side. She pressed her case even further, adding that her boyfriend, the general manager, could not find the time to do it himself.

It was the first time since she had caught him in her web of deceit that she heard a sound of hesitancy in his voice, and a flash of doubt appeared on François' face, a sudden realisation maybe meeting this woman was not an accident after all? Elena sensed she had gone too far, quickly sidestepped the conversation, and smoothly redirected her inquiries towards François' private life.

However, no matter the consequences, she had already said too much to let the man slip from her lure. This might be her one and only chance. People might talk if she tried that ruse again with someone else! With an emotional undertone in her voice, she remarked how he had fascinated her with his technical know-how and impressive ability to explain everything. Elena decided to finish the conversation, thanking the man for his time and bidding him goodbye.

At that moment, Elena knew François had been completely caught in her web. His face lit up with pride, and he offered to continue the conversation if she would like to the following day. Elena smiled generously and agreed to meet him at the same time and place. Giving him a peck on the cheek, she excused herself by having to attend a business meeting.

On her return to Louis' office, Elena felt absolutely drained and, at the same time, excited about her progress. Stretching herself out on his office couch, she instantly fell asleep.

Now she needed time to prepare her next move with as much finesse as possible and decided to skip their regular lovemaking that night. They had been at it every day since they had met and, on some occasions, more than twice. Appearing busy himself, Louis saw no reason to object.

Elena was impatiently pacing the floor while waiting for her friend Jean-Philippe to arrive. The awareness of being close to completing her mission filled her with excitement and tension. Could it be possible that she might be able to hold Erick in her arms in one or two days? What could be expected down in the belly of the monolith, maybe a tortured Erick or even his dead body? Erick reconstructed as a machine man? Was she prepared for all these unimaginable possibilities and ready to deal with them? And how would she get him out of the building if he were still alive? All these dreaded thoughts came over her at once. She was afraid of losing her self-control.

Now, more than ever, she was aching for Jean-Philippe's calming influence, hoping he might have some valuable suggestions on how to proceed, providing clarity and keeping her cool during her mission's final steps. She also needed to think about a backup plan. Any kind of rational thought was more than welcome under the circumstances. Also, some of her men were to be put on standby in one of the safe houses in case she needed help with Erick's extraction from the plant.

Another major problem was smuggling weapons into the building without being detected by the security system. The more scenarios Elena imagined to try to avoid detection, the more she realised the impossibility of it. There were not only the electronic barriers to be considered, which everyone had to pass, including the executives and Louis himself. Elena would have to consider the constant presence of heavily armed mercenaries at the entrance, the elevators and every level she traversed.

Reflecting on all these diverse circumstances, Elena had no doubt she would have to rely entirely on her skills, ingenuity and ability to improvise as she went along. On that subject, even Jean-Phillip's exceptional creativity failed to devise a workable solution.

However, he surprised her again by suggesting a simple but effective way to compensate for her lack of weaponry.

As always, anticipating Elena's need to overcome unforeseen complications, he had organised a few syringes containing a powerful tranquilliser. Gratefully pocketing the items, Elena wondered what else this man could provide in emergencies? Again, she was thinking that if his reasons for helping her were not as selfless as she had expected, what could be the ulterior motive involved?

Still, Jean-Philippe kept up with his surprises, handing her a roll of duct tape with the casual remark, 'Hard to come by these days, but highly versatile when on a mission full of unpredictability's.'

When entering the canteen the following day, Elena saw the technician blushing with excitement. She had no doubt he had been waiting for a while, eagerly to see her again. He sat upright, his shoulders unusually straight, and rushed off to get their coffees as soon as she had sat down. Elena responded with a seductive smile to soften her target for the next attack.

However, she could not help but feel sorry for using this simple man to aid her dangerous mission. While quietly sipping her coffee, she mulled over how to convince François to involve himself in the procedures she had in mind.

A rudimentary plan had taken form during the consultation with Jean-Philippe the night before. After leaving her friend's premises, she met up with a team of her closest associates among the sewer rats, explaining her strategies' rough outlines giving them directions on how to proceed and position themselves in the vicinity of the monolith. She decided not to wait any longer and to move as soon as François was ready to follow her wishes.

Elena made a show of passion out of her interests in the science labs, and at first, François appeared keen to please

Elena in any possible way. She added with a conspiratorial tone in her voice that she would make it worth his while if this might cause any trouble for him, suggesting flippantly he supply her with one of those white lab coats and pretend she was one of his assistants.

At that bold suggestion, François suddenly gasped for air, explaining quietly that agreeing to her demands would amount to industrial espionage. It could cost him his job and maybe even his life if he were to be found out.

Now at a point of no return, Elena had no intention of sparing the man's consciousness. Dropping her friendly girl act, she told him bluntly, 'I am a wealthy woman! I am willing to reimburse you handsomely for any inconvenience or the possible loss of your position. After that, you will never have to work again in this place. How much gold,' pronouncing the word *gold* with a seductive undertone, 'would be sufficient to make the deal worthwhile for you to show me around the restricted areas?'

As anticipated, Jean-Philippe's judgment on general society's attraction to the yellow metal was right on the mark. As if by magic, at the mention of the word gold, François' facial demeanour changed instantly. Not doubting François' expression, Elena placed a small but visibly weighty bag on the table.

'This bag contains ten ounces of gold,' she whispered, adding that if she succeeded in her quest, he would receive the same amount again afterwards, delivered to him in two days at a place of his choosing.

The prospect of such riches changed the man instantly from a compliant servant into a greedy opportunist. With a sly expression, he put his hands inside the bag, feeling for the bars of gold before swiftly storing them in his lunch bag.

Now, nothing was holding him back, as if he was driven by a sudden energy boost. He demanded an extra ounce to bribe the person in charge by issuing magnetic security cards allowing Elena to enter the following four lower levels without limitations.

There was no more time to waste. Doors were beginning to open. Now she had to act on the spur of the moment.

François told her he would need about thirty minutes to an hour to organise the identity card. After that, he would take her down the elevator as far as his security clearance permitted. From then on, she would have to proceed on her own. They would meet again in the corridor opposite the canteen toilets, where she could change into a white lab coat.

Before François left for his errands, Elena reminded him quietly not to get any ideas of disappearing on her, telling him she had recorded their conversation word by word. François made no reply and scurried away.

Elena's nerves were on edge.

Time appeared to move in slow motion. What if François decided to inform the security administration? But then again, she was convinced, after seeing how the man's face had lit up when gold was mentioned, that he had, without a doubt, chosen riches over responsibility.

While waiting, Elena tried to imagine delving into the unknown territory of the lower levels. Without carrying weapons for either defence or attack, she had to be ready to use deadly force without hesitation against anyone who stood in her way. All her actions would be dictated by the situation at hand. So, it was best not to have preconceived ideas on how to react; rationality could hamper her instinctive responses.

On his return, François voiced doubts about having the nerves to go through with their deal. Elena replied coldly that he was now inextricably involved, and any change of mind might expose his treason and even cost him his life. Coming to terms with the fact he had no way out, François accepted the situation quietly and showed no further resistance.

During their downward excursion, Elena tried to remember every turn while they traversed endless corridors or when they had to change lifts for reasons of restricted areas. She soon had to give in to confusion, momentarily letting go of her concern about finding her way back through the maze.

Armed guards were positioned at all lift shafts and corridor intersections but displayed self-assured carelessness. Easy pickings if she needed a weapon, Elena thought.

After descending to the last level, which François had permission to enter, he said his goodbyes and wished her good luck. Before he turned, Elena advised him to leave the premises immediately and, for good, reiterated once more they would meet again at the agreed location as planned.

She watched him walk away. He had resumed his former stance again, shoulders hunched over, displaying the demeanour of a lost soul.

Elena doubted she would see him again.

36

Descent into hell

Three levels further down, Elena decided to take a close look at the factory floors she was passing through. There appeared to be no difference in the machinery display and assembled items, as in all other above-ground-level workshops, without hinting at anything sinister. She expected to see products that might reveal more of what the administration was so secretive about, only to be disappointed.

Surveying the location, Elena thought it might be helpful to study the floor charts on display, considering whatever lay before her, she would have to make her way back along the same corridors. The charts were conveniently displayed next to the elevator shafts. Unfortunately, as Elena had been warned, her activation pass for using the elevator was discontinued at ground level. Her moment of truth had arrived. From now on, she would have to improvise. She needed a new identity pass to travel further down.

Elena hid in one of the toilet cubicles in the nearest amenity station, waiting for a single staff member's presents, knocking the woman unconscious with a jab to the temples, paralysed her using one of the tranquiliser syringes and then locked her up in a cubicle.

Elena could only hope she had obtained a valid security pass to enter the restricted areas for the sections further down.

In case of failure, she would have to repeat the procedure, increasing the risk of discovery.

To her relief, the pass worked on the next elevator's console. After descending one level down, she stepped out into a vast, brightly lit corridor fronted with glass walls on both sides, allowing an unobstructed view of the beyond workshops. There were no more assembly lines of the standard type like she had seen above. Instead, individual teams worked on one object, attaching robotic arms and legs to a metal frame. In the workstation next to it, a team completed the structure with the overlay of an armoured suit.

On this level, the lift's positions changed again. To Elena's annoyance, she saw a group of heavily armed security guards loitering nearby. What if her newly acquired pass failed to open the lift in front of the men? Walking on without holding her steps, she calculated the risk of taking them out. Would she be able to neutralise them without causing too much commotion? At this moment in her exploration, a violent confrontation could spell the end of her mission.

Elena chose to walk past them, smiling gingerly and opting for the console in front of the unguarded fire stairs further along the corridor as the less risky option. To her relief, the pass worked, and she walked unhindered down to the next level.

The floor layout appeared to be similar to the one above. However, as she watched, Elena saw that the assembled metal carapaces were nearly complete, displaying four prosthetic limbs and a fully armoured bodysuit. Only the heads were now missing.

Satisfied with her observation, Elena went down another floor using the fire stairs again. Here she was suddenly overcome with dread. The odour of a butcher's shop permeated the air, causing cold sweat to run down her back.

What if…? She fought off the dreadful thought, fearing she might become paralysed and be unable to complete her mission.

Every discovery she had made so far steadily increased her anxiety level. What she saw now confirmed her worst nightmare. The assembly lines in the workshops above displayed only robotic contraptions without the vital parts of human heads and torsos. Here, motionless, possibly drugged human beings, some with missing forearms or entire limbs, were being fitted into those contraptions.

Elena was troubled to find an accurate description of these creatures with all-powerful bionic limbs featuring various weapons arrays, reminding her of the monster Erick had fought. How much of humanness was left in them?

Several assembly stations surrounded a sizeable cubicle from which tubes led into the back of lifeless torsos. There was blood everywhere, and some of the cyborgs were being dissembled, having obviously turned out to be failures.

Elena's nausea kept increasing, but so did her anger, further heightened when she saw a trolley nearby in the hallway, piled up with severed human limbs covered only partially with a blood-stained sheet. She concluded a similar fate had possibly befallen Erick! Unless he had not died, he also must have been butchered and assembled to become part of a machine. For a moment, she was torn between a complete meltdown and a fit of massive explosive anger. However, if she now failed to control herself and acted out violently, all her efforts would be for nothing. Thoughts of revenge and mayhem were to be put off for the right moment. Elena had to focus; despite her assumption about Erick's possible fate, she needed to continue her search for him, even if the outcome was only to end his suffering.

As before, Elena surveyed the floor layout on the display board next to the staff rooms, feigning an absent-minded look as if she had lost her way to avoid any possible scrutiny by a passerby. However, after lunch, everyone was back at his or her workstation.

She did not have to look too hard. The name of that particular storeroom was marked in red as a highly restricted area and described as a 'Depository for cyborgs awaiting final tests'. Such a bland description only proved that the administration had no intention of hiding what they were up to, being convinced of its fail-safe security apparatus shielding them from any possible moral scrutiny.

To add one more difficulty, the storerooms were located at the other end of the building, nearly 500 m away. Elena would have to traverse meandering corridors in between, and on the way, with no choice but to ask people for directions. Nearing her destination, she saw two heavily armed guards minding the entrance she was aiming for. This time there was no chance of avoiding them.

One aspect of the remote location played out in her favour. She found herself in a quiet corridor. The hum from the factory floors above was barely audible, and human traffic was non-existent.

She could finally get physical, welcoming the situation that would help to relieve the tension captivating her mind.

She noticed there were two security cameras focused on the entrance of the storeroom. It meant those two guards needed to be lured away from the door. After what she had witnessed,

Elena was in no mood to handle these guards sensibly but simply intended to kill them. More disconcerting to her was the hand identification console protruding from the wall.

But first things first, she thought!

To attract the attention of the two stooges, she used her 'young, attractive woman fainting' act to lure them away from the door and out of the range of the cameras. In her experience, such an act was foolproof. Without wasting time on humanitarian considerations, she killed them both with two powerful jabs to their Adam's apples, breaking the larynx instantly. Then she eliminated the cameras using the newly acquired weapons by shooting at them from an unobservable angle. At the same time, Elena counted on the inertia of those behind the monitors, who might at first assume a technical failure before taking action.

As expected, her ID card was useless on this particular hand identification console. She smashed it with the butt of the handguns, fusing the bare wires to open the door and ripping out all the remaining cables to eliminate the possibility of anyone trying to open the door from the outside. To avoid early detection, she pulled the two dead guards through the opening, closed the doors from the inside.

As soon she entered the storage facility, Elena was overcome by an unbearable, nauseating stench. She had trouble keeping the rising bile down before she spotted a battery of gas masks hanging in an alcove next to the entrance. The audible air conditioners made no difference to the overwhelming smell of human waste. The cause of the stench became only too apparent as soon she inspected the stored merchandise. The ample space held endless rows of cyborgs, each hanging in their own cubicles. And leading into their backs, noses, and chests were several feeding tubes. Most of them had had both of their forearms replaced with bionic contraptions, which held all kinds of weaponry attachments. The same armoured corsets Elena had seen assembled in one of the upper-level workshops were strapped around their torsos.

Looking down the length of the rows of cubicles, Elena estimated there could be more than a thousand cyborgs in this depositary alone. And this might not be the only storeroom. She had no doubt these cyborgs represented part of the secret weaponry on which Jean-Philippe had speculated.

Elena donning one of the breathing masks, forced herself to walk along the rows of mutilated bodies, filled with rising fury and, at the same time, scared of the moment when she would come across Erick's dismembered body, but still holding onto a sliver of hope that he might still be a sane and complete human being kept locked up somewhere else.

The cubicles were numbered, but it was difficult to identify any individual features. All heads were shaven and displayed a drugged expressionless sullenness, eliminating any personal characteristics. Even the differences between men and women were barely recognisable.

The horror about the collections started to strain her psyche and infused her mind with irrational responses. She assumed the conversion of humans into cyborgs focused on healthy bodies, regardless of gender. If Erick was held in this facility, she had to find him as quickly as possible. However, considering the hundreds or even thousands of subjects on display, it would be lucky to find him quickly. So far, she had not even thought about how she would get him out of there and overcome all the possible obstacles on the way back to the entrance.

While absorbed in her contemplation, she could suddenly hear loud banging from the direction of the entrance. The cavalry had arrived and was clearly trying to break down the door by force. It was time to take care of business at the gate.

On her way back, a plan began to form in her mind. The only way to force Louis to fulfil her demands was to threaten him by disrupting the cyborgs' life support, potentially leading to their destruction.

Elena expected the switchboard for the regulating system for the plant room to be near the entrance. She was somewhat irritated with herself for not having thought about it beforehand. Time was now in short supply, and judging from the sound of grinding metal on metal, the breakthrough at the door was imminent. Near the entrance, she saw a door marked as a tech room, and on the inside, all kinds of flashing green and red lights, buttons, and leavers. It was all she needed to know for now.

Elena shot the first man who dared to crawl through the opening, hoping it would discourage further intrusion. Under the circumstances, she was convinced there would be no gunfire in return because of the possible damages any stray bullets could inflict on the merchandise. Nor did she expect they would dare use tear gas for the same reason.

The death of the first intruder was obviously not a sufficient deterrent when a second security guard, after having widened the opening further, jumped through with a gun at the ready. She wounded him in the legs, forcing him to retreat screaming. No one was willing to risk their life after that, and possibly no one either knew what to do next.

Elena shouted her demands that Louis and nine executives be brought down as hostages. She gave them fifteen minutes to comply. Otherwise, she would start by eliminating one cyborg for every additional minute wasted, warning them that if they still refused to cooperate and were unwilling to meet her conditions, she would blow up the tech room and destroy the entire cyborg army.

Elena was sure, under such dire circumstances, Louis would willingly negotiate to avoid risking the loss of his most valued products.

What she had witnessed had enraged Elena to the point of no return! She did not care anymore about the consequences of her actions and was prepared to go under with all guns blazing.

37

Pyrrhic victory

In less than fifteen minutes, the group of hostages arrived. Every one of them was trembling with fear, their arms held up, appearing puzzled and shocked about the situation, except for a pale and confused-looking Louis, who crawled first through the opening and was now briskly walking towards Elena, stuttering:

'Darling, what is going on here? Are you hurt?'

Elena raised her gun and ordered him to stop, telling him coldly that she was not negotiating and expected her demands to be executed immediately. Warning everyone not to behave foolishly, adding if their ID cards did not match the person they were meant to represent or any of them carried a concealed weapon, she would shoot them point-blank.

She then ordered them to strip naked and shake out their clothes. There was a short moment of hesitation among the group. Elena raised her gun and eliminated a cyborg. The garments came off quickly after that. One man had a small handgun strapped to his chest, and two short knives dropped down when he shook out his pants.

In response and as a warning to the others, Elena shot the man in his right arm. After taking the blades and the gun, she told them to get dressed only in their white lab coats, put on gas masks and bind each other's wrists together with duct tape before lying on the floor.

She demanded they hand over the man who had been brought in eight weeks previously with the last delivery of slaves, wearing a prosthetic arm, and that this man is transported immediately to a specified destination.

Now convinced Elena had been stricken by a bout of madness, Louis believed he could use his diplomatic skills to persuade her to stop the drama. He attempted to confuse her with questions about their love for each other and her mental well-being.

Taking no notice of his pleading, Elena coldly commanded him to give his orders and not waste any more time with useless words, assuring him that from now on, for every ten minutes' delay, she would shoot one more cyborg. And as a warning, she immediately did just that.

In anticipation of the unexpected, Elena had previously organised one of the safe houses to be prepared for the arrival of Erick and his instant transition into the safety of the underground.

Louis finally understood he had been played all along! He knew his former lover well enough when she was serious. Without further hesitation, he ordered his technicians to check out the intake of the particular day, find the man in question and transport him to the agreed location.

To assure her the transfer had been successful, Elena had given her people at the safe house a code name and message to be returned to her. She demanded to see the man before he was shipped out to ensure they delivered the right individual.

Elena gasped when she saw Erick's drugged, mutilated body and expressionless face. It was challenging not to lose her resolve or let her feelings get the better of her by becoming emotional. In a threatening gesture, she pointed the gun at

Louis and told him to order his men to hurry and to relieve her tension, she eliminated another cyborg, causing Louis to shake with rage.

Having witnessed his former lover's ruthless determination, Louis changed his tone, calling her names and threatening that she would not leave the building alive.

Elena, seething with hate and lust for revenge after what she had seen and what they had done to her beloved Erick, kicked Louis hard into his groin, forcing him to sink to his knees, coughing and swearing.

'How do you control these cyborgs?' she asked him, putting as much menace into her voice as she could manage and lifting her foot again, ready to give him another kick if the answer should displease her.

'The remote-control devices are in the cupboard next to the gas masks,' he muttered through his clenched teeth. Elena ordered a technician to step through the door and hand one of the devices over. She would have liked to ask for instructions, but any distraction could endanger her control over the situation.

It was time to put the second part of her plan into motion. She demanded a bus to be delivered to the main entrance of the building and parked in the direction of the oncoming traffic to take her and the hostages to a destination of her choosing.

'What if I refuse to play along?' Louis sneered at her, still hoping he could outplay her on the long way towards the gate. In response and without warning, Elena shot him point-blank through his left upper arm, adding coldly, without caring about his screams, that he would bleed to death if he did not speed up the procedures and fulfil her demands as she had asked. Louis, becoming finally aware he had no chance of outmanoeuvre her and now fearing for his life, commanded that Elena's instructions be followed up without delay.

After she had received the message of Erick's save delivery, Elena also strapped on a gasmask and ordered the hostages to group around her, making sure no one could tell who was who before they left together the storage facility. The group, forming a tight circle around Elena, moved along timidly while she held her gun firmly onto Louis' back. She demanded the last remaining security guards to clear the way, threatening that if she saw anyone wielding a gun or trying to block their way, she would eliminate the hostages one by one.

As everyone in the group was wearing the same outfit, a possible sniper on standby would have had difficulty singling her out.

Progress was slow, taking a hard toll on Elena and the hostage's nerves. Cries of lament and sobbing could be heard. The corridors appeared endless, and there were numerous opportunities for an ambush along the way before they reached the first of many elevator shafts. But fear for the life of their chairman kept any would-be assassin out of the way.

Entering and exiting the lifts were complicated manoeuvres to control and could prove dangerous. The hostages could have easily crushed her in the tight space of the elevator. However, she counted on their fear and lack of imagination not to try any foolish moves. After all, these were executive characters, spineless and self-interested. None of them would risk playing the hero to help the other.

When they arrived in the foyer, Elena was surprised by the large crowd already gathered in front of the building, kept at a distance by a chain of patrolling guards.

Being acutely aware of the dangerous moment when she would have to exit the building, Elena had taken appropriate measures against any possible assassination attempt. As soon as she stepped onto the forecourt, three bodies still clutching their rifles were suddenly flung down from the opposite buildings surrounding the plaza onto the street, their smashed bodies dispersing the horrified and screaming crowd of onlookers below.

Louis grunted in dismay. He had just witnessed the failure of his last attempt to turn the situation to his advantage. The sewer rats had done their job as instructed. A few quick moves with their knives solved the problem. They had had plenty of time to prepare before they saw the assassins arrive and take up their position.

It was when all secretly held hopes of release evaporated from the group of hostages. Their shoulders slumped forward, resigned to their fate; moving on like sheep, they entered the bus without resistance.

So far, Elena was pleased with the outcome of her plan. No one had considered her instruction to park the bus in the wrong direction. She closed the doors and waited until she heard the sound of an approaching motorbike, snaking its way with agility through the crowd.

The bike stopped suddenly next to the folding bus doors, and the driver aggressively revved up the motor to disperse the public around him. At that moment, Elena swiftly swung herself into the back seat before the bike raced on, pushing its way through the stunned bystanders.

None of the mercenaries had dared to shoot at her with such a large crowd present. Unfortunately, the cars on standby to follow the bus were all parked in the opposite direction, and the crowd surrounding them made any manoeuvre to turn around impossible.

38
The death of a hero

Demoralised, distraught and depressed, Elena could barely manage to hold herself together. Despite the successful outcome of the mission itself, she felt no triumph.

After all these weeks, often pushing herself close to a mental breakdown, living entirely in the hope of freeing her friend and finding him alive and well, Elena was now faced with this most horrific outcome of a physically and mentally butchered Erick. It was too much for her! In her mind, it would have been better for Erick to be killed in action instead of delivered to her in this vegetable state. She could not even cry or scream to relieve her pain in one way or the other. All she felt was an empty dullness in her heart.

Elena would have liked to sit beside his mute body and talk to him to try to reach inside that unresponsive mind of his. But for now, she was at a loss about dealing with the unpredictability of his cyborg existence. She also did not dare use the remote control for fear of whatever unexpected reaction it might bring.

So, it was decided to lock Erick up, or what was left of him, until Elena was emotionally stable. They chose one of the most secure places, a chamber that had been hewn into the rocks and barred with a reinforced steel door. Exhausted as she was after her mission, Elena did the previously unthinkable: she took drugs to shut out reality.

Hours later, she was woken up by a loud banging on her door. Dazed and disorientated, she had trouble finding her way around in the absolute darkness before she could open the door.

Seemingly panic-stricken, one of her lieutenants informed her that Erick had broken out of the locked chamber and was nowhere to be found. At first, Elena felt tempted to use the remote control to locate his whereabouts, but on second thoughts, rejected the idea because of not knowing what the consequences would be.

With her mind somewhat revived after her extended sleep, Elena began to have suspicions about the corporation's unimpeded delivery of Erick to the underground. Could they have tricked her by attaching a tracer onto Erick to find a way to enter the underground system and possibly launch an invasion?

Now she blamed herself for ignoring the usual security procedures. Despite being overwhelmed by the intensity of the previous day's mission, there was no excuse for not having searched Erick's body for any possible tracking device. The question was, had sufficient time passed for the enemy to mobilise their troops? Undoubtedly, it was expected that they were already on the move. Elena had no doubt they were now in great danger. There was no time to waste!

Elena was not surprised when she heard shootings and explosions soon after she had raised the alarm, even before she had finished the strategic meeting with her lieutenants. She gave the signal immediately and ordered everyone to arm themselves. All possible entrance points where invading troops could enter needed to be blocked off, and if impossible to defend, they were to be blown up. For such emergencies, detonators were always in place, but the locations needed to be reached before the enemy had broken through.

A breathless messenger arrived, reporting that the invading mercenary troops had overwhelmed defenders in several tunnels, and were now unopposed, penetrating deeper into the underground system. Elena, in anticipation of worse to come, rushed to her chambers to arm herself while at the same time warding off the rising panic about a possibly dangerous cyborg on the loose.

Explosions and gunfire could already be heard from the central tunnel leading into the great assembly hall—a dire warning to everyone, indicating how deep the attackers had advanced into the compound. For a short moment, Elena was conflicted about whether she should assist her troops in organising a counteroffensive or search for Erick and neutralise him for good.

The decision was made for her when a bloodied lieutenant appeared, informing her that the defenders in the main entrance tunnel were in retreat towards the great hall of the invading troop's overwhelming firepower. If they lost control over the great hall, the enemy would have no difficulty clearing out the smaller tunnels one by one and, in the process blowing up the whole underground system.

From her vantage point high up in the command centre, Elena observed the carnage with horror. The armoured cyborgs, invincible to the defender's inferior weaponry, were relentlessly pushing on, their heavy machine guns mowing down everything in their path. Behind them, a large troop of heavily armed mercenaries took cover from the enemy fire.

The confrontation with the cyborgs coursed some of the sewer rats, overcome with fear and panic, to flee into adjacent tunnels. Others had thrown themselves in death-defying viciousness against the enemy and, realising the uselessness of their guns against the cyborg's armour, were using battle axes and crowbars instead. In close combat, it proved the machine men were still lacking in agility and vulnerable when attacked with brutal force at the joints of their prosthetics.

Observing the fighting strategies of her soldiers in close combat, Elena ordered snipers to target those weaknesses in their attacker's body armour. They managed to eliminate a few of the cyborgs with some well-aimed shots.

Still, there were too many of them to make a decisive difference in slowing the enemy's relentless advance.

Not only were the sewer rats unable to stem the tide, but to their horror, the attacker's strategy took on a new dimension when some of the cyborgs, using their clawed hands and feet, began to climb up the sheer walls towards the command centre on top.

The men and women surrounding Elena were suddenly overcome with panic and called for reinforcement to protect their strategically important location.

However, having previously experienced a similar situation where the whole underground was in danger of being conquered and destroyed by the enemy, a radical solution on how best to protect the underground had been decided on and perfected.

The city's mercenary troops eliminated most of the defenders during the last great invasion. In that desperate moment, it had been decided to flood the lower part of the tunnel system where most of the invaders had gathered in triumph, drowning their own fighters and the enemy alike.

As was expected, such an extreme solution was not taken lightly and was only implemented with great reluctance. The resulting loss of many lives and damage left behind on the underground had to be considered.

Nonetheless, defeat was perceived as unacceptable for the sewer rats. It would undermine their reputation of invincibility, inviting renewed attacks by the competition, especially those warlords ruling over the outer circles.

The strategy was simple and straightforward in execution. First, the main tunnel would have to be blown up and sealed off to stop the enemy from escaping and any further reinforcements from entering. This would include the sacrifice of those defenders still trapped in minor tunnels on the lower levels and those trapped behind the enemy lines.

Elena had no doubt the loss of life coursed by flooding the system would lead to a renewed leadership contest in the aftermath of the carnage. Despite her fears, she had little choice but to give the order.

However, the command centre, positioned high above the sheer walls of the great hall, which had always been perceived as unassailable, was now under attack! At this point, the cyborgs climbing up the wall were getting close to the balustrade and were being given protection by machine-gun fire from the ground. Their advancement appeared unstoppable. If they reached the top of the wall and destroyed the communication facilities, all connections with their troops would be lost.

When the first cyborgs had climbed over the balustrade, all that was left for Elena and her soldiers were to use heavy iron bars and battle axes to fight back. Even so, they had dislocated some cyborgs with massive rocks, but those who had dared were exposed and taken out instantly by the mercenaries firing from the ground.

Soon the defenders had no choice but to retreat, overwhelmed by the relentless onslaught of cyborgs and more to follow. All that was left for them to do was to hide in the bunker behind the command centre. They would make their last stand and perish in heroic defiance as soon as the attackers' relentless gun blasts had broken down the heavy steel door.

Unfortunately, the flood had not come in time to save their group from being annihilated. Elena could smell the odour of disappointment and defeatism all around. She sent out her last call for help reminding everyone to fight at all costs, and issued an order to hold off the advances in the great hall until the floods arrived before the line's connections were severed.

All small tunnel openings that could not be defended had to be sealed with explosives. Once the mercenaries realised they were cut off from outside support and were forced to fight a rear-guard battle in the main tunnel, the pressure on the defending troops in front did ease. As soon as the sirens could be heard, warning of the approaching floodwaters, everyone was to take the flight to higher ground.

Despite their dire situation, the men and women in the command bunker sighed with relief when they heard the sirens.

When the water flooded the hall, chaos broke out. The defence lines broke down immediately as everyone was desperate to escape the possibility of drowning, forcing the sewer rats to fight their way through to higher ground with extreme viciousness. Some managed with the rising waters licking at their heels, and those left behind threw themselves at the enemy in a suicidal manner, knowing they would either be killed or drowned.

Mistaking the defender's retreat as a victory, the mercenaries began to raise their guns in confident triumph, paying no attention to the roaring sounds of the approaching danger. The cyborgs went under first, being too heavy to swim. The mercenaries had to let go of their weapons to stay afloat in the rushing torrent, offering now easy pickings for the snipers aiming at them from above. In no time, the great hall was filled to one-third of its height with stinking sewage and hundreds of floating dead bodies of defenders and enemies alike.

The drama on the ground of the great hall was over in a few minutes, all in contrast to the desperate situation above on the ledge.

With relentless determination, the cyborgs blasted away at the rock wall surrounding the door. It was only a matter of time before the masonry would disintegrate. The trapped companions watched anxiously how, one by one, the hooks holding the iron bracing in place, gave way. Sharing a last embrace, they extinguished the lights and positioned themselves on both sides of the door, ready to hack away at anyone who stepped into the dark space. With only minutes of their lives to spare, adrenaline was feeding their killer instincts.

All of a sudden, the battering stopped. Gunfire could be heard from the opposite direction.

The trapped defenders started to cheer, filled with sudden hope, believing their own soldiers had finally come to their rescue. Everyone tried to get out at once to join the fray. But the door was blocked by several dead cyborgs, making it impossible to rush out quickly.

When they finally managed, they fell on the five remaining attackers who were still firing into the opening of a side tunnel, hacking viciously away at their enemies' backs, dismembering the cyborg's limb by limb and throwing the pieces over the balustrade into the gurgling waters below.

Seeing no sense in such blood sport, Elena walked cautiously towards the dark opening, where she could make out the shape of a large body lying on the ground. Coming closer, she saw a cyborg without body armour, bleeding profusely from many fatal wounds. Elena had no doubt that it was Erick. She kneeled beside him, taking his head in her hands and shouting his name. At last, he opened his eyes; there was a brief moment of recognition before all life left him.

Later on, Elena could only theorise about what had happened. Being disconnected from the feeding system and drug-induced coma, Erick might have regained consciousness and instinctively taken up his old role as Elena's protector. When he had finally located her at the command centre, he must have come across the attacking cyborgs, and Erick had done what he always did; defend his friend at all cost!

Despite repeated urgings, Elena refused to move from the spot, overwhelmed by the pain that had been growing during those interminable weeks was now to be released. Her unearthly screams reverberated through the underground, letting go of all the emotional restraints that had kept her together until now. She continued holding and caressing Erick's head, which was showered with an endless stream of tears.

Notwithstanding the damage and the significant loss of lives among their people, the sewer rats' victorious roar filled the caverns for hours. Elena was mistaken if she had expected to be deposed as leader soon after the battle. She was more than surprised when she heard her name shouted in reverence to her heroic stand against the enemy and her skilful handling of the defences.

Elena realised again that there was still much to learn about these people. Contrary to her beliefs, life did not count much for those down and out, but having been victorious over their greatest enemy, was worth more than anything! Such a triumph raised their confidence and self-esteem. Elena showed no interest in the victory celebrations while overcome by emotional exhaustion and held entirely in the thrall of her sadness.

She sat for days beside Erick's body, which had been laid out in his former living quarters. Ice cubes, to prevent his decomposition, were repeatedly replaced. Elena refused to leave his side despite her friends begging to put him to rest but finally gave in when overcome with fatigue.

As for the sewer rats, mourning their dead carried very little meaning. Dead bodies were unceremoniously sold off to the pig breeders in the outer suburbs.

They entombed Erick with his personal belongings in his old chamber. The room was filled with rocks and sealed with a plaque commemorating his heroic death.

One positive conclusion could be drawn from the whole disastrous outcome of Elena's mission: the cyborg program had clearly not yet reached the point of perfection, as their vulnerability in battle had proven.

The time was drawing nearer to prepare for the assault on the city, especially on the corporation!

Elena saw no more reason, nor felt any need, to return to the city. Jean-Philippe had played his part and might be under investigation by now. Such circumstances would make it too dangerous for her to be seen near him.

An immediate and exciting new adventure for the sewer rats was still to come. As soon as the clean-up had been completed, they would start to prepare for the assault on the Madame's compound.

One issue had been solved to all underground members' satisfaction: the dead mercenary had left plenty of high-quality weapons behind.

The End

About the author

My name is Michael Ernest Wilhelm Chapus; born in the eastern part of Germany to a German mother and a French father in the early 1950s.

My birthplace was a small medieval settlement surrounded by hilly woodlands. I remember those places as my childhood paradise, the cradle of my fantasies and dreams.

In the early 1960s, my family emigrated to the western part of Germany.

After finishing high school, I embarked on an apprenticeship in cabinetmaking. These three years were the most challenging in physical and mental terms. But the most formative years in my educational history! My master, a man of exceptional integrity, set me on my path of being critical of people who avoided the truth for financial gain.

A short stint at the national service followed. Sharing a room with eight other privates for more than a year teaches you a lot about human nature.

Studies in engineering and architecture followed. It was a time of unrestrained freedom, meaningful friendships and a new intellectual awakening. Berlin, I had arrived! Life in a big city, for the first time, is a challenge for mind, body and spirit! I embraced the abundance of culture with all my heart.

The architect's career was short but intense. After having entered the fray with enthusiasm, my idealism withered quickly. I was suffocated by competing egos, corporate greed and being witness to unrestrained corruption. At thirty-two, after having suffered suicidal tendencies for two years, I left Germany, never to return.

Australia felt like home from day one! The sun and its people were essential to my healing process.

My new goal was to achieve a life with maximum freedom, simplicity, meagre possessions and no reliance on securities!

It did not take long to realise the only existence a society can accept without looking down on you was to be an artist! Allowing you to think freely, read as much as you like, and experiment without the restraints of conventions. I chose my new direction without hesitation and embarked on a painters' career.